continued . . .

"I look forward to the next Emma adventure with her wonderful grandmother. Enjoy!" —*Once Upon a Romance*

"A unique voice." —*Kirkus Reviews*

GHOST
in the
GUACAMOLE

SUE ANN JAFFARIAN

BERKLEY PRIME CRIME, NEW YORK

THE BERKLEY PUBLISHING GROUP
Published by the Penguin Group
Penguin Group (USA) LLC
375 Hudson Street, New York, New York 10014

USA • Canada • UK • Ireland • Australia • New Zealand • India • South Africa • China

penguin.com

A Penguin Random House Company

GHOST IN THE GUACAMOLE

A Berkley Prime Crime Book / published by arrangement with the author

Berkley Prime Crime Books are published by The Berkley Publishing Group.
BERKLEY® PRIME CRIME and the PRIME CRIME logo
are trademarks of Penguin Group (USA) LLC.

For information, address: The Berkley Publishing Group,
a division of Penguin Group (USA) LLC,
375 Hudson Street, New York, New York 10014.

ISBN: 978-0-425-26249-8

PUBLISHING HISTORY
Berkley Prime Crime mass-market edition / January 2015

PRINTED IN THE UNITED STATES OF AMERICA

10 9 8 7 6 5 4 3 2 1

Cover illustration by Robert Crawford.
Cover design by Diana Kolsky.
Interior text design by Kristin del Rosario.

Acknowledgments

My undying gratitude to my agent, Whitney Lee; my editor, Faith Black; and all the good folks at Berkley who take my words and bring Granny Apples and all her friends to life between the delightful covers of a book.

A special thanks goes out to Lupe Lopez, who helped me with Spanish words and culture, and to David J. Hatch, Esq., who helped me iron out some of the legal details of the story.

· CHAPTER ONE ·

THE eye sockets of the skeleton were small wells of black ink, conveying both mystery and mockery. "That thing gives me the creeps," Granny announced as she studied the figurine in Emma's hands.

Emma smiled then whispered to the ghost of her great-great-great-grandmother, "That's funny, Granny, considering that you're dead."

"I may be dead, but you don't see me showing off my bleached white bones, do ya?" The diminutive ghost, dressed as always in pioneer garb, sniffed in disgust. "It's like showing your backside to the world."

Emma shook her head in amusement and turned the small figure in her hands over several times to inspect it. It was of a horse and rider, both skeletons. The rider wore a sombrero and a grimace of big white teeth. Around the horse's bony neck was a tiny garland of silk flowers. "Phil might like this," she told Granny. Reaching out, she picked up another skeletal figurine, this one holding a gun in one hand and a bottle of tequila in the other. It was also wearing a large colorful sombrero. "Or do you think he might like this one instead?"

The ghost shivered, even though she couldn't feel temperatures—hot or cold—and pointed to two figurines on the shelf: a skeletal bride and groom dressed in wedding finery. "Maybe you should get those," she said to Emma. "You can put them on top of your wedding cake if you and the cowboy ever get hitched."

Emma put down the dolls in her hands and picked up the bride and groom. "These are pretty cute."

"Puppies and kittens are cute," groused the ghost. "Babies are cute. Those are downright creepy."

"These are called Day of the Dead dolls, Granny," Emma explained. "*Día de los Muertos*—Day of the Dead—is a big holiday in Mexico. It's a day when people celebrate and remember family and friends who are deceased." She smiled at the ghost and whispered, "Not everyone is as lucky as we are to have our dead relatives with us all the time."

"*Humpf*," snorted Granny. "I can't tell if you're being sarcastic with that remark or sincere."

Granny's real name was Ish Reynolds. She'd died in the late 1800s at the end of a rope, having been hanged by vigilantes who'd thought she'd killed her husband—a murder for which Emma had proved she'd been framed. For a hundred years, Granny had searched for someone to prove her innocence, a search that had been frustrating and fruitless until she met Emma at a séance and convinced her to help. It was also this connection that had triggered Emma's awareness of her talents as a medium. Ish and her husband, Jacob, had lived in Julian, a mining town in the mountains north of San Diego, which today is a charming tourist destination known for its apples. Granny had only been in her forties when she died, having received her nickname of Granny Apples due to her fame as a pie maker. In time, after her death, she did become a grandmother when her only child, Winston, married and had children, starting the line that led to Emma. As a sales clerk approached Emma, she bit back the laugh on the tip of her tongue. She handed the wedding pair to the clerk. "I'll take these."

Granny watched the transaction with interest. "Is there something you're not telling me?" Emma only smiled as she took her change and package from the clerk.

Bright colors, lively music, and the smell of onions sizzling with sharp spices put Emma in a festive mood as she strolled down the small street lined with shops, restaurants, and kiosks.

"Are we in Mexico?" the ghost asked as she drifted alongside Emma.

"No," Emma whispered. She put a hand to her Bluetooth earpiece as she spoke to give people around them the impression she was on the phone instead of speaking to herself. It was a trick she often used when speaking with Granny while out in public. "This is Olvera Street in downtown Los Angeles," she explained. "It's the birthplace of the city."

"Interesting," said the ghost. "It looks like it could be in Mexico."

Emma tried hard to remember the last time she'd visited Olvera Street. Her daughter, Kelly, had been in grammar school—third or fourth grade—and had been on a school field trip. Emma had come along as one of the chaperones. Quickly she did the math. Soon Kelly would begin her senior year at

Harvard, so it had been about a dozen years since Emma had stepped foot on the short but busy brick-paved street.

It was a Tuesday in late July and the small street was booming with tourists and workers from downtown offices on lunch breaks. On the weekend it would be packed as the tourists were joined by locals looking for a fun weekend outing. Emma stopped at a booth to look at pairs of huaraches lined up like soldiers ready for marching orders. She'd once had a pair she'd picked up on a trip to Mexico. For years she'd worn them on weekends, but they had finally fallen apart and had to be tossed. Glancing over the various styles and colors, she picked up a pair and looked them over. With a smile that showed a couple of silver teeth, the woman working the kiosk encouraged Emma to try them on. After checking her watch to make sure she had time, Emma slipped out of her flats and into the huaraches. They weren't quite right. She chose a couple of other styles and slipped into them until she found exactly the right style and fit. She looked down at the open-toed sling-back shoes in natural leather. The woven leather would need time to soften and break in, but she knew they would soon become comfortable friends to her feet. She looked back at the woman, returned the smile, and pulled out her wallet.

"Did you come here to shop?" asked Granny when the clerk left to get Emma's change.

Emma shook her head. "I'm meeting someone for lunch."

Emma left the shoe stand with her new shoes in a bag and continued her way down the lane, stopping here and there to look at various wares until she reached her destination—Restaurante Roble. It was a good-size restaurant and one of the few on the street with a proper dining room and patio and waiters in pressed black pants and bright white shirts. Most of the other dining options were geared toward take-out or grabbing quick bites.

Emma quickly looked around as she approached a hostess standing at a podium. "I'm meeting a friend for lunch," she told the young woman. "But I don't think she's here yet."

Emma figured the hostess wasn't much more than eighteen or twenty tops since her oval face still held a trace of the plumpness of childhood. Through lips the color of rubies, the girl flashed a wide smile of bright white teeth at Emma and at the two men in business suits who'd come up to the entrance behind her. The hostess was wearing a traditional Mexican costume of a long flouncy black skirt encircled with strips of green and red ribbon and white lace secured at her waist with a wide red sash. Her top was a short-sleeved white blouse adorned with intricate embroidery. A red ribbon secured her long glossy black hair at the back.

"Are you Emma?" she asked in a soft voice, her brown eyes wide and luminous with inquiry. The name tag attached just below her right shoulder said *Ana*.

"Why, yes, I am," Emma answered with surprise.

"Follow me, please," Ana told her. Before leading Emma away, Ana told the two men that she'd be right back to seat them and flashed another smile. Emma doubted the men minded the wait after that.

Emma followed the girl to the far end of the patio to a round table that could easily sit six. On the table was a *Reserved* sign. As she took a seat, she noted that all the tables near her also had similar signs. On the other end of the patio, most of the tables were filled with patrons.

"Ms. Ricardo will be with you in just a few minutes," the hostess informed her as she handed Emma a menu. "May I get you something to drink?"

Emma started to order an iced tea, her usual drink of choice, but changed her mind. "Ana, do you have limeade?"

"Yes," Ana said, offering up another bright smile. "It's made fresh daily right here."

"I'll have that," Emma said.

Ana left the table and stopped a waiter—a small dark man who looked to be in his early fifties with his dark hair pulled back into a tidy braid. She said something to him in Spanish and indicated Emma. A minute later he returned with an icy goblet of limeade, which he placed in front of Emma. His name tag read *Hector* and up close Emma noticed that his hair was laced with gray and his white shirt was actually embroidered white on white. She recognized the shirt as a *guayabera*, or Mexican wedding shirt. Behind him was a tall young man dressed in the same manner toting a basket of chips and two small bowls containing salsa and guacamole. His name tag read *Carlos*. The younger man put the items on the table and left.

"Will there be anything else, *señora*?" Hector asked.

"Nothing, thank you," she responded pleasantly.

With a slight bow, Hector left her table, but not before Emma noticed him frowning at the empty tables around her.

The limeade was perfect, not too sweet yet not too tart. Emma preferred limeade over lemonade on hot summer days. She took several sips and smiled. Ana had said that Ms. Ricardo would be with her shortly. She only knew the first name of the woman she was meeting. It was Rikki. If Ms. Ricardo and Rikki were one and the same, then Emma was about to have lunch with Rikki Ricardo. She couldn't wait to tell Phil, knowing he would get a big kick out of it.

Granny settled into the chair next to Emma. "I love Mexican food," said the ghost with a breezy wistfulness. "There was a woman in Julian in my day who taught me how to make some of it. My man Jacob enjoyed it, too, especially her tamales, which I could never get just right. What are you ordering?"

"I don't know yet, Granny," Emma whispered, glad the tables around her were unoccupied. "I'm here to meet a woman from my yoga class."

"Yoga? You mean all that bendy stuff you do?" The ghost rolled her eyes.

"Yes. She asked me if I'd meet her here today for lunch. She said it was about a ghost."

At the mention of ghosts, Granny's interest sparked to life. "Oh boy," the ghost said with glee. "We haven't had any excitement since Vegas."

"And that's how I like it," said Emma, "uneventful and unexciting."

Granny stuck out her chin. "Speak for yourself. You try being dead for over a hundred years. It gets real boring real quick."

Ignoring the remark, Emma said, "I sensed some spirits as I walked through the street just now, but nothing seemed disturbed or unhappy about them."

"Yeah," said Granny. "I got the same feeling. Everything seems pretty calm on that front."

"And," Emma continued, "Rikki's concern might not have anything to do with Olvera Street."

Rikki had approached Emma at the end of their Thursday evening yoga class—a class Emma took every week in Pasadena if she was in town.

"You're Emma Whitecastle, aren't you?" the woman had inquired just as Emma left the yoga studio. Emma had seen her in class many times. She was petite but strong and sturdy with great flexibility.

"Yes, I am," Emma had answered.

The woman adjusted her rolled yoga mat under her left arm and offered her right hand. Emma took it. "I'm Rikki," the woman said, shaking Emma's hand. "Can I speak to you for a moment?" Before Emma could say anything, Rikki added, "It's about ghosts and I was hoping you could help." When Emma stiffened with wariness, Rikki quickly added, "I know who you are. You're the medium on TV. My family could really use your help with something. We'd be willing to pay you."

"I don't know how much help I can be," Emma had demurred. "Maybe you should contact my colleague and mentor Milo Ravenscroft. He's much better at contacting spirits than I am. They generally just come to me or I stumble upon them. I can give you Milo's number."

Rikki shook her head. "No, I'd rather it be you. We may not know each other well but at least you're not a total stranger." The woman gave Emma a shy smile. "My mother sometimes watches your show. She was quite impressed to learn that I took yoga with you."

After coordinating their schedules, they agreed to meet for lunch on Tuesday, although Emma was surprised when Rikki had insisted on a restaurant on Olvera Street, a tourist spot.

"Is that her now?" asked Granny.

Emma looked up from the menu to see a woman around thirty speaking to Ana, then heading their way. She'd had short black hair when Emma had last seen her, but now it was cut even shorter in a trendy style that made her large brown eyes look even larger. She'd worn no makeup on Thursday night, but today her face and eyes were beautifully done. Like the waiters, she wore black pants and a white top, but her top was similar to the feminine embroidered blouse Ana was wearing.

"Yes," Emma whispered to Granny, barely moving her lips. "That's her."

"Emma," Rikki said with a big smile when she reached the table. She shook Emma's hand with warmth. "Thank you so much for coming today." She pulled out the chair next to Emma and sat down. It was the same chair Granny had been sitting in and Rikki sat down on top of the ghost.

"*Humpf!*" groused Granny, moving to hover behind Emma. "I hate that."

Ignoring Granny, Emma said to Rikki, "I haven't been to Olvera Street since my daughter was in elementary school. I'd forgotten how cute and fun it is." She held up the bags containing her purchases. "I even did some shopping. Do you work here?"

"I'm one of the owners of this restaurant and I also man-age the place. My family has owned it since the late 1920s," Rikki told Emma with great pride. "It started out as a hole-in-the-wall café. My great-grandfather waited the few tables and my great-grandmother did the cooking—everything from scratch. Over the years it expanded to become the largest restaurant on Olvera Street."

Emma looked down at her menu and took note of the oak tree depicted on the front. She tapped it with a manicured nail. "Isn't this the same logo that's on Roble products in the grocery store? Any connection?"

Rikki nodded with another wide smile. "That's us. Over the years we've gone from a tiny cantina to a large Mexican food brand. We've even launched two food trucks that are doing great. *Roble* means oak tree. My great-grandfather named the restaurant for the huge tree that grew on their property back in Mexico."

"We use those products all the time at home," Emma told her with a chuckle. "My boyfriend loves your salsa verde. He slathers it on almost anything he can. He'll be tickled that I met you. In fact, I bet he'll insist that we come here for dinner sometime soon."

Rikki blushed a bit. "I'm sure with your TV show and your background with the rich and famous, you meet a lot more interesting people than us restaurant folks."

"Don't sell yourself short. *Rich and famous* doesn't always translate into *interesting*. Besides," Emma told her with a wink, "now I can tell people I had lunch with Rikki Ricardo."

Rikki laughed and her blush went deeper. "Yeah, you'd think I would get used to that over time, wouldn't you? Would you believe my sister is Lucy Ricardo?"

"No!"

"It's true," Rikki said with a playful grin. "We're named after our maternal great-grandparents, Lucinda and Ricardo Duarte, who lived in Mexico, not after the old TV characters. It was something my mother promised her mother she'd do right before my grandmother passed when my mother was young. There was supposed to be a boy in the family, but after a few miscarriages following Lucy's birth, my parents decided I'd be the end of the line, so they named me Ricarda. Our parents never call us Lucy and Rikki, but everyone else does."

There was a slight pause in their conversation, so Emma got down to business. "So why do you think you're being haunted?"

"Let's order first," Rikki said. "Are you allergic to any-thing or dislike anything?"

"I'm mostly a vegetarian," Emma told her, "but I do eat fish. In fact, I love it."

"Got it," said Rikki. "Then let me order your lunch for you. Something special. How spicy do you take it?"

"Medium, please."

Rikki got up. "I'll be right back. Then we can talk about ghosts."

Emma watched Rikki as she disappeared into the restaurant and wondered what kind of ghost was involved. Picking up a chip, she dipped it into the fresh salsa and bit into it. It was delicious and the chips were fresh and crispy with just a hint of salt, not coated with it like in some restaurants. She tasted the guacamole, and it was so wonderful she wanted to eat it with a spoon.

Granny settled herself in the chair next to the one Rikki had occupied. "Let me get this straight," the ghost said with knitted brow. "She and her sister were named after the guy on that old TV show who sings 'Babalu' and his nutty red-haired wife?"

Emma whispered back, "Not named after but they have similar names to those characters. Is *I Love Lucy* another show you watch with my father?" In spite of being a ghost, Granny loved watching TV, especially with Paul Miller, Emma's father. Crime dramas and NFL football were Granny's favorites.

"Not with Paul," Granny clarified. "I watch it with your mother. Elizabeth and I have seen some of those shows over and over but they're always a hoot."

Emma shook her head. Granny had become an important part of their family and kept company with all of them, even with her father and Phil, neither of whom could see or hear her. Over the years, both men had learned to sense when she was near and talked to her like she was breathing flesh and bone even if they could not hear her responses.

When Rikki came back out, the man named Hector stopped her. He seemed perturbed and gestured toward the empty section of the patio where Emma was sitting. He spoke to Rikki in Spanish in a low but angry voice. Rikki squared her shoulders and responded back in the same tone.

"You don't understand Spanish do you, Granny?" Emma asked the ghost, trying to keep her lips from moving since she'd removed her earpiece upon entering the restaurant.

"Nothing beyond *adios*, *gracias*, and *cerveza*," responded the ghost. When Emma shot her a sharp look, Granny added, "What? Like you've never heard Phil order a beer?" The ghost turned her attention back to Rikki and Hector. "That's who we need now, ya know. Phil speaks Spanish. I've heard him."

"Yes, he does, Granny," Emma confirmed. "And so do both Milo and Tracy. I really must take the time to learn it, but that's not going to help us now."

When Rikki left Hector and returned to the table, Emma gave her a warm smile. "I hope everything is okay? I can move if you need this table."

"Everything is fine," Rikki assured her as she sat down again. "And stay put. Hector is worried we're losing business by having these other tables empty. I blocked them off so we could have some privacy. But there's no line for lunch today and there's plenty of room inside the restaurant." She inhaled deeply, held it, and blew it out, then repeated the calming exercise again. "Sometimes Hector forgets who's in charge."

"Is he family?"

Rikki shook her head. "No, but close enough. He's worked here since he was a kid. He came over the border illegally when he was just ten or so. He was an orphan and showed up here starving and begging for food. My grandfather took him in, found a family to care for him, put him in school, gave him a job, and eventually helped him gain citizenship."

"Wow," Emma said. "That was really lovely of your grandfather."

"Yes," Rikki agreed. "He was like that. He did the same for a couple of other orphans over the years, but only Hector remained with the restaurant. The others moved on to careers in other fields." She watched Hector as he consulted with Ana over something, then sighed deeply. "Hector and my dad were tight, like brothers. I think he was disappointed that he didn't get more in the will. I think he was expecting to get a piece of the business."

"But he didn't?"

"No," Rikki answered. "Both my father and grandfather were generous to him in their wills, but neither gave him any interest in Roble Foods. Since its humble beginnings, the family business has been just that—the family business. My father convinced my grandfather to incorporate decades ago but only he, my grandfather, my uncle Tito, and my mother were on the board and only family members held shares. For a Mexican family, we're very small. Uncle Tito never married and had no children. He died when I was still in college. It was just after Uncle Tito died that they elected Lucy and me to the board, and when Lucy finished with her MBA, she became involved in the day-to-day operations of the corporation and helped expand it deeper into the retail market. When our grandfather died, he was not replaced on the board. Since my father's death, only Lucy, our mother, and I remain on the board. We've talked about bringing Hector on to the board and even selling him stock, but we can't seem to agree among ourselves about his capacity or how much stock to sell him or much of anything else, so we're in a bit of a stalemate. The Crown Corporation had approached my father about selling the business to them shortly before he died. That went by the wayside after his death, but Lucy still wants to sell and opened up dialogue with them again. I'm dead set against it, and our mother is torn between us. One day she wants to sell. The next she doesn't. The company cannot be sold without unanimous consent."

Rikki turned her attention fully on Emma. "Which segues right into why I wanted to meet with you, Emma."

Rikki stopped speaking when their food arrived, carried by Carlos, the young man who'd served Emma her chips. He placed a sizzling plate of grilled shrimp and vegetables in front of Emma. Also on the plate were chunks of grilled fish, rice, and beans. He placed a similar plate in front of Rikki.

"Thank you, Carlos," Rikki said to him. "Could you also bring me a limeade? In fact, just bring me a glass and a pitcher of the limeade. That way we can do our own refills."

"Sure," Carlos said. When he tucked the tray under his left arm, Emma noticed a smattering of tattoos snaking out from under the short sleeve of his *guayabera* down past his elbow. "Anything else?" When he spoke, he didn't look at either of them but straight ahead, his jaw tight.

"No, Carlos," Rikki told him. "That's it. Thank you."

When Carlos left, Rikki gave up another deep sigh. "Between Hector and Carlos, I can't seem to win today. Shortly before you arrived, I spoke to Carlos about wearing a short-sleeved shirt instead of one of our longer-sleeved ones."

"But it's awfully hot out to wear long sleeves," Emma noted.

"True," Rikki agreed, "and personally I don't mind it. In fact, I have a couple of tattoos. But our customers don't like seeing the tattoos, especially the *gringo* summer tourists from out of town. They tend to equate them with gangs, although Carlos is a good student and on his way to college in September. He'll also get much better tips if he covers the tats. Carlos has worked for us for a couple of years and knows that covering tattoos with our longer-sleeved shirts is one of our policies. And our long-sleeved shirts don't come all the way down to the wrist, so they aren't that uncomfortable in summer."

"Your hostess seems quite young. Is she also a student?"

Rikki glanced over at Ana, who was in the process of seating a couple on the other side of the patio. "Yes. Ana is Hector's daughter. She's been working here summers and school holidays for several years. She starts her second year at the University of Arizona in September."

Emma started in on her food. So did Rikki.

"Boy, that looks good," said Granny. "Nod once if it is," she said to Emma.

Emma nodded while she chewed a big bite of the shrimp. "This is delicious," she said to Rikki after she swallowed.

Rikki smiled. "The shrimp and fish are marinated in citrus juice and spices before being grilled. It's one of our specialties and a guarded secret of the chef." With her fork, she pointed to the left side of Emma's plate. "That's grilled cactus. I hope you like it. And the pinto beans are vegetarian."

"It's all scrumptious," Emma said with enthusiasm. "I'll definitely have to bring my boyfriend here. He'll love it."

Carlos brought a pitcher of limeade and a glass for Rikki.

He placed it on the table and left without a word. Emma could see that his silent anger bothered Rikki.

After taking another bite, Emma opened the conversation back up. "So back to the ghosts. Do you think this place is haunted?"

"I'm hoping it is," Rikki said in all seriousness. Picking up the pitcher, she refreshed Emma's glass then poured herself a glass of limeade. After taking a drink, she said, "I want you to contact the ghosts of my father and abuelito. That's my grandfather. I believe they are still here in the restaurant or at least visit it from time to time. Since Lucy and I are in a deadlock, I'm in bad need of their advice on how to change her mind."

"Tell her no."

Emma almost dropped her fork. The voice had come out of nowhere. It was male and not faint or tenuous, but bold and determined. The words were not a request, but an order.

"We're not alone," Granny cautioned Emma. "The spirit's over there." Granny pointed to the railing separating the restaurant from the street. Emma glanced over to where Granny indicated but could only see a shaky shimmering cluster of light, not a full outline of a spirit.

"You okay, Emma?" asked Rikki.

"Ah, yes," Emma answered as she quickly regained her composure. "I'm fine. I just remembered something I forgot to do before leaving home," she lied.

Emma turned her attention away from the railing and focused back on Rikki. "As I told you after yoga class, I'm not well versed in calling spirits to me. I more or less stumble upon them or connect with those that are already present." Emma stuck a piece of grilled fish into her mouth and chewed without tasting. She cast a look at the railing but still didn't see anything beyond a faint shimmer.

"I got this," Granny told Emma. The ghost left the table and floated over to where she thought the other spirit was hovering.

Across from Emma, Rikki tapped the table top with the tip of her right index finger. "I do believe my father and grandfather are here. I just need someone to connect with them so we can communicate. I'm sure they would never want their legacy sold like a sack of oranges on a highway divider."

"Tell her no," the voice said again. "She's to listen to her sister and sell it all. As soon as possible."

Granny approached the shimmer. "Don't be so rude to Emma. Show yourself if you want help."

Not wanting to rouse Rikki's suspicions, Emma tried not to focus on Granny and the spirit. She continued eating. After another couple of bites, she asked Rikki, "Why does your sister want to sell the business?"

"She says she wants to move on and do other things with her life, like be free to travel the world while she paints." Rikki scoffed at the idea. "Don't get me wrong," she quickly added, "Lucy is a pretty good artist, but I don't think she's touched her brushes in years. And believe me, she's not wired to be foot-loose and fancy free. She's been uptight and controlling since we were kids." Rikki speared a shrimp but didn't put it into her mouth. "We were both made to work here during vacations. Lucy hated it, while I thrived here. When our father started the commercial food end, he all but forced her to run it for him. She seemed happy enough to do that as long as she didn't have to participate in the restaurant end." Rikki put her fork down and spread her arms in a wide encompassing arc. Her brows were knitted in defiance. "This restaurant, this street, and its people are in my blood and I'm fiercely proud of that."

"Why don't you compromise with Lucy?" suggested Emma.

"Let her sell off the commercial food end and you keep and operate the restaurant end?"

"I did suggest that," Rikki told her, "but Lucy said the potential buyers want it all or nothing."

"She has more than one buyer lined up?"

Rikki nodded. "Lucy told me that there is another company interested and both want it all."

"Maybe you can change their minds on it," Emma said with encouragement. "Open negotiations and see if you can reach a compromise."

"According to Lucy, that's not going to happen." Rikki picked her fork back up and popped the shrimp into her mouth. When she was done chewing, she said, "That's why I need you. I know my father and grandfather are here. I need them to help me convince Lucy not to sell or to at least let me keep the restaurant end."

"No," said the unknown spirit. The shimmer came closer to the table.

"Show yourself if you want help," Granny told it again in a stern voice. "Or go away."

After a short pause, the hazy sparkles came closer and started to gain an outline. It was definitely a man. He was of compact stature and middle-aged with thick silver hair and a gray mustache. He wore clothing almost identical to the waiters in the restaurant. Emma looked at him, then at Rikki. They had the same broad face and sharp jawline.

"Do you have a photo of your father and grandfather?" Emma asked.

"So you're going to help me?" Rikki's voice swelled with hope.

"I don't know yet," Emma answered truthfully, "but it helps if I can see a photo of the people."

Rikki nodded in understanding and pulled a cell phone out of a pocket of her pants. After scrolling through some photos, she turned the phone toward Emma. "Here's a photo of my father with my mother. It was taken just before he died. I don't have one with me of my grandfather, but he and my father looked a lot alike."

Emma studied the photo, then quickly shot her eyes at the spirit standing next to the table. Granny looked over Emma's shoulder at the photo. "Yep," Granny pronounced. "That's him."

"What was your father's name?" Emma asked Rikki.

"Felix," Rikki answered. "Felix Guillermo Ricardo. His father was Paco Miguel Ricardo."

Granny looked at the spirit of Felix Ricardo. "Is Paco going to be joining us?"

Felix shook his head. "My father no longer has interest in earthly matters."

"But you do?" asked Granny.

"In this matter I do," answered Felix.

Emma listened to the ghosts' conversation while keeping her attention on the photo and Rikki. She didn't want to arouse Rikki's suspicions about the presence of any ghosts—her father or Granny. "You look a lot like your father," she said to Rikki. "Same jaw and facial bone structure."

Rikki smiled. "Yes, and Lucy looks like our mother. Her name is Elena."

While the man was compact and wiry with a broad face, his wife was taller and thickly built with a delicate face. Emma studied the photo one last time before handing the phone back to Rikki.

Rikki took the phone back. "So are you going to help me? I really need to convince Lucy to not sell our family's heritage to the highest bidder."

"No," the ghost of Felix Ricardo said again with great passion. "Tell the stubborn child to sell like her sister wants." Felix drifted in his agitation, then came to hover close to Emma, almost putting his face next to hers. Emma tried to remain still so she wouldn't put Rikki on guard. "Tell her to sell it all!" he yelled. He pounded the table with a fist. It created no sound or impact. Had he been alive, the same gesture would have caused the dishes to hop and their drinks to spill.

Emma glanced at Granny, trying to convey for her to question the spirit since Emma couldn't herself. Granny read the almost imperceptible gesture with accuracy.

"Calm down," Granny told Felix. "Getting all huffy won't help Emma help you. If Rikki wants to keep the family business, why not let her?"

Felix straightened up, his eyes flashing between Granny and Emma. "Because she'll die if she doesn't sell," he told them. "Just like I did."

CHAPTER TWO

"TELL me, Rikki," Emma said. She'd taken another couple of bites of food even though she was no longer hungry. She was stalling for time while she sorted out what Felix had just said and its implications. "How did your father die?"

Rikki pushed her plate away. "It happened here in the restaurant. In his office upstairs. He was working there alone and had a heart attack. Apparently he fell while trying to get help and hit his head hard on the edge of his desk. I found him crumpled on the floor but it was too late to do anything." Rikki looked upward, toward the canopy that protected the patio. "The coroner said it was actually the blow to his head, not the heart attack, that killed him."

"Is that true?" Granny asked Felix, but the ghost didn't respond. Instead, he drifted over to Rikki and tried to put a cloudy hand on her head to comfort her. It only slipped through her solidness.

Granny and Emma exchanged a quick look of curiosity

before Emma said to Rikki in a soft voice, "I'm so sorry for your loss, Rikki. When did this happen?"

"Not quite a year ago," Rikki answered. She didn't look at Emma when she spoke. Running a finger down the side of her glass, she stared instead at the trail it made in the condensation. When she finally looked up, her eyes were damp. "I miss him so much, Emma. We were very close. He taught me everything about running a restaurant and made me the manager of this place about three years ago. When I suggested using food trucks to reach more customers, he gave me total control over implementing the idea and was so proud when they became an instant success."

"I'm sure he's still very proud of you," Emma told her. She glanced up at the ghost, who was looking at his youngest daughter with both pride and sadness.

"Help her," the spirit said to Emma, taking his eyes off the top of Rikki's head for an instant. "Help her by convincing her to sell the place. You'll be saving her life." With a final attempt at patting Rikki's head, he disappeared.

Rikki was about to say something when a woman ran up to the railing from the street side and leaned over it toward them. "Mom told me what you're up to, Rikki," the woman said as she shook a finger at them.

The woman looked vaguely familiar to Emma, but she couldn't place her on the spot. It was Granny who put the pieces together. "Isn't that the woman from the photo?" The clue gave Emma clarity. The woman wasn't Elena Ricardo but Lucy Ricardo, Rikki's older sister. She looked exactly like her mother, with a plump lush body and pretty face, made less lovely at the moment by her anger.

Before Rikki could say anything, Lucy strode along the railing and entered the patio, brushing past Ana like a tornado hell-bent on destruction, her high heels punctuating the pavement with each riled step as she made her way to her sister's table.

"So this is the crackpot you're bringing into our family business?" Lucy said the words at Rikki, but pointed a finger at Emma as she spoke. She had long red nails, Emma noted. Acrylic nails freshly and expertly done.

"Who's she calling a crackpot?" Granny asked, approaching the table, her hands on her slim hips, a scowl on her hazy face.

Emma wanted to caution Granny but didn't dare with Lucy Ricardo watching her with an intensity ready to erupt into a blaze.

Rikki stood up, her jaw as set as her sister's. "Now hold on, Lucy. This woman is my guest, so treat her with respect."

The physical difference between the two sisters was made more obvious as they stood facing each other. The waif-like yet athletic stature of Rikki was dwarfed by Lucy's larger, rounder, and softer body. Even if Lucy had not been wearing heels, she would have been almost a head taller than Rikki. Lucy was prettier than Rikki in a more classical sense with her delicate face and thick dark hair worn in a feminine shoulder-length cut. Lucy was also dressed in an expensive and stylish designer suit in a dark rose that enhanced her brown skin and clung to her plump curves in such a way as to enhance her figure rather than point out its flaws. Based on the photo Emma had been shown, the sisters had been divided squarely between their parents in the looks department. The only physical similarities were their large brown eyes and the set of their mouths when angry.

"I don't need an introduction to any scam artist," Lucy shot back.

"Now wait a darn minute," Granny protested. The ghost moved between the two sisters and faced Lucy. "You can't talk about Emma that way."

"It's okay," Emma said, meaning the words for both Granny and the Ricardo sisters. She dabbed at her mouth with her napkin and stood up. "I'll just go."

"No," Rikki said to Emma. "Please don't. My sister has no right to insult you that way." She turned to look at Lucy, not realizing an angry ghost stood between them. "You will apologize to my guest, Lucy."

"The hell I will," the older sister said. To show she meant business, she plopped her large designer handbag down into one of the nearby chairs and looked straight at Rikki in defiance.

Hector rushed over. "What is going on here?" he asked in hushed English. He switched into Spanish for his next words, which Emma judged by his tone and look contained a sharp scolding. He glanced over at the other side of the patio, where diners were watching the face-off with interest, as if it were a show staged for their benefit.

Both sisters looked over at their customers, then at each other, neither giving in. Finally, Rikki said, "Sit down, sis. I don't know what Mom told you, but at least hear me out."

Lucy was clearly thinking about the invitation to sit. She glanced over at the curious patrons and studied Hector's glare a moment, then finally removed her handbag from the chair and sat down.

"Please, Emma," Rikki said, indicating for her to take her seat. "I'm sorry, but please stay."

"Please, Emma," said Felix Ricardo, echoing Rikki's words. He'd appeared once again, this time between his two daughters. "It's too late to help me, but not them."

"Tell us what happened to you," said Granny, floating over to him. But instead of answering, he faded away again.

Emma considered her options and decided to stay, if for no other reason than to possibly find out more about Felix and his death. She wanted to know why selling Roble Foods would save the Ricardo sisters. Had the stress of the business driven Felix to his grave, or was there more to it than that? She took her seat. Granny hovered right behind her. "Do you want me to try and find that Felix spirit again?" Granny said into Emma's ear. Without a word, Emma gave her a very slight nod and Granny disappeared.

"How about some coffee?" Rikki said to Emma and Lucy. When neither answered, Rikki asked Hector to arrange for three *cafés con leche* to be brought to the table. Hector gave the Ricardo sisters a final warning scowl and left. Rikki retook her seat.

Rikki indicated Emma. "Lucy, this is Emma Whitecastle, a famous medium and TV personality. I've asked her to help us contact Abuelito and Dad. I believe they can help us resolve our issues."

"I don't need to hear about any mumbo jumbo," Lucy insisted, keeping her voice low. She glared at Emma as she spoke to her sister. "You may have Mom fooled, but not me." She turned her face to Rikki. "This is just some cheap trick to keep me from selling Roble Foods. But it won't work." She started to say something else but stopped when Carlos appeared at the table with the three *cafés con leche*. He placed them on the table, one in front of each of them, and started to clear Emma's and Rikki's plates.

Lucy put out a hand and pointed at Carlos's bare left arm. "And this is how you run this restaurant?" she asked. "By hiring *cholos*?"

"I am not a *cholo*," answered Carlos, his jaw tight and chiseled in contained anger.

For a minute, Emma thought Carlos might fling the dishes back down on the table, but instead he took a deep breath. Emma knew that *cholo* was a term for a tough Latino male who dressed in baggy pants, wife-beater T-shirts, and flannel shirts. Usually *cholos* were also gang members.

"I'm sorry, Carlos," Rikki told the young man. "You'll have to excuse my sister's ignorance."

"I'm not the ignorant one," Lucy said to no one in particular.

With a slight nod, Rikki dismissed the young waiter. He took the dishes and left them, but as he passed Ana and Hector, who'd both been watching from a distance, he snapped something at them in Spanish. From Ana's look of surprise and Hector's scowl, Emma surmised what the young man said wasn't very pleasant. When he disappeared into the restaurant, Hector followed him. Emma wondered if Carlos had just given his notice.

"Exactly what did Mom tell you, Lucy?" Rikki asked her sister.

Instead of answering, Lucy concentrated on sipping her coffee. Emma's first impression of the older sister was that she was smug and imperious, totally opposite Rikki in more than just looks.

Lucy put down her coffee. The cup hit the saucer with a sharpness that echoed her disapproval. "Mom told me that you were trying to contact the dead in order to change my mind about selling the company."

"Not the dead, Lucy, Dad and Abuelito. It's their company. They built it from nothing and I want to hear what they have to say about the sale. I'll bet they wouldn't be too happy with you right now."

Lucy tilted her head back and laughed. "You've been hanging around Olvera Street too long, little sister. You've got *Día de los Muertos* on the brain. All those ghoulish dolls have finally twisted your thinking."

Lucy turned her attention to Emma. "Or did you put this nonsense into her head?"

"Leave Emma out of this," Rikki told her sister. "It was actually our mother who suggested I have someone help me contact either Dad and Abuelito."

"Well, Mom's nuts," pronounced Lucy. "She's always been a little off the rails, and you know that. We may not often see eye to eye, Rikki, but I've always thought of you as being stable and sensible." She picked up her coffee and took a quick sip. "Now I'm not so sure."

Looking around, Lucy caught the eye of Ana and waved her over. She said something to the young woman in Spanish, and she left and disappeared into the restaurant.

"Ordering food to go?" Rikki said, still simmering over her sister's remark. "Not good enough to eat here with your crazy sister?"

"It looked to me like you've already eaten." Lucy drained her cup and set it down, more gently this time. "Besides, I have to get back to the office. I have a company to run and a company to sell."

"You can't sell Roble Foods without my consent," protested Rikki. "And I'll never allow you to sell, especially to Crown. That big conglomerate would just suck the life out of it."

"Like I've told you, Rikki, Crown is not the only company attracted to Roble. In fact, they very recently withdrew their interest." Lucy slapped a smirk on her face. "But Fiesta Time is very interested."

"Fiesta Time?" Rikki was obviously not pleased with the news. She clenched her fists as she glared at her sister. "Selling to them would be like spitting on Dad's grave."

Carlos came out with food packed to go and placed it on the table, leaving before anyone could say anything to him. Emma was glad to see that he hadn't quit his job in a huff of anger. Maybe Hector had calmed him down. Maybe he could also work some magic with the Ricardo sisters.

Lucy stood up and fished her car keys out of her purse. "At least if we sell to Fiesta Time, Roble Foods will stay in Mexican hands."

Lucy glanced at Emma and tilted her head so that she was looking down her nose at her. "I'd appreciate it, Ms. White-castle, if you'd keep your nose out of our business. This doesn't concern you one bit." She slung her bag over her arm, picked up her plastic bag of take-out food, and started to leave.

Rikki jumped up from her seat and grabbed Lucy by both of her shoulders before she could take two steps. Spinning her around, Rikki stood on tiptoes to get nose to nose with her sister. "I won't let you do this, Lucy. I won't let you sell our family's legacy to anyone. Mom and I will continue to stonewall you."

Lucy slipped out of her sister's grasp and took a step back. A smug smile crept across her face. It was the sort of smile that raised Emma's hackles, but she kept her seat. "Today Mom's having a good day," Lucy announced. "Today she's siding with me."

Hector approached again to calm the noise down so it wouldn't bother the other diners, but Rikki held up a hand to silence him.

"Doesn't matter," Rikki said to Lucy, her jaw set and her eyes flaming. "You need my vote to make it happen, Lucy. I will block this sale, and I can keep it up forever."

"Not if I take you to court over it," Lucy said in a quick comeback. "I'll sue you to break up the company and force the sale if I have to."

The threat of fighting over the business in court only enraged the diminutive Rikki more. "Over my dead body will I let you win, Lucy. I swear that to you."

Lucy's smug smile spread wider. "Get in my way, Rikki, and you might just get your wish."

CHAPTER THREE

AFTER Lucy left, Rikki sat back down in her chair with a heavy thud. With elbows on the table, she rested her face in her hands as if the weight of her head were too much to bear. "I don't know what's gotten into Lucy. Ever since Dad died, she's been determined to divorce herself from everything our family's built."

"Why don't you buy her out?" Emma suggested. "Let her go her way and have the family retain Roble Foods. I'm sure you could find someone to run the corporate end for you."

"When she first told me she wanted to sell, I suggested that. I even suggested she leave to pursue her own dreams and retain her stock. I know several people capable of taking over the reins of the company management-wise. Tomas Mendoza is our chief financial officer. He's not on the board and isn't an owner but is Lucy's right hand and has been with the company for several years. They met while getting their MBAs. Lucy was the CFO and stepped into the CEO spot when Dad died. The board promoted Tomas to CFO. He's doing a great job and Lucy likes him. And he'll be family soon enough."

Emma leaned forward. "What do mean by soon enough? Is he dating Lucy?"

Before Rikki could answer, a tall man in an immaculate suit approached the railing. "Are you okay, Rikki?" Without waiting for her reply, he quickly went to the entrance of the restaurant and entered, nodding to Ana as he strode past her. Emma noticed that as he passed the young coed, Ana lifted her chin and her chest and gave him a beaming smile. He seemed to have a similar effect on a couple of women passing by the restaurant at that moment. Hector had just come out of the restaurant. The man stopped, said something to Hector, and shook his hand. For the first time since she arrived, Emma saw Hector flash a hint of a genuine smile. Pleasantries exchanged, the man came up to their table. "Are you okay?" he asked Rikki again, placing a hand on her shoulder. "I was told that Lucy came down here on the warpath."

Instead of answering, Rikki turned to Emma. "Emma, this is Tomas Mendoza. The person I was just telling you about." She made the introductions.

Tomas held out a hand to Emma and shook hers warmly. "Call me T.J.," he told her. "Everyone does."

Emma smiled and did a quick study of T.J. Mendoza while he turned his focus back to Rikki. He wasn't a handsome man. His nose was too crooked, his chin and eyes too small, and his face slightly pockmarked by the ghosts of acne past. Tall and slender in build with wide shoulders and good posture, he exuded take-charge masculinity and competence like a heady scent. In reaction to his presence, Emma found herself straightening her posture just like the much younger Ana had. When she caught herself doing it, she chided herself with an inward eye roll. In spite of his perfectly tailored designer suit and freshly shined shoes, Phil would have tagged T.J. a man's man.

Almost immediately, Carlos appeared and placed a *café con leche* on the table in front of T.J., who thanked the young waiter in Spanish and offered his hand. After a slight hesitation, Carlos shook it. T.J. said something else to him and the boy beamed. T.J. turned to Emma. "I was just telling Carlos how proud we are of him. He'll be off to college soon with a scholarship."

"So Rikki told me," Emma answered. She smiled at Carlos. "My daughter is about to start her final year of college. Before you know it, you'll be almost done, too. Enjoy it."

"Thank you, *señora*," Carlos said shyly, the anger of earlier either forgotten or masked. "I will." He picked up Lucy's abandoned cup and left.

T.J. slipped out of his suit jacket and draped it over the back of the chair next to Rikki. "It's pretty warm today." He sat down and lifted the cup of coffee to his nose. "But never too warm for a *café con leche*." He smiled then said to Rikki, "Is your sister gone?"

From the way he looked at Rikki, it was clear to Emma that she was the Ricardo sister T.J. was dating, not Lucy as she'd originally speculated.

"Yes," Rikki told him. "You just missed her. Did Isabel also tell you why she was upset?" She glanced at Emma and explained, "Isabel is the executive secretary at Roble Foods and one of Lucy's minions. In fact, she's Queen Lucy's top handmaiden." T.J. shot her a reproving look but she shook it off. "The Queen is what most of the office over there calls Lucy," she explained to Emma.

T.J. took a sip of his coffee before answering. "No, I was just told that Lucy got steaming mad after a call to your mother. Was the reason for her anger your plan that involves Emma here?"

"It sure was," Rikki admitted. "Mom told her about my meeting today and what I was hoping to accomplish. She told me she's selling the company even if it's over my dead body. She's threatening to take me to court to force the sale."

"Can she do that?" Emma asked T.J.

T.J. shrugged. "According to the shareholder agreement, a sale of stock can only be made to family members unless there is unanimous agreement between all stockholders. It could be structured as an asset sale instead of a stock sale, but again there's language in place that it can only be done with the approval of all board members. In this case," he explained, "the shareholders and board members are identical—Lucy, Rikki, and their mother, Elena. Without unanimous consent, any potential sale is at a stalemate. Lucy could file a lawsuit as a shareholder claiming Rikki is not living up to her fiduciary duty as an officer and board member and is causing harm to the company, but she'd also have to prove that the company is being financially damaged by Rikki's actions." He laughed. "Since Roble Foods is doing better than ever, that would be a very hard sell to the court."

"How do you feel about the sale?" Emma asked him, wondering if he'd answer truthfully in Rikki's presence.

Before he could answer, Carlos approached the table and said to Rikki, "Excuse me, but Hector said you're needed in the kitchen."

After Rikki excused herself, Emma repeated the question to T.J.

T.J. took another sip of his coffee and leaned back

casually in his chair. After a bit he answered, "Frankly, either could be good for me personally. I have a very good job that I love at Roble Foods, so if the company isn't sold, I'm good. If it is sold, Lucy would probably leave and the new owner might keep me on to run the place."

"You mean as CEO?" Emma asked.

"It's possible, depending on whether or not they intend to run it separate from their own company. Or if they merge it into their own organization, they also might make a place for me. The third possibility is that there's a sale and I'm canned. In that case, I'd leave with a very nice severance package per my employment contract, which would leave me with a cushion while I pursue other options."

"So the sale would not affect you that much?"

"Oh, it would affect me a great deal, Emma, but it wouldn't necessarily be a negative impact in either circumstance."

Emma was impressed. T.J. seemed a very pragmatic man. He'd looked at his situation from all sides with intelligence rather than emotion. But his answer still didn't tell her on which side of the fence he was sitting.

"Seeing that you're rather neutral when it comes to yourself, as a businessman which way would you go?" she asked.

"Great question, Emma." T.J. took another sip of his coffee and leaned forward. "But I'm not going to answer you as a businessman, but as a man in love." He gave her a shy smile. "Rikki, like her father, loves this company. It's her life. I don't want it sold because it would break her heart. I've tried to influence Lucy to sell off just her part since she's so set on getting rid of it, but she's not budging. She's determined to remove Roble Foods from all their lives."

"Do you know why?"

He shrugged and loosened his tie a bit. "She claims it's because it's stolen so much from them—time, their father, her dreams. Lucy never wanted to be a business executive, even though she's quite good at it. Her father pretty much forced her to be a business major and get her MBA and take her place running the company. He did the same with Rikki but funneled her into the restaurant end. Rikki loves and thrives in the business. Lucy despises it."

"Rikki said something about Lucy being an artist."

"Yes," he answered simply. "She loves to paint and is quite good. She wants to do it full-time, not as a hobby when she has time, as she does now. She thinks of herself as a modern Frida Kahlo. Lucy has made it clear that as soon as the company is sold, she plans to travel the world painting and sketching."

"It still doesn't make sense," Emma said. "Why get rid of the company when she can just sell off her stake in it and do what she wants?"

"Spite, Emma. After their father died, Lucy's resentment of Roble Foods became so deep she won't even entertain that option. It's like a big ugly bleeding gash to her gut. I've known Lucy Ricardo a long time, longer than I've known Rikki. She's always been very spiteful and vengeful. Even in school when someone got in the way of something she wanted, she'd never find a way around them. She'd roll right over them to reach her goal, whether it be a plum assignment or project, a business deal, or even the affections of a man."

"Did you two ever date in school?" Emma asked.

He nodded. "For a very short time, but we soon discovered we were much better friends than lovers. At Roble I often act as a buffer between Lucy and the rest of the company, and that's okay, but in my personal life I prefer the sweeter nature of Rikki. She's still a sound and tough busi-nesswoman, but Rikki also has a good heart and treats employees with kindness and respect."

Emma thought about the way the two sisters handled the situation with Carlos's tattoos. Even though the waiter didn't care for Rikki's discipline on the matter, he took it much easier than Lucy's harsh accusing words.

Emma turned her cup around on its saucer as she readied herself to ask the next question. "And what do you think of Rikki asking me to assist her?"

A slow, embarrassed smile crept across his face and he looked toward the entrance to the dining room, as if hoping Rikki would return at that very minute and save him from answering. Almost a full minute later, he turned back to Emma. "After she told me her plan, I watched a couple of old episodes of your show online. Very impressive. I like that you often present both the paranormal and scientific sides of your topics and handle them with an even hand."

"Thank you," Emma answered. "My goal isn't to force the paranormal issue, but to let viewers make up their own minds. There's still a lot I'm learning and a lot I don't believe in myself."

T.J. smoothed down his tie and leaned closer to Emma before speaking. "But you do believe that people can com-municate with the spirits of the dead?"

"Yes," Emma answered with conviction. "I do and I have done it myself." She wanted to add that she does it every day, but she wasn't ready to disclose that she was that close to the spirit world, specifically that she was besties with a ghost. "When it first happened to me," she continued, "I didn't believe it, but over time there has been too much evidence and too many interactions with the other side for me to ignore."

T.J. nodded as he digested her words. "You know that Mexicans hold a deep belief in the spirits of their dead?"

"Yes," Emma answered. "I know that *Día de los Muertos* is a big celebration in Mexico and even here in the Latino community."

He ran a hand over his chin. "*Día de los Muertos* was celebrated long before Christianity came to the people of Mexico. In fact, the observance can be traced back almost three thousand years. We celebrate and remember our dead on those days and many believe the dead return to earth during that time."

"Do you believe the dead return on those days?" Emma asked, her eyes meeting his.

T.J. pointed to himself and chuckled. "Me? No. I believe the dead are dead. But Rikki does believe the spirits of our loved ones can walk among us. She's hoping you can call out the spirits of her father and grandfather now and not wait until the end of October for *Día de los Muertos* for them to make an appearance. Can you do that?"

Emma thought about the ghost of Felix Ricardo already making his appearance. "I have already felt the presence of Felix Ricardo today," she admitted. "But I haven't told Rikki."

Coming to attention in his chair, T.J. Mendoza stared at Emma. "You've already made contact with Felix?" His question was said in jest. "That's fast work." His dark eyes studied her and Emma knew he was looking for deception.

"I said I've already felt his presence," she clarified, not taking her eyes off his. "But for argument's sake, what if Felix does communicate with me and tells me to advise Rikki to sell Roble Foods?"

T.J. broke eye contact with Emma and again relaxed in his

chair. After casually draining his coffee, he put the cup down and leaned again across the table. This time his eyes held anger and a fierceness she'd not seen before. "So that's your game, Emma Whitecastle? You will tell Rikki whatever the highest bidder tells you to tell her? Did Lucy already get to you with a nice fat wad of cash to say that to Rikki?" He shook a finger in the air. "It would be so like Lucy to do something like that. Elena probably told her about you right after Rikki set up today's meeting, giving her time to make contact."

Emma bristled. She was used to people not believing in her gift, but being called a swindler along with a fraud was too much. "I beg your pardon," she said to T.J. in a voice laced with ice. "You may or may not believe in the living being able to communicate with the dead, but I will not tolerate you claiming I'm for sale."

He flashed her a slick grin. "I checked you out, Emma, and not just your show. You used to be married to Grant White-castle, that ass on TV. He and that sleazy talk show of his make a mockery of decent people by sensationalizing their problems and tossing them into the public feeding frenzy." He shook his head in disgust. "You're no different." He paused. "So what did Lucy pay you or offer to pay you?" he asked. "I'll double it for you to tell Rikki what she wants to hear."

Emma threw her napkin down on the table and stood up just as Rikki came back out onto the patio. "I'm sorry, Emma, but we had an emergency with a supplier. Do you have to leave?"

Emma gave T.J. one last frozen stare before turning to Rikki. "Yes, I'm afraid I must run along." She picked up her purse and her packages.

T.J. got to his feet. "It was interesting meeting you, Emma." He didn't offer his hand and Emma didn't offer hers. Rikki didn't seem to notice the coldness between the two.

As Emma walked toward the exit, she thanked Rikki for the meal.

"Can we set up another time to meet?" Rikki asked with eagerness. "I'd really like to try and reach my father and grandfather as soon as possible."

Emma did her best to push T.J. Mendoza and his accusations out of her mind and concentrate on Rikki and what Felix had told her. Felix had said Rikki was in danger if she didn't consent to the sale of the restaurant. He'd also hinted that his own death was suspicious. If Rikki Ricardo was in danger, Emma wanted to help her, or at least find out why Felix had said such a thing. But she certainly didn't want to be accused of being a fraud with a price tag. She didn't need the headache.

"I have a very busy schedule coming up," she told Rikki. "So I may not be able to do it as soon as you might like. Let me think on it."

She could tell Rikki was disappointed by her answer, but nodded with understanding just the same. Emma glanced back at the table. T.J. was still standing, watching the two of them. If she did meet again with Rikki, she'd want to do it without his interference, but she also doubted he'd allow that. He was on alert, ready to protect Rikki, and certainly not ready to accept any communication from Felix Ricardo as being real.

· CHAPTER FOUR ·

"I SHOULD punch that guy in the nose," Phil Bowers said after Emma told him about her meeting with the Ricardos and T.J. Mendoza. "How dare he imply that you'd make crap up for the highest bidder."

They were cuddled on the sofa in the den of Emma's parents' stately home in Pasadena. Emma split her time between this house and the home she'd built in Julian, which stood on Granny's old homestead across from Phil's ranch. Phil had had a meeting in Los Angeles that day and was staying the night in Pasadena before heading back down to San Diego. Like Emma, he also had two homes—the ranch, which he shared with his aunt and uncle, who raised him after his parents died, and a stylish condo overlooking the ocean in San Diego near his law practice. Phil had taken Emma and her parents out for dinner. The Millers had gone up to bed after returning home while Phil and Emma had settled in on the sofa to watch the news and enjoy a glass of wine.

"I'd like to punch his lights out myself," said Granny, who was hovering nearby. "It's a good thing I wasn't there."

After Emma relayed Granny's comment and pointed Phil's attention in the right direction, Phil said to the ghost with a grin, "And what would you have done, Granny, passed through him a dozen times? That would show him."

The tiny ghost put her hands on her hips and moved closer to Phil. "No need to get uppity about what I can and can't do, cowboy. It's the intent that's important."

Emma laughed and acted as translator. Finished with that chore, she turned back to the ghost. "Did you have any luck finding Felix Ricardo, Granny?"

"No, I didn't, but I'll keep trying. So," said the ghost, nearly bouncing with excitement, "does that mean we're on the case?"

"There is no case, Granny," Emma told her.

"Yeah, yeah, yeah," said Granny with sarcasm. "You say that every time and every time there turns out to be a case."

"I don't want to get mixed up with that crazy family and all their intrigue," Emma said. "I barely know Rikki, and I didn't like being called a cheat and a fraud."

"The cheat I understand," said Phil, "and I object to that, too, but you get called a fraud all the time, Emma. It comes with doing what you do, and you've never seemed to mind it before."

"True," Emma said, "and I really don't. I understand that communicating with spirits is difficult for people to understand, and I can hold my own against the nasty remarks. It's not that different from when I was married to Grant and our lives, both the truth and lies, were splashed across the tabloids. It's just that except for Rikki, I don't really like these people, especially Lucy. I understand T.J. wanting to protect Rikki, but Lucy was just plain nasty and combative."

"People can get that way when they're forced to follow someone else's dream and not their own," Phil explained. "If she really wants to make her mark on the art world and feels she can't as long as she's connected to the family business, I can see why she is so resentful of Rikki's standoff. Although I don't understand Lucy's refusal to simply cash out and leave it behind, especially if the rest of the family is willing to let her do that."

"That would seem the simplest solution and a win-win for everyone," Emma agreed. "It's like Lucy won't be happy until she destroys the business."

Granny paced the den. "What about the way Felix dropped that bomb about his own death and that the same might happen to Rikki if she didn't sell?"

"I didn't like that, Granny," Emma said. "Not one bit." She took a drink of wine and sorted through her thoughts like sorting dirty clothes from clean. "It sure sounds as if Felix didn't die from his fall during his heart attack like everyone thinks. And it's the only thing keeping me from deciding to ignore the Ricardos altogether. I want to know if the threat to Rikki's life is real. If it is, maybe we can stop it or at least warn her."

"Now that's the tough-minded Emma I know." Phil pulled her tighter to him. "Just so long as you don't end up in danger."

Emma looked at Phil like he'd lost his mind. "Are you going soft in the head, Phil? Every time I look into one of these situations, I end up in danger. And often you do, too. Or did you forget about those bullets flying around just a few months ago?"

"It keeps the spice in the relationship," he said and kissed her with a loud smacking noise. "I just don't want you getting yourself in danger without anyone to watch your back."

"I've got her back!" announced Granny.

"Granny's got my back," repeated Emma to Phil.

Phil turned his eyes to the place he last knew Granny was standing. "And I appreciate that, Granny." Emma pointed several feet away, by the fireplace, and Phil adjusted his focus. "I really do. But you can't physically protect her like I can."

"I need you both," said Emma, quickly seeing that Granny was preparing to argue with Phil. "Granny's my eyes and ears and, Phil, you're my muscle. What more does a girl need?"

"I think," said Granny, somewhat mollified by Emma's words, "that you should go back to the restaurant and investigate the place where Felix died. I think he hangs out there sometimes. Didn't Rikki say she often feels his presence?"

After Emma filled in Phil, she said, "Yes, Granny. That's a great idea. Maybe I just need to make one more contact with Felix to determine the severity of the situation. If I believe Rikki to be in real danger, I'll warn her."

Emma got up from the sofa and retrieved her purse from the kitchen, where she'd dropped it. When she returned to the den, she was holding her cell phone and one of the packages from Olvera Street. She handed the bag to Phil. "Here, I bought you something." While Phil investigated the contents of the bag, Emma started texting someone.

"Who are you texting?" asked Granny.

"Rikki," Emma answered. "I'm seeing if I can stop by tomorrow early in the day before the restaurant opens and gets busy. She probably won't see this tonight, but at least she might in the morning."

Phil's deep laughter broke the quiet. In his hands were the bride and groom Day of the Dead dolls. "Is this your way of saying it's time we take the plunge?"

Emma gave him a quick kiss. "Consider it an informal proposal."

"Not a formal one?" he asked with a grin.

"I'll leave that up to you," she said, looking at him with the slyness of a fox. "I'm just saying I wouldn't be opposed to it."

"Well, it's about time!" Granny said with enthusiasm.

Emma's phone vibrated. "It's Rikki," she said with surprise, looking down at the message. "She said for me to stop by Restaurante Roble tomorrow at ten and that she's excited to see me again." Emma looked up. "Maybe I should tell her to be alone and not tell T.J. or Lucy about the meeting."

Phil put the Day of the Dead dolls down on the coffee table and shook his head. "I doubt she'll say anything to her sister, but you tell her to leave T.J. out of it and it will sound suspicious, like you are definitely trying to flim-flam her. I'm sure T.J. has already warned her about you."

"I agree with Phil," said Granny. "Best to act normal. If that guy's there, we can take him." The ghost bounced from foot to foot with the raised fists of a boxer.

After Emma translated, Phil said, "I'm coming with you tomorrow." When Emma started to protest, he added, "I'd already cleared my calendar for tomorrow in case my meeting today needed more time. And the rest of the week I was planning to spend in Julian, so I'm free to stay here and help. I'd also love to see Olvera Street again. I haven't been there in decades."

"Yeah," agreed Granny. "I can be the brains and Phil the brawn."

Emma knew better than to argue when Phil and Granny joined forces. Quickly she responded to Rikki's text, saying she'd be at the restaurant at ten in the morning. She left off any mention of T.J. Mendoza or Lucy Ricardo. A minute later, Rikki confirmed the meeting.

"Okay, that's done." Emma picked up her wineglass from the coffee table and took a drink. "Tomorrow we'll try to contact Felix, see what he has to say, and convey the information to Rikki. Then we're out of there."

"What?" asked Phil with disappointment. "We're not staying for lunch?"

"Okay," Emma agreed. "We'll have lunch and *then* we're out of there."

Granny floated over and pointed to the figures on the coffee table. "Just make sure you two don't end up looking like those guys."

Emma looked down at the skeletons dressed in wedding finery but did not relay Granny's words to Phil.

· CHAPTER FIVE ·

"WHEN we're done here," said Phil as they made their way from the parking lot to Olvera Street, "let's play tourist and check out Union Station across the way. As often as I've taken the train up from San Diego, I've never taken the time to look around the station, and it's a beauty. In fact, if we don't feel like Mexican food or lingering at Roble, there's supposed to be a great restaurant inside the station called Traxx."

"You're on," Emma told him, linking her arm through his as they walked. "After all, who knows what will happen today, but Rikki is going to be disappointed either way."

Phil glanced at her. "How do you figure?"

"If I don't contact Felix," Emma explained, "she'll be disappointed. If I do and tell her he wants her to sell the family business, she won't be happy either. It's a no-win in either circumstance."

"Good point." Phil pulled his cell phone out of his pocket.

"Who are you calling?" she asked.

"I'm looking up Traxx. With those odds, we might as well make lunch reservations with them."

Emma laughed. "Put the phone away and let's just wing it. You know how spirits have a way of surprising us."

"Speaking of surprising spirits, where's Granny this morning?"

"She went on ahead to the restaurant to see if Felix is there."

Unlike the day before, Olvera Street was very quiet. Most of the kiosks and storefronts were still closed, locked, and shuttered, especially the smaller ones. A few people milled about getting their businesses ready for the day. Some were sweeping the street, others setting up displays. The quiet held a peaceful old world charm that belied the fact that the bustling downtown of Los Angeles was just a short distance away.

"Here we are," announced Emma when they reached the restaurant.

Restaurante Roble, like many other businesses, was getting ready to start its day. Carlos and another young man, both dressed in their waiter's slacks but wearing white T-shirts, were rolling up security gates and cleaning off the patio tables. Nearby a stack of crisp white tablecloths waited to be placed on the tables along with the usual condiments.

Emma approached Carlos. "Hi, Carlos. I was here yesterday."

He glanced at her, then Phil. Without stopping his work, he said, "I remember."

"I have an appointment this morning with Rikki but I'm a few minutes early. Is she here yet?"

"Yeah, she's inside." Carlos stopped working. "Do you want me to go get her?"

"No, that's okay," Emma told him. "If it's all right, I'll go inside and find her myself."

With a shrug that said he didn't care either way, Carlos went back to his work. "Doesn't matter to me. She's probably with Chef Lupe." In Spanish he said something to the guy working with him, who studied Emma before giving her a friendly nod and tight-lipped smile from under a thin wispy mustache. He seemed around the same age as Carlos.

Once inside the restaurant, Emma whispered to Phil, "What did Carlos just say to that guy? I caught Lucy's name."

Phil leaned close and whispered back, "He called you the nice lady who made Lucy go loco yesterday."

"That's all he said? Seemed like more."

"Well," continued Phil, suppressing a grin, "let's just say he doesn't like Lucy very much and leave it at that."

Emma nudged Phil. "Something tells me you're going to be very useful today."

Phil grinned at her. "You mean I'm not most other days?"

"It's about time you two got here." Granny popped up in front of them. "Felix was upstairs in his office."

"Was?" asked Emma. "He's not still there?"

Granny shook her head. "He was losing energy, so I told him to go recharge and come back in a few minutes or so if he wants to help his daughter. He said he would."

"Thank you, Granny," Emma said to her. She turned to Phil. "Granny says Felix was here, but agreed to return shortly to help."

Inside, the restaurant was neat and compact. The décor was stylish and modern Mexican. Soft blues, greens, and pinks had been artfully used, along with artistic tiles that lightened up the heaviness of the dark wood tables and chairs.

"Emma!" called Rikki. She waved from the far end of the wide hallway where she stood with a man in a white chef's coat, indicating for them to approach. When Emma and Phil reached them, Emma realized it was a woman, not a man, with Rikki. She introduced Phil. Rikki, in turn, introduced them to Executive Chef Lupe Lopez. "This is the person who makes and guides our magic here."

Chef Lopez was a squat woman in her mid to late thirties, thick and brown as a redwood, with close-cropped spiked dark hair and a round serious face. Her voice held a trace of an accent.

"I greatly enjoyed the meal you made for me yesterday," Emma told the chef with a smile. "I had the grilled citrus shrimp and fish. The seasoning was perfect and the cactus delicious."

Chef Lopez gave her a slight bow. "Thank you. That's an updated version of what had been a long-time staple at Roble."

"I brought Chef Lopez in about a year ago," Rikki explained. "Right after my father died. I wanted her to freshen up the menu, adding healthier modern options along with the traditional dishes. She's done a great job. She also consults on the food truck menus, which is why they continue to be so successful."

"Mexican food is so much more than beef tacos and enchiladas," the chef said, her thick brows knitting to let them know how serious she was about the subject. Before anyone could answer, the chef excused herself. "I must get back to work and make sure everything is ready for the day."

After Chef Lopez left, Emma said to Rikki, "I love the décor. Is that also your idea of blending modern Mexico with tradition?"

Rikki nodded with pride. "Yes. The tables and chairs have been here forever and are as solid as rock. The walls used to be a dark neutral with lots of cheap Mexican ornaments hung on them. You know, like a lot of the stuff you see outside in the stalls." She took a deep breath. "The plans for the redecorating were approved before my father died. I'm sorry he didn't see how well it turned out." She glanced around the tidy room, then looked at Emma and Phil. "After he died, I almost didn't go through with the renovation, but Lucy encouraged me. Now I realize it was just to make the restaurant more attractive to a buyer."

"Chef Lopez didn't work for your father?" asked Phil.

Rikki shook her head. "Not here in the restaurant. She'd been brought in originally only as a consultant on the food trucks since we already had an executive chef. But Dad and I had hoped she would one day take over the restaurant kitchen, too. Raul Solano had been our executive chef for decades and Dad was encouraging him to retire. My father understood that we had to modernize both in decor and food to continue to grow. When Dad died, Chef Raul retired and that opened the way for Lupe."

Rikki started to lead the way back to the dining room. "Let's sit down. Would you like some coffee or something?"

"What I'd like," answered Emma, "is to see your father's office. Would that be okay?"

"Sure," said Rikki. "Follow me."

Rikki took them down the hallway and past the customer restrooms until they reached a wide back staircase. Across from the staircase was a huge pantry, its large door open to reveal shelf after shelf of food goods and gleaming refrigerators. They followed Rikki up the stairs. Upstairs was as large as the restaurant but divided into rooms. Rikki gave Emma and Phil a quick tour. "This is where we store paper goods and extra linens," she explained, tapping on a closed door. She opened the door across from it. "Here is the employee bathroom and lockers for their personal items. This was once a large private residence and these rooms were the bedrooms and original bathroom." She went down a hall. "This is Hector Gonzales's office." She opened the door to another large room with a large oak desk, a few chairs, some file cabinets, a bulletin board covered with pinned papers, and a massive whiteboard with a schedule printed neatly across it. "I shared this space with him until I moved into my father's office."

At the end of the hall was an open door. Rikki took them through it. It was an office just a little bit larger than Hector's but less cluttered and configured differently. Shaped in a long narrow rectangle, it ran across the front of the building with two windows that looked out onto Olvera Street. The windows were open, and the sound of nearby traffic from the busy cross street could be clearly heard.

"You must have redone these rooms when you did downstairs," noted Emma. "They're all fresh and cheerful. Even the bath and locker room."

"Yes," Rikki said. "We weren't going to spend the money to do it, but since Dad died here, I knew I couldn't work in this office unless I fixed it up. Then it seemed foolish not to give the whole place a fresh coat of paint. I think it helped morale, too. My father was loved by his employees and the redecorating and painting gave closure to the tragedy for many of them." Rikki tapped the desk. Unlike the rest of the furnishings, it was a sleek modern design on which sat a laptop and scattered papers. Behind it was a lovely painting of Olvera Street. "I also moved my father's big desk into Hector's office. I couldn't bear using it knowing he'd died hitting his head on it. Hector loves the desk. I think it keeps my father's memory close for him."

Emma took a closer look at the painting. "Was this done by your sister? It's really good."

"Yes, it was," answered Rikki. "She did it years ago. I think she might have been in high school. It has always hung in this room but used to be between the windows. When Dad died, I asked Lucy if she wanted it back and she told me she didn't care if I burned it."

Phil went to the window and looked out, then turned to Rikki. "Emma told me you're the manager and Hector the assistant manager. How do you divide duties?"

"I do all the accounting and books and special menu planning with the chef," Rikki explained. She walked over to a large brown leather sofa against the far wall and picked up clothing carefully draped over one side. She took the clothing and hung it on a coat hook attached to a nearby door, which Emma guessed to be a closet. "My uniform for today," she explained. "Though I'd much rather wear these," she said, indicating the yoga pants and T-shirt she was currently wearing. She pointed at the sofa. "Please have a seat." Emma and Phil sat side by side on the sofa while Granny floated in and out of the room looking for signs of Felix's return.

Rikki rolled her ergonomic desk chair near Emma and sat down. "Hector oversees the employees except for the kitchen staff; that's done by Lupe. He also orders all supplies except for food and produce, also done by Lupe. Hector and I share front-of-the-house management during operating hours so that neither of us has to be here all day, every day. Hector's off on Wednesdays, like today. I'm usually off on Mondays. During our slow season, we try to give each other whole weekends off."

"But this is your busy season, right?" asked Phil.

Rikki nodded. "Summers and school vacations bring in more tourists. Several times during the year there are special events here on Olvera Street and no one gets a day off until they are over."

Emma put her bag down on the floor and leaned toward Rikki, gently patting her arm. "I know it might be difficult, but can you tell me about the day your father died?"

Rikki took a deep breath. "It was a Saturday in June, Father's Day weekend," she began, speaking slowly and swallowing a few times. "We were slammed with customers. Every table in the place was filled and people were waiting outside. Even though it was a busy time of year, Dad had given Hector the whole weekend off so he could go visit his oldest daughter, who had just had a baby. I was downstairs working with the staff. We were so busy I didn't even notice that I hadn't seen Dad in a while. When the rush was finally over, I went back upstairs and found him on the floor." She pointed to a spot near one of the windows. "Right there. I called 911, but he was already gone."

"You said yesterday he hit his head on the edge of the desk. That's quite a distance from the desk," Emma said, noting that Rikki's desk was set at an angle between the wall opposite the sofa and the far window.

"Dad's desk was positioned between the windows and took up a lot of the floor space in here. By putting my desk in this position, I get to look out the windows and open up more of the room."

Phil stood up and went to stand where Rikki had said she found her father. "So his desk was here?" He spread his arms to indicate the location. Rikki nodded. "Emma told me he had a heart attack and fell, striking his head on the corner of the desk, which would have been here?"

He looked to Rikki for confirmation and she nodded. "Yes," she told him. "He hit the rear right corner. It was quite sharp and struck him hard on his left temple and must have knocked him unconscious." She took a deep breath. "The coroner said he died from the blow, not the heart attack."

"Do you know if he was standing or sitting when he fell?" Phil asked.

Rikki gave it some thought before answering. "The police thought that when he started feeling unwell, he stood up and tried to go for help. That's when he fell and hit his head." She turned to Emma. "Why all the questions?"

"When connecting with a spirit," Emma explained, stretching the truth a bit, "it helps if we know more about the person's death." She turned to Phil and gave him a discreet look of warning, knowing he was playing detective. Emma didn't want to make Rikki uncomfortable before they had a chance to approach the subject of Felix's ghost.

"And no one heard his fall or came upstairs, not even any of the staff?" Phil continued, even though he gave Emma a nod of acknowledgment. "Even with the staff locker room right down the hall?"

"Like I said," Rikki answered, "we were inundated with customers. It was between shift changes and everyone was downstairs pitching in."

"Except for Felix?" Emma asked.

"Dad was downstairs earlier helping, then he got a call on his cell and took it upstairs, where it was quieter. That's the last anyone noticed him."

"Do you know who the call was from?" Emma asked, then added, "I'm sorry to pry, but I'm curious."

"No problem," said Rikki. "It was from my mother, but she said the call only lasted about ten to fifteen minutes.

Dad was gone close to two hours before I went looking for him."

"Tell her," came a voice that was more like a sound carried on a breeze.

Emma slowly turned her heard toward the sound but saw nothing.

"Tell her what I told you yesterday," the ghost of Felix Ricardo insisted. "Tell her to sell and let's be done with this."

CHAPTER SIX

THE spirit finally started coming into view. No, not one spirit, but two. Emma's first thought was that Felix had brought his father, Paco Ricardo, with him. But as the images of the two ghosts came more into view, she realized Granny was the second image.

"Look who I found floating about," Granny said with a pleased grin. "He was wandering around outside and seemed a bit confused."

Felix looked around the room, taking in each living person in turn, his eyes resting the longest on his daughter, who was watching Emma with interest.

"I was not confused," Felix told Granny, nearly snapping at her.

"All right. All right," snapped Granny back. "Don't get your *pantalones* in a bunch."

Felix did not take his eyes from Rikki's face as he explained, "Almost every morning before we opened, I would stroll Olvera Street greeting longtime friends and wishing them a good day." He turned to look at Emma, twitching his mustache before speaking. "I still do it most mornings. I will continue to do it long after this place is sold, even if they cannot see or hear me. I grew up with many of these people and have known their families for years. Like this restaurant, many of the businesses on this street have been here for generations."

"What are you looking at?" Rikki asked Emma. She turned to look at the doorway, but saw nothing.

"I thought I heard something," Emma semi-lied, not quite ready to tell Rikki the truth.

Phil was also looking toward the doorway. He couldn't see Felix or Granny, but knew from being with Emma and from the cool breeze coming from that direction that at least one spirit had entered the room. He moved back against the wall, by one of the windows, and leaned against it to watch. The windows were open, letting in the early morning breeze before the heat of the day took over and they were closed to allow for the use of the AC. Granny floated up to him. "Look, Phil, Felix has a mustache just like yours, but he's got a lot more hair on his head." Sensing a spirit near him, Phil looked to Emma for some sign of explanation.

Emma suppressed a smile but moved her gaze back to Felix. She'd tell Phil what Granny said later when they were alone. Or maybe not.

"My father's here, isn't he?" asked Rikki, getting up from her chair. She pointed to the doorway. "And he's there, where you're looking."

"Sit down, Rikki," Emma told her gently. When Rikki hesitated, Emma added, "Please."

Seeing Rikki's hesitation, Phil added, "Listen to Emma

if you want to communicate with your father, Rikki. Ghosts can be skittish. She knows what she's doing."

Looking back and forth between Emma and Phil, Rikki finally relented and sat back down, but she swiveled her chair so that it faced the doorway. She pointed at it. "He's there, isn't he?"

Emma took a deep breath, then admitted, "Yes, he is."

Rikki leaned forward, trying hard to see what she could not. "Daddy," she said to the doorway. "Is that really you?"

"Sí, mi hija." Felix's face softened and he came closer. Like the day before, he tried to touch her head and face but his hand only went through her. *"Aiiii,"* he said to Emma, his face drooping with sadness. "It is so frustrating to not be able to touch my baby girl." Emma smiled at him with understanding, knowing how much Granny often wanted to hug family members and couldn't.

Rikki turned to Emma. "I feel like he's right here." She gestured close to herself with her hands. "I mean, like right *here* next to me."

"That's because he is, Rikki," Emma told her. "He's to your right."

Rikki reached out a hand and touched the air to her right, then pulled her hand back as if she'd touched something hot. She swiveled to face Emma. "Wait a minute," she said, her face turning hard in a flash. "You're not playing me, are you?"

Emma shook her head slowly from side to side. "No, Rikki, I'm not."

"T.J. told me last night to stay away from you. He said you're a sleazy fake who's been paid off by my sister."

Granny moved forward, her face pinched with anger, her hands on her hips. "Don't you go calling my Emma a fake or sleazy."

Phil straightened and stepped forward, too, standing next to Granny, although he didn't realize it. "I can assure you that Emma is neither a fake nor sleazy," he said to Rikki in a firm tone.

Emma held up a hand toward Phil and Granny to stop them, then said to Rikki in a calm even voice, "T.J. is wrong. I have not been paid off or in any way compensated or bribed to be here today or to tell you certain things. You asked for my help and I'm here to give it."

"If this T.J. is so concerned," asked Phil, "why isn't he here today for this meeting?"

Rikki grasped the arms of her chair hard with her hands and looked down at the floor. "Because I didn't tell him about it." She looked up, first at Phil, then at Emma. "I knew he was upset after meeting you but we didn't discuss it after you left because we both had work to do. He told me at dinner that he thought you'd been paid off by Lucy to convince me to sell. He even confronted her about it when he got back to the office."

"After witnessing your sister's temper yesterday," Emma said, "I'm sure that didn't go over well."

Rikki shook her head. "To say the least. Isabel called me to say they were fighting about it right in the office, yelling and everything."

"Isabel is the secretary at Roble Foods?" Emma asked, remembering the name from the day before.

"Yes," Rikki confirmed with a nod. "She said even with the door of Lucy's office closed, people could hear the fight. She said T.J. then stormed out. At first Isabel thought he might have quit or Lucy fired him. She wasn't sure, but thought I should know." A pause, then a confused smile. "It felt almost like Isabel was relishing telling me this. She usually doesn't even acknowledge my existence."

"Did either of those things happen?" asked Phil.

"No, but after Isabel's call I half expected Lucy to call me and give me an earful, but she didn't. A bit later I called her both at the office and on her cell, but never reached her. I left several voice mails for her to call me, but she never did. I couldn't reach T.J. either until almost dinnertime. He said he left the office and went for a drive to cool down."

"You didn't work the dinner shift here?" Phil asked.

"Olvera Street isn't open late so neither are we except on Friday and Saturday nights, which is nice. It gives us and our staff a reasonable family life. Still, I left earlier than usual and went home to wait for T.J. Hector was here to cover things until closing." Rikki looked at Emma and gave her a sad half smile. "T.J. and Lucy haven't agreed on this sale thing, but there is one thing they do agree on and that's that I'm a stupid idiot for bringing you into it."

"Aren't we getting way off track here?" asked Granny, moving to stand near Emma. Granny cocked a thumb in the direction of Felix Ricardo. "He's looking kind of hazy again. He might have used up all his juice taking that stroll down memory lane this morning."

One look at the other ghost and Emma knew Granny was right about Felix starting to fade. His shoulders sagged and his mustache drooped. His authoritative posture of before had dissolved into sadness. Maybe it was from low energy, as Granny suggested, or maybe it was despair upon hearing how his daughters were battling. Next Emma looked at Phil. He shrugged, letting her know the next step was her call.

"Rikki," Emma began as she turned to face her. "The last thing I want is to be caught in the middle of a family drama, but forgetting for a minute about Lucy and T.J., tell me, what do you believe?"

Rikki turned her face toward the spot where Emma had said the spirit of Felix stood. She stared at it almost a full minute before saying, "I don't know what I believe, but I know what I want to believe." She held out a hand, palm outward, to the empty space. Felix placed his palm against hers and smiled, although neither could feel the other. "But I have no way to prove it," Rikki said with sadness.

Emma shifted in her seat, then said, "Every morning your father walked up and down Olvera Street greeting his friends and neighbors, isn't that true?"

With knitted brows, Rikki turned to Emma. "That's right, but how would you know that?" Before Emma could say, Rikki added, "But that's something Lucy could have told you. Anyone who knew my father knew he did that."

"He still does it, Rikki," Emma told her. "Even in death, he still checks on his friends on the street."

Rikki brightened considerably, then her face fell just as fast. "It is something he might do, but you saying it doesn't mean anything." She rested her elbows on her knees and leaned forward until her hands held her chin. The position made her look like a young girl instead of an adult business owner responsible for employees.

"She always sat like that when she was trying to figure something out," Felix told Emma with a small smile, even as he started to fade more.

"You father just said you always sit like that when you need to think deeply about something," Emma told Rikki.

Rikki snapped her head up and stared at Emma, then turned away. "Easy guess about a habit."

Felix floated closer to Emma. "Ask her about the time she ran away," he said. "She was about eight and had a big fight with Lucy over something."

"Felix just told me that you had a fight with Lucy when you were eight and ran away," Emma relayed.

Rikki's gaze returned to Emma's face, eyes large with wonder.

"Mrs. Chan who ran the dry cleaners in Chinatown just a few blocks from here," continued Felix, "found her hiding in the back of her store, soaked and cold from the rain. We took our cleaning there for years, so she knew Rikki and called me."

Emma relayed the story. Rikki's brown eyes got rounder and larger with each word.

"I took her for sweet and sour soup to warm her up and to talk." Felix moved closer to his daughter. "Ricarda loved sweet and sour soup, even as a child. She begged me not to tell her mother or Lucy, and I never did. I never told anyone."

Emma nodded to the ghost, then looked at Rikki. "After picking you up from Mrs. Chan's, your father took you out for sweet and sour soup and promised he'd never tell anyone. He says he never has."

Rikki broke down and began sobbing softly. "Oh, Daddy. You are here."

Granny sniffed and wiped a hand across her tearless face. "Poor child."

"I must go," Felix said to Rikki. "But I'll come back. I promise."

Just before fading into nothing, the ghost turned to Emma and pointed a filmy finger at her. "This doesn't change anything," he said with determination. "Tell her to sell. Tell her to take the money and start a newer and better restaurant somewhere else."

"Your father had to go," Emma told Rikki as soon as Felix was gone.

"No!" Rikki looked up, her face puffy.

"Don't worry," Emma told her. "He may be back, though I don't know when. Ghosts can only materialize a short time before they need to go away and recharge their energy."

"Some ghosts," clarified Granny. "I've got this sticking around thing down pretty good, if I say so myself."

Emma smiled inwardly at Granny's comment. Over time, Granny had learned to stick her earthly presence longer. Sometimes it was a good thing and sometimes annoying. Returning her focus to Rikki, Emma said something that was weighing on her mind more than ghosts and their energy. "Rikki, I have a serious question I need you to consider and answer truthfully."

Rikki got up from her chair and covered the distance to her desk in just a couple of steps. She grabbed a couple of tissues from a box on the corner and mopped her face with them. After blowing her nose, she moved behind the desk and tossed the used tissues in a small wastepaper basket. Several minutes of silence passed before she turned back to Emma, leaned against the edge of her desk, and said with a determined nod, "Fire away. I'll be truthful, even if it kills me."

Emma looked at Phil. He gave her a look of encouragement. Granny floated over to stand next to Rikki. Looking at Emma, Granny said, "Give it to her straight, Emma. Candy coating it won't help her or her father."

Emma took a deep breath and smoothed the summer shift she was wearing over her legs. On her feet were the huaraches she'd bought the day before. She and Granny were almost always of the same mind when it came to giving people the straight-up truth in these situations, whether people had trouble believing it or not, but Emma wasn't totally sure how Rikki would respond to Felix's request. "Rikki," she began after clearing her throat and looking up, "your father came to me yesterday while I was here having lunch with you."

Rikki stood up straight and stared at Emma in disbelief a few seconds before speaking. "He did and you didn't tell me?"

"I wasn't sure how you would take it," Emma responded.

"Is that the question you needed to ask? If I could *take it* or not?"

"No, Rikki. That's not the question." Emma put her hands palms-down on her thighs and plunged forward. "My question is, if your father tells me to tell you something that I know you won't want to hear, do you still want to hear it?"

Rikki shook her head like a confused puppy. "What kind of a question is that?"

"A darn good one," chimed in Granny as she moved closer to Rikki.

Phil left the window and also moved closer to Rikki. "What Emma is saying is, what if your father isn't on the same page as you about the company? Isn't that why you're having Emma contact him?"

Looking first at Phil, then Emma, Rikki said, "I want my father's advice."

Emma stood up and joined them at Rikki's desk. "Rikki, you told me you want Felix's advice on how to convince Lucy not to sell Roble Foods."

"Yes, that is what I want," Rikki confirmed. "He's always known best how to deal with her pigheadedness."

"But," Emma continued, "what if Felix sides with Lucy on this? What if he tells you to sell it all?"

Rikki crossed her arms in front of her in defense and narrowed her eyes with suspicion. "Has he told you that, or are you preparing me in case he does?"

"He has told me to tell you to sell," Emma told her. "In

fact, he's emphatic about it. He wants you to take the money and start over someplace else."

"Leave Los Angeles?" Rikki asked with surprise.

"He didn't clarify that," Emma said, "but he wants you to leave here—this restaurant and this location."

Rikki stalked to the window. After looking down on the street for almost a full minute, she turned back to Phil and Emma, her face set hard as stone. "Now I know T.J. is right about you. My father would never agree to the sale and especially not to our family abandoning this street. It's part of our heritage. You said yourself that even in death he still walks it every day to check on his friends."

"True, but yesterday he told me to tell you to sell it," Emma told her. "He told me again today that you need to sell."

"And you folks need to leave," Rikki replied, pointing at the door.

"This girl is as pigheaded as her sister," groused Granny.

Phil held out a hand toward Rikki. "Please, Rikki, listen to Emma. She's telling you the truth."

Rikki looked at Phil. "Did you hear my father say that?"

Phil shook his head. "No, I didn't. I can't see or hear spirits, but I know that Emma can." He frowned at her, taking a tougher stance. "You came to her, remember? She has no interest in how this plays out, sale or no sale. She just wants to help you."

Rikki was quiet for a few seconds, then said, "Please leave, both of you, now."

Emma went back to the sofa to pick up her purse. Granny followed her. "Stubborn or not," the ghost said to Emma, "you can't leave without telling her everything. She at least needs to be warned."

Again Emma agreed with Granny, but she needed to piece

together exactly how to say the words to Rikki, who was now on the defensive and angry. After a slight nod to Granny, Emma slung her bag over her arm and indicated to Phil that it was time to leave. Before they reached the door, Emma turned to Rikki and dropped a bombshell. "You know how to reach me if you want more help, Rikki, but I'm going to leave you with this to consider. Yesterday, when Felix came to me, he was adamant that you sell the business. He said if you didn't, you might die, just as he did. Today he was still determined that you sell and for the same reason."

Rikki's rigid arms fell limp by her sides. Emma and Phil were nearly out the door when she found her tongue. "Are you suggesting that my father was killed?"

Emma turned to her. "I'm just relaying what he said to me."

"But who would have done such a thing? Everyone loved my father and the police said he fell when he had a heart attack."

"He didn't say anything more than that, Rikki. He's only spoken to me briefly and I haven't had the chance to question him about it. I was hoping to do that when he returned."

Rikki shook a finger at Emma. "I don't believe it, Emma Whitecastle. You're a scammer just like T.J. said. You're trying to frighten me into selling and using my poor dead father to do it. If my sister is behind this, I'll see her rot in hell!"

CHAPTER SEVEN

"THAT went well," Phil said as they walked back down Olvera Street. "Guess we're lunching at Traxx after all."

Emma didn't say a word. When they reached Los Angeles Plaza Park at the end of Olvera Street, she became even more sullen and distracted but didn't resist when Phil directed them left down Paseo de la Plaza. Granny had disappeared when they left Rikki. They continued walking in silence until they reached Alameda Street. Emma started across the busy street and would have walked right into traffic if Phil hadn't gotten a good grip on her arm to hold her back.

"Hey, where do you think you're going?" he asked her. "The cross light is red."

Although Emma stopped when Phil grasped her arm, she didn't look at or even acknowledge him. She stared ahead, almost in a trance.

"Emma, what's the matter?" he asked.

She didn't answer but her face puckered as she fought back tears.

"Emma," Phil said to her.

When the crosswalk light came on, Emma moved forward across the wide street. Phil walked with her, keeping a tight hold of her arm. When they reached the other side, he guided her into Union Station.

Opened in 1939, Union Station is a stately building of great beauty, both inside and out. The architecture and furnishings skillfully blend Spanish Colonial, Mission Revival, and Art Deco. It was a busy day with passengers going to and from train platforms or sitting scattered in the boxy mission-style chairs in the main waiting room.

Phil guided Emma to a section away from most of the waiting passengers and sat her down in one of the chairs. He bent down in front of her on the terra-cotta tile. Her eyes were open but her face was screwed up in horror only she could see. "Emma," he said gently, "come back to me." When she didn't respond, he clutched her right shoulder with his left hand and shook her firmly. "Come back to me," he ordered, again keeping his voice low and gentle. "You belong here."

Finally, she turned her blue eyes to his. Recognition entered them like a slow-filling cup until she shook off the stupor and returned to the present. She looked down to her lap. Phil's right hand was holding both of her hands, his knuckles nearly white with intensity.

"I'm okay, Phil," she said to him. She gave him a small smile to confirm her words.

"Where did you go, Emma? What did you see?" He took the seat next to her but continued to hold on to her hands. "Was it Felix? Did you see his death or who killed him? Did you see something else happening?"

She shook her head. "No. Nothing to do with the Ricardos." She looked around. "Can you get me some water, Phil?"

"Sure, but you stay put." He got up and crossed the waiting room, walking quickly across the wide inlaid center strip to a small concession stand on the other side. In just over a minute he returned with a bottle of cold water, twisting the cap off on the return trip. "Here, sweetheart." He handed her the water and sat next to her again.

After taking a long drink, Emma said, "It was horrible, Phil. Shortly after we left Olvera Street, I started feeling awful, like I was being squeezed in a trash compactor or something like that."

"Were there lots of spirits coming to you?" he asked.

"No, I didn't see any spirits, but I felt them. Pushing and closing in on me. They were crying for help and begging for their lives but in another language. I didn't understand them, yet I did." She looked confused. "They were dying horrible deaths."

Phil looked surprised. "Did you recognize anything at all? See anything at all?"

Emma took another drink while she searched her memory. "I think they were Asian, maybe Chinese. The words sounded like Chinese anyway." She shrugged. "We are close to Chinatown." She closed her eyes and took a deep breath. "Hanging," she said bluntly after a few seconds without opening her eyes. "Some of them were or had been hanged."

"Hangings? You're sure?" When she nodded, Phil slumped in his chair and closed his own eyes. When he opened them, he turned to her and took her hands again. "What do you know about this area? You know, the history of this area of LA?"

Again she shrugged. "Just what I learned in school. This is where the first settlement occurred. Settled in the late 1700s by the Spanish, I think. The mission on the other side of the plaza was built shortly after."

"That's correct. Anything else?" he urged.

"I know the modern Olvera Street marketplace we visited today wasn't established until the 1930s. I read that online before visiting Rikki yesterday."

"Nothing else, Emma?" Phil asked, not taking his eyes off her face.

She gave it more thought then shook her head. "They just taught us the basics in school. Why? What do you know?"

"In college," he began, "I did a paper for a class based on Los Angeles immigrants, going back to when LA was first settled. The ground we're on today was where the original Chinatown was located."

"Not over on Broadway?"

"No, that came later." Phil cleared his throat and looked into her eyes. "You really have a remarkable talent, Emma. A remarkable, real, and terrifying talent."

"Tell me, Phil." She stared back at him. "Tell me right now what I saw."

He patted her hand, but didn't let go of it. "In 1871, the Chinese Massacre took place on this spot."

Emma sat up straight. "A massacre?"

He nodded. "A very large mob of white men rioted and attacked Chinatown, beating and torturing people, ending with the lynching of eighteen Chinese."

Emma's mouth hung open. "Right here?"

"Pretty much here and the immediate vicinity."

"But why?"

"According to historical accounts," he explained, "it

started when a white rancher was killed during fighting between two Chinese factions."

"Gangs, even then," said Emma with sadness.

"Yep." He squeezed her hand tighter. "But that was then and you are here now. I know you can't always control these trances; I just hope they don't become frequent. It worries me to no end."

The color had returned to Emma's cheeks, and she felt less drained. "Trust me, Phil, I wish what I had sensed had something to do with the Ricardos. In the past these episodes did have something to do with the matter at hand. Maybe the tragedy of the place was just so strong it engulfed me." She took another drink of water. "I'll have to tell Milo about this and see what he thinks."

"Good idea." Phil held out his hand for the water. Emma handed it to him and he took his own long drink. They sat there side by side in silence for several minutes before Phil asked, "How are you feeling now? Still feeling crushed?"

"No. I'm feeling quite myself now." To confirm her words, she gave him a soft, tender kiss. "I'm sorry if I frightened you, Phil."

"Not the first time," he answered, then laughed softly. "And I'm sure it won't be the last." He patted her hand. "You still in the mood for lunch or should we head home?"

"A little lunch would perk me up." To add support to her words, she got to her feet and looked up at the ceiling of the waiting room, taking note of the inlaid wood beams and ornate metal chandeliers. "So much beauty built on top of such horror and ugliness."

Phil stood up beside her. "Much of this city was built on violence, and even today supposedly innocent people like Felix Ricardo can get caught in the crosshairs."

Once they were seated at a table in Traxx and handed

menus, Emma asked, "Phil, why did you describe Felix Ricardo as *supposedly innocent*?"

Phil lowered his menu and looked over the top of his reading glasses at her. "Just keeping the options open for other possibilities. Just because he may have been murdered doesn't mean he wasn't involved with something shady that got him killed and put his family in jeopardy."

Emma closed her menu and placed it on the table. "You're right, Phil. I hadn't thought of that."

"No, but I'm sure you would have in short order." Phil tossed her a wink and went back to reading his menu. "See anything you like?"

"The quinoa stew," Emma said.

"You want to split the beet salad?" he asked.

"Sure," she answered without thinking, her mind now focused more on the other possibilities Phil had raised instead of her stomach.

When the waiter returned with their iced tea order and some bread, Phil ordered the quinoa stew for Emma, the chicken posole for himself, and one beet salad. "I'm not saying Felix was crooked, but something got him killed," Phil continued after the waiter left with their orders. "And it sounds from what you told me that it might have something to do with that sale."

Emma nodded as she took a drink of her tea. "I just hate the way I left it with Rikki. I don't feel right about having to defend myself, but I also don't want to walk away from this if she's in any real danger."

Phil reached over and took Emma's hand. "Give her a bit of time to think it over. She does believe her father was there. That's half the battle. I'm sure she'll be mulling over how he died now, too. You can't force her to listen to you."

"I know you're right." Emma squeezed his hand. "Let's have a lovely lunch, look over this incredible building, then head home. How about taking in an early movie later? We haven't done that in a long time."

"Sounds good, but will walking around here bother you? You know, the spirits and all."

"I honestly don't know," she told him, her own voice unsure, "but on the way back to the parking lot I'd like to walk around the plaza more."

"There's a small plaque posted nearby memorializing the massacre. Would you like to see it?"

"Yes," Emma told him. "I would like to see that, but you may have to keep an eye on me."

He squeezed her hand before letting it go. "Don't I always?"

After lunch the two of them walked around Union Station, taking in the graceful architecture and design. Leaving there, they crossed Alameda and turned left on Los Angeles Street until they came to the Chinese American Museum and the plaque about the massacre in front of it. Emma bent and touched the bronze plaque, which was hot from exposure to the sun. Once again she felt the presence of horror and death, but not crushing like before.

"You okay, Emma?" Phil asked with concern.

She stood up and smiled, not at him but at the plaque. "Yes. I'm fine. I think earlier they just wanted me to know they were here."

"The museum is quite interesting; would you like to go in?"

She nodded and together they entered. After the museum, they strolled arm in arm around Los Angeles Plaza Park. Phil bought them each frozen juice bars from a vending cart, and they sat on a park bench facing the entrance to Olvera Street to enjoy them.

"You're still bothered by what happened with Rikki, aren't you?" Phil asked.

"Not really," Emma answered.

"Come on," Phil said, giving her a small nudge. "You haven't taken your eyes off the entrance to that street since we sat down. Are you hoping to see Felix or someone living?"

"Okay," she confessed. "I am bothered by it. I wish Felix would say more about why he wants Rikki to agree to the sale. As it is now, it's just him ordering her to do it and her digging in her heels against it, swearing Felix would never say that. If I could give Rikki a solid reason from her father, it might clarify things."

"Aren't you two a couple of cozy old farts," said a familiar voice coming out of thin air.

· CHAPTER EIGHT ·

EMMA snorted and started coughing at the unexpected comment.

"You okay?" asked Phil once again with concern. "Is it the spirits?"

Emma wiped the juice trickling down her chin with a paper napkin. "It's Granny," she explained. "She just called us a couple of old farts."

"That's right, Granny," Phil agreed. He had an arm around Emma's shoulders and tightened it, bringing her closer to him. "We're a couple of happy old farts." He kissed Emma on the side of her head. "Getting happier with every day."

"Where have you been, Granny?" Emma asked after snuggling closer to Phil.

The ghost materialized next to their bench. "I've been off trying to find Felix but haven't yet. I tried to come back earlier but there was this awful block in my way. Like you were walled off from me."

"Was that a couple of hours ago?" Emma asked.

"You know ghosts have no idea of time," Granny said with a sputter. "I tried to contact you but it was like I got no signal."

Emma told Phil what Granny said, then added, "I'll bet that was when the other spirits were around me."

Phil looked in the direction Emma indicated. "Emma went into another one of her trances," he told the ghost. "The spirits of some murdered Chinese were letting her know they were present."

"I don't like them trances," the ghost said with concern. "Do they want you to help them?"

"No, Granny," Emma told her, "they don't want my help. I think they just wanted me to know they were here. Phil and I visited the plaque to their memory and paid them respect and they left."

"Good," said Granny, "because we have work to do on this case."

"Granny," Emma began, looking at Phil while she spoke to the ghost, "there is no case. I connected with Rikki's father, as she asked, and I told her what he said, as he asked."

"Granny," Phil said, looking at Emma while he spoke, a ploy they used often, "Emma and I discussed this at lunch. There's really little we can do."

"You discussed it without me?" The temperamental ghost stamped her foot on the pavement but for all her effort no sound was created. "I thought we were a team."

Emma leaned closer to Phil. "Granny's upset because we didn't include her in the discussion." Emma then turned to Granny, not caring if anyone noticed. "Granny, you weren't there. But basically it boils down to when someone orders you out, you go. To pursue this now would really be rude and might even cause us trouble."

"And what if that young woman gets hurt or even dies?" Granny demanded, moving to stand directly in front of them. "How would you feel then?"

"If something happened to Rikki, Granny," Emma told the worked-up spirit, "I would feel truly terrible, but we've already told her she's in danger."

"Emma's right, Granny," Phil said, understanding the conversation without translation. "We can't lock Rikki up or wrap her in bubble wrap like a china cup to keep her safe. And Emma certainly doesn't need a restraining order slapped on her."

"What's a restraining order?" asked the ghost.

"A restraining order," Emma explained, "is when someone gets a court order forcing you to stay away from them, and if you don't, you can go to jail."

She turned to relay Granny's question to Phil, but he waved her off with a casual hand. "I'm following the gist of things just fine from your side." Phil turned straight ahead, as Emma had done when she last spoke to Granny. "Granny, I didn't meet this T.J. guy or Lucy, but from what Emma's told me, either of them wouldn't hesitate to get Emma into legal trouble to serve their purposes."

The ghost looked down and softly kicked the pavement with the toe of her boot. "Well, we sure wouldn't want that." She looked up at Emma and Phil. "But I'd sure feel better if we knew more about how Felix died and who did him in."

Emma nodded. "I'd feel better knowing more about Felix's death, too, Granny. But we can't go poking around asking questions without raising suspicion from the Ricardos and T.J. It could have been most anyone who contributed to his death."

"Except his wife and Hector," noted Phil. Both Granny and Emma turned to him. "Didn't Rikki say," he continued, turning his attention on Emma, "that Felix had just spoken to his wife on the phone and that Hector was off that day?"

"That's true," agreed Granny. "But it doesn't mean they didn't know about a plan in the works."

"Good point, Granny," Emma said after giving it more thought. "Mrs. Ricardo and Hector still might have known of a plan to kill Felix, but how it happened doesn't feel planned, at least not entirely. If someone wanted to bump off Felix, they could have done it in other places and times without the high risk of being seen."

"I agree with Emma," said Phil. "Killing him with a knife or gun while he was going to or from his car or somewhere else would have been much easier for a killer. This has an emotional feel to it. Maybe a confrontation gone bad."

"If that's the case," Emma said, thinking more about it, "then it would have been done by someone who could easily come and go in the restaurant without raising suspicion."

"Emma's right," said Granny with conviction. "Rikki didn't say anything about someone special being there that day, so it had to be someone who was supposed to be there."

"That's a pretty wide field," noted Emma. "All the waitstaff, kitchen staff, the hostess—none of them would have raised suspicion."

"Neither would that T.J. fellow or Rikki's sister," Phil pointed out.

Emma's phone vibrated. She pulled it out of her purse and looked at it. "That's interesting," she said after reading the message. "It's a text from Tanisha's father."

Both Granny and Phil looked concerned. Tanisha Costello was Kelly Whitecastle's best friend in Boston. She wasn't a student like Kelly, but a young journalist who lived in the area. "Is everything okay with the girls?" asked Phil.

"I dropped in on them yesterday," Granny reported. "And they were both doing fine. Kelly was getting ready to start that summer intern job with Quinn, and Tanisha had just returned from an assignment. Aren't they living together this summer?"

"Yes, they are living together for the summer, at least during the time Kelly is in the country, but this has nothing to do with the girls," Emma told them while still looking at her phone. "Gino wants me to call him in the next few days to discuss something to do with a new book he's researching."

"Gino Costello is a crime fiction writer," Phil noted. "Maybe he wants to pick your brain about some of your adventures solving murders."

Emma shrugged. "Maybe."

"Have you ever met him?" asked Phil.

"Not yet," Emma answered. "I've only spoken to him on the phone and that was just once. As you know, I invited him and his wife to come out to Julian that week Tanisha was visiting but they couldn't make it." Emma looked up. "But you've met him, haven't you, Granny?"

"Not officially so that he'd remember me," said the ghost. "It's more like I've been around and he doesn't know it. Tanisha keeps me under wraps when he visits. But I was around last fall when he bailed the girls out of that trouble. He's a big burly man. Looks more like he spends his time working outdoors instead of at a computer all day."

Emma gave Phil Granny's description of Gino Costello. "Yeah," he agreed. "I've seen him on some talk shows, and he is a big tough guy. He doesn't look like Tanisha at all."

Emma laughed. "Kelly tells me that while Tanisha and her dad don't look alike, they are very much alike in personality—stubborn and determined."

"That's a good description from what I've seen," Granny added. "They're both bullheaded, especially around each other."

Phil laughed himself after Emma gave him Granny's report. "I would love to meet Gino Costello," he said. "I'm a big admirer of his work."

"Down, fan-boy," said Granny, her arms crossed in impatience.

A snort escape Emma's lips. "Granny just called you a fan-boy."

"That I am," confessed Phil with a slight grin. "I've read every book he's written and his short stories."

Emma wrapped her empty Popsicle stick in a napkin. "Guess I'll give him a call later and see what he wants."

"And what about this case?" Granny persisted. "How are we gonna handle it since we're not exactly supposed to be involved?"

Getting up, Emma took Phil's Popsicle stick from him and deposited them both in a trashcan a couple of steps away. When she returned, she said, "I really am worried about Rikki." She looked to Granny. "Since Phil and I can't be involved directly, Granny, maybe you'll have to go under-cover and report back."

"Really?" the ghost said, hopping up and down. "You mean like a stakeout? I love doing those."

"Yes," Emma confirmed with a smile, noting Granny's excitement. "Maybe you can hang around the restaurant to see if anything odd is going on and who seems suspicious. If Felix returns, question him about what happened. Also stay close to Rikki as much as you can and let me know if she seems in any danger." Emma turned to Phil. "Can you think of anything else for Granny to do?"

"I wish we had two Grannies," Phil said, getting up from the bench. "Then we could send her to keep any eye on Lucy, too."

"I'll try to connect with her if I can," Granny said. "You know, just try to pop in, but I may not have had enough contact yet to zero in on her."

"Do what you can, Granny," Emma told the ghost. "Anything will be a big help."

The tiny ghost snapped to attention, giving Emma what had become a customary salute. "You got it, Chief."

As the ghost started to fade, she muttered, "Too bad I'm not still alive. Then I could do a real stakeout and sit in a car eating junk food and pee in a soda can."

· CHAPTER NINE ·

AS they headed to the parking lot where they'd left Emma's SUV, Emma told Phil about Granny's last comment. When they finished laughing, Phil said, "Maybe you should try recruiting other spirits to help you snoop. You could build a small army of them like those minions in that cartoon. It would be better than surveillance equipment."

Emma shook her head in mock horror. "No thanks. I've got my hands full with Granny."

"I heard that," came Granny's voice from thin air. "The cowboy's right—it might be a good idea to get me a little help, as long as you remember who was here first."

Emma swung her head toward the direction of the voice. "Granny, I thought you'd left to check on Rikki and the restaurant."

"And I did," the ghost snapped as she came back into view. "Or don't you want to know what I just saw?"

"Granny already has something to report," Emma said

to Phil. He moved in closer and Granny joined them, the two live people huddling with the ghost.

"That T.J.'s back," Granny began.

"Are you sure?" asked Emma. "You weren't there when I met him."

"Well, this guy showed up and that Carlos kid called him T.J.," answered Granny, her hands on her hips. "Or should I go back and ask him for ID?"

"Don't get snippy, Granny," Emma told her. "Tell us what happened."

"Right after I popped back into the restaurant, I saw Carlos slip out a back door."

After telling Phil, Emma checked her watch. "It's after the bulk of lunchtime business. Maybe Carlos went out to take a break."

"Emma's right," added Phil. "He could have been taking a break after the rush."

Granny stamped her foot. "Do you two want to hear this or not?" Emma motioned for her to continue.

"Anyway," continued Granny, "I thought he was acting a bit sneaky, so I followed him. He walked to the end of the street, crossed it, and met some guy who was standing out of the way by some trees. The guy was nicely dressed in a suit and Carlos called him T.J."

After Emma relayed the information to Phil, he asked, "What trees, Granny?"

"Those trees," Granny said, pointing to the far end of the parking lot where they stood. The public parking lot was on Main Street, sandwiched between the historical La Iglesia de Nuestra Señora la Reina de Los Ángeles and Cesar E. Chavez Avenue. Across Main were a few businesses that butted up against the backside of Olvera Street. On the other side of the fence bordering Chavez was a thick stand of trees.

"Those trees right there?" asked Emma, pointing toward the area Granny indicated.

"You deaf?" snapped Granny. "Carlos just got there, but who knows how long their little powwow will take."

Ignoring the remark, Emma said to Phil, "Granny said that Carlos met T.J. by those trees at the end of the parking lot. Just now."

Phil surveyed the trees. They were too far away to see anything, and with all the traffic in the area, they probably wouldn't even hear a shouting match. "Stay here," he said to Emma. "I'm going to mosey on over there and take a look." Before she could say anything, Phil took off at a trot across the lot in that direction.

"Glad he didn't actually mean *mosey*," Granny said. "Secret meetings like that don't usually take very long."

Emma nodded, but didn't take her eyes off Phil. "Granny, please go on over there and keep an eye out."

"You read my mind," Granny said and disappeared.

Once Granny was gone, Emma slipped behind the wheel of her vehicle and started it up. After backing out of the parking space, she eased the SUV in the direction Phil had headed, being careful not to move too fast and attract attention. She was also glad she drove a hybrid with its quieter engine. It was midafternoon. There weren't many cars down at the far end of the lot since it was a weekday, even if it was summer. On the weekend the lot would be full. The inside of the vehicle was hot and stuffy, so she snapped the AC on low.

Keeping her eyes on Phil, Emma watched him slip in and out of the few cars at the far end, using them for cover, and was glad he'd worn quiet tennis shoes instead of his usual heavy cowboy boots. She urged her SUV closer but edged to the left, away from Phil, just in case anyone on the other side noticed her through the trees. Phil turned and saw her and held up his left hand for her to halt. She did and saw that in his right hand he held his cell phone in the direction of the fence.

"They're still there," said Granny, popping inside the SUV.

Emma squelched a tiny yelp and put a hand over her heart. "Granny, why do you always scare me like that?"

"I'm a ghost, Emma. It's what we do. It's not like I can wave a hankie to announce I'm on my way. I'm either here or I'm not." She watched as Emma dug her wallet out of her purse and pulled out several bills. "What are you doing?"

"Getting money ready to pay for our parking in case we need to make a quick getaway." Emma pulled the parking ticket from behind the visor and put it with the money.

Granny looked at her and shook her head in disbelief. "If bullets start flying, you're going to wait in line to pay for your parking? Just crash through the gate," Granny told her. "That's what they do on TV."

"This isn't TV, Granny." Still, Emma thought, Granny was right. Changing the subject, Emma asked, "Did you see anything significant?"

"The T.J. guy handed Carlos an envelope, which he tucked into his waistband," Granny reported.

"Did you notice if it was thick or thin?"

"Looked kind of bulky to me, like it was stuffed with cash." The ghost buzzed with excitement. "It's probably a payoff. You know, for Carlos killing Felix."

Even though her mind had made the same initial leap, Emma dismissed it. "Let's not jump to conclusions, Granny. Besides, Felix died a year ago. A payoff wouldn't be going down now for a job that old."

"Maybe T.J.'s on some sort of installment plan," Granny suggested. "It can't be cheap to hire a hit."

Emma glanced over at the ghost, thinking she was being sarcastic, but one look at Granny's set jaw as she eagerly watched Phil let Emma know that Granny was serious about her remark. "Maybe," Emma said hopefully, "it's not cash."

Granny flashed her a look of disbelief. "Get real, Emma! What else could it be that they would need to meet in secret? Surprise birthday plans for Rikki?"

As usual, Emma was surprised by the dichotomy of a ghost dressed in pioneer clothing talking slang. It was something she didn't think she'd ever get used to. Granny's speech was peppered with it, picked up from watching television and hanging around Kelly and her friends. And it wasn't always modern slang. It could be from any era from the TV shows and movies that the ghost enjoyed. For a whole week not too long ago, Granny went around mimicking Marlon Brando in *The Godfather* until Emma and her mother about went nuts. Phil and Emma's father laughed together about it, thankful they couldn't hear the ghost.

"In the movies," Granny continued, "secret meetings with envelopes usually mean drugs or payoffs." Emma had to admit, she couldn't argue with that logic any more than she could argue with paying for parking while under fire. "Maybe T.J.'s paying Carlos to bump off Rikki or someone else," Granny continued.

"Let's see what Phil says," Emma said. "He's coming back now." Emma nudged the SUV closer, meeting Phil partway. As he opened the door and hopped into the passenger's seat, Granny popped into the back.

"Was it a bribe?" the ghost asked Phil, forgetting for a

moment that he couldn't hear her. She turned to Emma. "Ask Phil if it was a bribe." The front half of the ghost spilled over into the front seat between Emma and Phil.

Emma headed for the parking attendant, glad she didn't have to crash her Lexus SUV through the gate. "Granny told me she saw T.J. hand Carlos an envelope."

"That he did," Phil answered as he checked his phone. "I hope I got it." He fiddled with the screen on the phone. "The trees hid them from the street well enough and I could see them through the chain link fence, but not clearly. I was afraid to get too close. I hope the zoom worked." He glanced at Emma. "But one of them was definitely the kid from the restaurant who didn't like Lucy."

He found the photo and held the phone out to Emma while they waited their turn at the parking lot exit. When Phil leaned toward Emma, his body merged with Granny's, imposing his face onto her hazy head. The image spooked Emma and she shivered and turned away.

"What's wrong?" Phil asked.

Emma turned slowly around and was relieved to see that Granny had moved back and Phil's face was again his own. "Just caught a chill," she told him. "Probably too much air-conditioning after spending the day outside."

She glanced at the photo and could see two men on the screen. Phil enlarged the picture for her. "Could you hear anything?" she asked.

He shook his head. "Just bits and pieces. It was all in Spanish but the traffic muffled a lot of it."

Granny looked at the photos over Phil's shoulder. "That's them. And see, T.J. is handing something to Carlos." The ghost pointed at the screen. One of the photos had captured an envelope being handed off.

"I think," Phil added, "that Carlos's last name is Fuentes. T.J. called him that a couple of times in what little I did hear."

"So now we know that Carlos is Carlos Fuentes," Emma said. "At least we won't have to ask anyone for that information."

When it was their turn at the pay station, Emma lowered her window and paid their parking fee. Just before exiting the lot, she said to Granny, "Granny, why don't you go back to the restaurant and keep an eye on Carlos. Maybe you'll be able to see the envelope and what's in it better if you follow him."

"You got it," said the ghost. "But don't you two go making any important decisions about the case without me."

"We won't," agreed Emma, trying to keep impatience out of her voice.

"You promise?" Granny pushed.

"I promise," Emma agreed, "but you'll have to check in regularly so we can run things by you."

When Granny left, Phil asked, "What was that all about?"

"Granny made me promise that we wouldn't make any important decisions about this matter without her."

Phil laughed. "She's a pistol, that's for sure. Makes you wonder what she was like when alive, doesn't it?"

"I'll bet she kept Jacob on his toes," Emma said, smiling at Phil.

"Just like you do me?" He reached over and stroked her arm with affection.

"What can I say?" Emma replied with a slight laugh. "It runs in the family."

· CHAPTER TEN ·

THEY rode in silence while Emma maneuvered the SUV through a couple of miles of downtown traffic and onto the 110 Freeway heading north. Emma's home was less than ten miles away, but you never knew how long it would take with traffic. It could be a fifteen-minute drive or an hour's drive. Midday traffic was heavy but not clogged, and they made it back to the house in twenty minutes. In a couple of hours that same drive time would at least double.

Emma and Phil were comfortable with their silence without either feeling awkward. They often spent long stretches of time together reading and watching TV without a word between them, letting the occasional touch or smile speak for them. Emma enjoyed that about Phil Bowers. Grant Whitecastle, her ex-husband, always needed noise or action around, and he always demanded her attention when they were together. Being a TV star had made him a runaway narcissist. Or maybe he was a narcissist who had found his place in the limelight of show business. Either way, she'd often found it exhausting to be around him and was glad their daughter seemed content and comfortable in her own skin instead of craving praise and approval from others.

When they got to the house, they found Emma's parents at a table in the shade of the back patio enjoying cold drinks. Paul Miller was playing ball with Archie, their black Scottish terrier. Paul would toss the blue rubber ball as far as he could into their large landscaped backyard and the dog would dash off to retrieve it, dropping it at his feet and barking with excitement until he threw it again.

"Archie," Elizabeth Miller said to the animal, "it's much too hot for you to keep that up." But the animal didn't listen, hopping around until Paul threw the ball again.

"Is Granny with you?" Paul asked when Phil and Emma came through the back gate to join them. "She's good at wearing Archie out."

"No, Dad," Emma said. "She's off snooping around for me."

Elizabeth indicated a tray with a frosty pitcher on the table. "I made up a batch of gin and tonics and there are a couple of extra glasses here. I thought you two might be along soon. Would you like some?"

"That sounds great, Elizabeth," Phil said just before disappearing into the house.

Elizabeth put some ice from a nearby ice bucket into two tall glasses and poured liquid from the pitcher into each. Emma took one, took a long drink, and gave a sigh when she was finished. "That is so good, Mother. Thank you." With her other hand she tapped the large crystal pitcher and smiled. "But you made quite a bit of the stuff. What were you going to do with it if Phil and I didn't come home?"

"Drink it all ourselves," her father answered with a laugh. "We're staying home tonight, so what's the harm in getting a bit tipsy?" He looked at his wife and winked. "Maybe we'll even turn in a bit early."

"Paul!" Elizabeth scolded, but there was color in her cheeks and a shy smile on her lips. "If you have a couple of those, you'll be on the sofa snoring like a freight train in no time."

Emma took another long drink and smiled to herself. Her parents were still deeply in love after almost fifty years of marriage and still openly flirted with each other. It had been wonderful growing up in such a secure loving home. The only rough patch she remembered was after her older brother, Paulie, was killed in an accident. He'd run out into the street to get a ball and been struck by a passing car. The driver of the car had been overcome with almost as much horror and grief as her parents. Paulie had been eleven at the time. Emma had been nine. Only once, shortly after Emma discovered her medium talents, had she been able, with Granny's help, to contact Paulie's spirit and bring him to Elizabeth for a short visit. Although decades after the accident, it had done Elizabeth a world of good and helped heal the hole in her heart.

As her father reached out and took his wife's hand, Emma wondered what residual issues Kelly would have from living with Emma and Grant during their tumultuous marriage. Emma harbored a lot of guilt over that, even though it had been Grant who had been publicly cheating throughout most of the marriage. She knew Kelly wasn't that close to her father, even though she did see him when she was home and occasionally took short vacations with Grant and his second wife, Carolyn, and their son. Kelly adored Oscar, her half brother, but had no use for Carolyn. Kelly had come to love

Phil, and Emma noticed that her daughter tended to go to Phil, not Grant, when she needed solid fatherly advice. Kelly also enjoyed Phil's two sons and got together with them on occasion without Phil and Emma as if they were her real brothers. Emma looked again at the entwined hands of her parents and smiled, knowing in her heart that she and Phil would have that kind of solid marriage.

"Did you leave any of that stuff for me?" asked Phil as he came out of the house with his laptop.

In answer, Emma pushed his full glass in his direction. "Get it now, cowboy, before it's gone. Dad's threatening to drink the entire batch."

Phil took a seat at the patio table and took a long pull from his glass. "Now that's tasty," he said when he was finished. He fired up his computer.

When Archie returned the ball again, Paul Miller didn't pick it up but instead told the panting dog to go lie down. The dutiful Archie wandered over to his water dish and lapped with gusto before curling up in a shady spot. Paul turned to Phil and said, "Are you going to try and get some work done? If so, maybe Emma's office might be best."

"No," Phil answered. "I'm going to see if I can get some hits on a search of people Emma and I are . . . ah . . . interested in."

"Interested in?" Paul parroted. "You mean investigating, don't you?"

"Dad," Emma said, looking at him with a set jaw, "you sound like Granny. We are not investigating anything. We're just curious about some of the people we've met recently."

"Uh-huh." Paul Miller stretched his long legs, a physical attribute Emma had inherited from him, and said, "Honey, you can say that all day long, but no matter how you slice it, what you do is investigative work. You investigate facts for your show and on the side you investigate the history and often murders of ghosts. Saying it's not investigative doesn't change the facts."

"Nor does it change the danger," snapped Elizabeth. Emma's mother, clearly agitated, rose from the table and started fussing with a nearby planter of flowers, snapping off dead blooms with the finality of an executioner.

Phil and Emma exchanged looks, both knowing that the usually pleasant and calm Elizabeth did not like her daughter's involvement with unknown ghosts and murder victims. Granny Apples was one thing. She was family and harmless, but some of the other ghosts Emma had investigated had led her into tense and even dangerous situations.

Emma looked at her father, who met her eyes and jerked his chin in the direction of his wife. Emma knew that look and gesture. It meant her father wanted her to address the issue with Elizabeth directly and immediately and not expect him to be the middleman. He had held that position all her life, expecting Emma to fight her own battles or plead her own case when she and her mother were in disagreement, which was happily not often. Emma had raised Kelly with the same independence, seldom interfering when Kelly and Grant had personal issues. Father and daughter had to carve out their own relationship, just as Emma had to do with both of her parents.

Emma took a long pull from her gin and tonic. "Mother," she began, getting up from the table and going to Elizabeth, "I'm sorry. I know it's difficult for you and Dad when I find myself in the middle of a situation that goes sideways, but I don't look for trouble intentionally."

Elizabeth moved to another planter and started removing

the dead buds from the flowers on that plant in silence. Without a word she walked to a nearby trash container and deposited the dead leaves and petals. "I know you don't, Emma," she said in a small voice. "Any more than Paulie intentionally ran out in front of that car." She dusted her hands together to remove any loose dirt before turning to look at Emma. "But in both cases, it's danger that could have been avoided."

Her mother had played the Paulie card. She seldom did but knew full well it would make Emma feel like crap. It was Elizabeth's way of saying she'd already lost one child and wasn't about to lose another, even if Emma was a full-grown adult. Emma studied Elizabeth's lined face. Even in her seventies her mother was still very beautiful. Elizabeth was small and compact and in the last year had stopped coloring her hair so now it was a shiny natural platinum silver. She wore it in a tidy and feathery short cut for easy care when she and Paul traveled, which they did a great deal.

When Emma remained silent, Elizabeth pointed an index finger at her. "Bullets, Emma. I'm talking about bullets. It's bad enough when you go into trances and lose yourself in the history of these spirits, but not too long ago you were in the middle of gunfire."

"No one ever shot at me, Mother," Emma pointed out.

"No, not directly, but one day you might not be so lucky." Elizabeth starting tearing up. "And I just couldn't bear that." Emma knew her mother did not cry lightly or often. The tears were real, not an emotional ploy.

Emma put a hand on each of her mother's shoulders. "Mother, I do try to be careful, and Phil and Granny look out for me."

"Granny's already dead, Emma," her mother remarked in comeback, "and I couldn't bear to lose Phil either, and neither could his aunt and uncle. They worry, too, you know."

When Emma remained silent, Phil started to speak, but Paul held a hand up in his direction and gave him a nod, telling him to wait. This was between mother and daughter. Phil complied and went back to working on his laptop while keeping an eye on the two women.

"Mother," Emma finally said, her voice even and kind. She dropped her hands from Elizabeth's shoulders and leaned against one of the patio posts. "I didn't ask for this ability, or gift as Milo would call it, any more than you did." She paused, then added, "Any more than Kelly did or Tanisha Costello, and I know you are concerned about each of them, too."

Elizabeth had locked her eyes on her daughter, letting her know that she was listening. With the addition of the two young women into the mix, she took a deep breath but remained silent.

"You choose," Emma continued, "to only interact with Granny, and that's okay. Kelly and Tanisha might also choose to limit their interaction with the dead. But my abilities are much more developed than any of you at this point. Why? I have no idea." Emma shrugged. "But they are, and the more this happens to me, the more I believe that they were given to me to help people, both the dead and the living, and I feel I must follow this path. The TV show I do is fun and interesting, but it's more on an intellectual level, not a personal one. So even if that were canceled, I know in my heart I would still assist people or spirits who came to me for help. It's who I am." She paused, then said as a punctuation, "It's who you and Dad raised me to be."

Instead of pinching more dead buds, Elizabeth gently

caressed several of the flowers in the planter near her as she sorted her thoughts. The other three remained quiet, letting her have her space. The only sound was of ice tinkling in a glass as Paul raised his to take a drink.

Finally, Elizabeth turned her face back to Emma. "Just promise me that you will be extra careful and not take any unnecessary risks?"

Emma sighed with relief. "I will do my best, Mother."

"And I'll be with her every step of the way," added Phil.

Elizabeth looked over at Phil and smiled. "I know you will, Phil. It gives both her father and I great comfort to know that you and Tracy and Milo are looking out for her. And Granny, too." She turned her eyes to Emma again and said, "That doesn't mean we don't worry, but it is a comfort."

Emma stepped forward and wrapped her arms around her mother. "I'll do my best to stay safe and make you proud."

When the embrace ended, Elizabeth looked at her daughter. "You always make us proud, dear. Always." After a couple of seconds, she clapped her hands together in a single soft slap, indicating the end of the drama. "Now, why don't we freshen our drinks while you tell us about your latest ghost."

"Are you sure you want to hear about it?" Emma asked.

"Yes, dear, we do." Elizabeth moved back to the table and picked up the pitcher. She held it in midair a moment, then said with determination, as if making up her mind then and there, "If we can't stop you, maybe we can help you."

· CHAPTER ELEVEN ·

ONCE Emma and Elizabeth were back seated at the patio table, Emma told them about the Ricardos, the sale of the restaurant, and the request by Felix to convince Rikki to sell. She also told them about Felix's death and their concern that it might not have been an accident.

"Dad," Emma began, turning to her father, "Rikki told us that the coroner said that Felix died from the blow to his head, not from his heart attack. Is that common?"

Her father, a retired heart surgeon, pondered the question before answering. "A lot of people fall when they are having a heart attack. They try to get help and can't make it. Did Felix have a history of heart trouble?"

Emma exchanged looks with Phil. "We never asked that question," Emma said, turning back to her father. "From what I've seen, I'd say he was in his mid-sixties or so when he died."

"You never know, he might have had a history of heart problems," Paul pointed out. "His death could have simply been a heart attack that had a tragic ending because of the fall and time that lapsed before anyone found him. Did his ghost say he was murdered?"

Emma gave the question careful consideration, rerunning in her mind her short encounters with the ghost of Felix Ricardo. A stillness covered the Miller backyard while everyone waited for her answer. The house was located on a small cul-de-sac, so not even traffic noise broke the peace and quiet. She could hear Archie's gentle snoring and the pecking of Phil working on his laptop. "No, he didn't, Dad, not exactly. He said that if Rikki didn't consent to the sale of the business, then she might end up in danger or dead like him."

"Maybe," said Elizabeth, "Felix meant Rikki would work herself into her grave. Your father and I have friends who own restaurants and they work night and day, even the very successful ones like the Ricardos. It's a very tough life."

"Your mother is right," added Paul. "Felix might be wanting a better life for his daughter before she ruins her health with stress and too much work. Didn't you say the sister wanted to go off and paint and live a more carefree lifestyle?"

"Yes, but Rikki seems to thrive in the business. And today Felix told me to tell her to take the sale money and start another restaurant someplace else."

"That's easier said than done," Phil said. "I'm sure whoever buys Roble Foods and the restaurant will have a noncompete clause in the agreement or a separate noncompete agreement barring the Ricardos from opening a restaurant or participating in any food service industry within a certain geographic area for a specified amount of time. And since Roble Foods is distributed in many supermarkets, the geographic area might be quite extensive."

Emma studied Phil. He wasn't looking at her, but continued

to plug away at the laptop. "So Rikki might be barred from working in the food industry altogether?" she asked.

Phil nodded and glanced at her before returning to his work. "Yep. Every contract and agreement is different, but if I were the buyer's lawyer, I'd push for an extensive noncompete. Your ghost might not have realized that when he suggested Rikki start another restaurant, unless he was thinking of her moving out of the area altogether."

"What are you doing?" Emma finally asked Phil.

He looked up from his laptop. "I'm running searches on some of the cast of characters to see if anything turns up, including criminal records, but it's difficult without a birthdate or social security number. It's like looking for a needle in a haystack. There are a lot of Carlos Fuenteses in the database, even narrowing it down to Los Angeles specific, so I narrowed the search by setting an age range. I'm coming up with nothing on him doing that. The hits I got were all older than the boy at the restaurant."

Emma scooted her chair closer to Phil. "What about T.J.? His name is Tomas Mendoza."

"Thomas or Tomas?" Phil asked.

"I'm pretty sure it was Tomas, no *h*," she told him, "but I have no idea what the *J* stands for. I'd put him at about mid-thirties in age."

"What about the companies that want to buy the restaurant?" Paul asked.

"I'm going to run a search on them, too," Phil told them. "One was Fiesta Foods. What was the other?" he asked Emma.

"It was Fiesta Time Foods," Emma said. "Or something like that. The other was Crown Corporation, but Lucy said they dropped their interest in Roble."

"Good, because Crown Corporation is huge," noted Phil.

"It's going to pop up all over the place. I might as well be searching for General Mills."

Phil started plugging in more information. "It says here that Fiesta Time, Inc., is a California corporation located in Montebello, so it's local." He flipped to another site and started checking information there. He followed that up with a visit to the Fiesta Time corporate website. A minute later, he told them, "And it's not a publicly held company that I can see." He maneuvered through the pages describing the products of the company. "Their products are similar to Roble's, but don't appear to be as widely distributed or as well known. And like Roble, they have a restaurant. It's located in Alhambra and is called Santiago's."

"So the smaller fish wants to gobble up the bigger fish?" asked Paul.

"Sure looks that way," Phil said. "But just because they're smaller doesn't mean they don't have the cash or credit to make it happen." He jabbed the computer screen with an index finger. "It says here that they've been around a long time catering to the Latino population in the Southwest. Roble had taken their name and products mainstream," Phil noted. "Maybe Fiesta now wants a piece of that action and thinks it can expand faster by buying the company already in that market."

"They also might have thought that without Felix at the helm, Roble Foods was vulnerable," noted Emma. "Rikki said something to her sister that selling to Fiesta would be like spitting on their father's grave. Maybe Fiesta had made a run at Roble before, or maybe there was bad blood between the two companies."

"If that's the case," suggested Phil, "with Felix now dead and gone, his enemy might be going in for the kill."

Phil moved through the pages of the Fiesta Time website

again. "Fiesta Time is owned by the Santiago family. I was hoping they would have their owners or management team listed, but they don't. A lot of companies do that and include photos. It would be good to see who we're dealing with on that end."

Emma raised her glass and took a good long drink. "As I've already said, I did what Rikki asked of me and I did what Felix wanted. There's nothing more to do unless Phil or Granny come up with something really off the wall, like with that packet of money or whatever it was that T.J. handed off to Carlos."

"That's what I'm doing now," Phil said, still working on the laptop. "I e-mailed the photos to myself so I could open them up on the computer and enlarge them." He worked over the keyboard and mouse, stopping every now and then to check the results before his fingers moved again. "My sons do this all the time. I wish they were here."

Emma took another long drink of the gin and tonic. Something was nagging at her about this, even though she kept telling herself she didn't need to pursue it any longer.

"You planning on getting drunk on that stuff?" Granny asked, popping up.

"Why not?" Emma answered, this time not jumping at the ghost's appearance. "Granny's here," she announced to everyone at the table.

"So I gathered from Archie's behavior," noted Paul. They all turned to watch the dog, who had snapped out of his snooze and was staring into space, wagging his tail with excitement.

"Because we have work to do," answered Granny, ignoring the dog.

"Did you find out anything more, Granny?" Emma asked.

"I followed Carlos back to the restaurant," the ghost

reported. "When no one was looking, he took the envelope out of his pants and put it in his locker. He looked inside briefly and it sure did look like cash to me. At least whatever was in there was green and made of paper."

"Granny said the envelope did contain cash," Emma told everyone.

"I'm glad she confirmed that," Phil said, "because it's not clear on these photos. They're pretty grainy enlarged." He turned the laptop in Emma's direction. Both Paul and Elizabeth got up and came to stand behind Emma to look. In the photos were two tall, slender men with dark hair—one young, one in his late thirties or forties. The older one was wearing a very nice dark suit and was handing something off to Carlos.

Emma pointed at the screen. "I don't think that's T.J. Mendoza."

"Are you sure?" Phil asked.

"Not entirely because they're still pretty far away. This man has the same build and height and even looks like him, but my gut response is that's not T.J." She turned to Granny. "Didn't you say Carlos called him T.J., Granny?"

"That's what it sounded like," the ghost said. "They were talking Spanish so I didn't know what they were saying, but I know for sure I heard Carlos say *T.J.* I thought he was addressing that guy."

"Can you enlarge the photos any more, Phil?" Emma asked.

"Not really."

"Maybe they didn't mean the man T.J.," suggested Paul. "Maybe the kid was referring to Tijuana."

"There's another possibility," agreed Phil.

"Go back," Emma told Phil. He moved back a couple of photos. "There," Emma said and pointed at the screen. It was a photo of the man in the suit turned slightly toward the camera.

Emma leaned forward, scrutinizing the screen a long time. Finally, she pronounced, "That is not Tomas Mendoza."

"Are you sure, honey?" asked her father.

"Yes, Dad, I am," Emma said with confidence. "He looks a lot like T.J. but he's better looking. T.J. is not a physically handsome man. It's his presence and confidence that make him handsome, not a pretty face."

"This guy's a looker," said Granny. "I remember that."

Elizabeth laughed. "Granny just called this man a looker."

"Hard to tell, Granny, from these photos," Emma said, "but I'll take your word for it. "And his hair is a bit different than T.J.'s. T.J. wears his long and wavy on top and brushed back. This man does, too, but his sides are also long. The sides of T.J.'s hair are trimmed closer."

"So Carlos was talking to this guy about T.J.?" asked Paul.

"It's very likely," answered Emma. "Unless he did mean Tijuana. Phil, are you sure you didn't overhear anything?"

"Unfortunately," Phil said, "the traffic on Cesar Chavez interfered. I caught a few words here and there and a couple of phrases. It sounded like the guy asked Carlos about school. He also told him the money was all there and that there might be more, or something like that."

Emma nodded. "Yes, Rikki told me that Carlos enters college this fall."

"Do you think the money was for schooling?" Granny asked. "You know, like a scholarship?"

Emma relayed the question to the group before answering. "I doubt it, Granny. If he was bankrolling Carlos's education, he wouldn't need to do it in secret with an envelope of cash. Even if he didn't want people knowing about it, he would probably still write a check."

"Unless the money is dirty, like drug money or something similar," noted Phil. "Then he might hand it out in cash, but I still don't understand the secrecy unless Carlos and this guy don't want people to know they're connected."

"Good point," Emma said. "Carlos got quite hot under the collar when Lucy inferred he was a *cholo* because of his tattoos, so maybe he's supersensitive about being linked to gang activities."

Granny struck a pose. Slouching, she crossed her arms in front of her, fingers on both hands splayed in two different imitations of gang gestures.

"What in the world are you doing, Granny?" Emma asked the ghost.

"This is how *cholos* look on TV," Granny explained. "What up, gangsta?"

Even though Elizabeth couldn't see Granny, she stared in her direction with an open mouth.

"What's going on?" Paul asked.

Elizabeth shook off the surprise and said to her husband in a low whisper, "We definitely need to monitor Granny's television time more closely."

"I heard that!" snapped Granny, now annoyed. "Don't listen to her, homey."

Emma shook off the interruption with a slow back-and-forth movement of her head.

"What is it?" Phil asked.

"I tell you later," she told him. "It will give you a good laugh, but for now, let's get back to business." Putting a hand on Phil's arm, she asked, "What was said about T.J.? That's the question here."

Phil shrugged. "I couldn't make anything out about the context, but I do think it was the man and not the city he was referring to. There was too much background noise at that moment, but his name was definitely mentioned. I can see how Granny thought this guy was T.J. from what was said."

Emma leaned back from the computer screen and took another sip from her glass while she pieced together what they knew so far. "We have Carlos Fuentes, a college-bound waiter at Roble meeting some mystery man in secret and taking a wad of cash from him. From what we can determine, this guy knows T.J., or Carlos would not have mentioned him." She put down her glass and leaned forward, willing the photos to say something she could understand. "Did you pick up anything about any of the Ricardos?" she asked Phil.

"Not that I could hear," he reported.

"So," Emma continued, "we have no idea if this meeting had anything to do with the Ricardo family or the sale of the restaurant."

"Maybe T.J. sent the guy to make the money drop," suggested Granny. "You know, so they wouldn't be seen together."

Emma nodded. "That's a good point, Granny." This time Elizabeth did the honors of translating Granny's comment to the two men.

"Yes," Phil agreed. "A very good point." He turned to the ghost. "Granny, what else did you observe following Carlos?"

The ghost thought about her answer for a minute. "Not much. After he stashed the cash in his locker, he went back downstairs and waited tables and helped tidy up the restaurant for dinner. His shift ended shortly after that. He changed out of his waiter's shirt, grabbed the money, and took off on a motorcycle parked at a nearby gas station. I think he knew the people at the station because he waved to them as he took off."

Emma relayed the information, then added, "They might be friends who keep an eye on his motorcycle while he's at work. Did you tag along, Granny?"

"I did. He went to a house in a residential neighborhood. I think it was his family's home. There was a middle-aged woman cooking and a couple of kids running around. Carlos changed his clothes, had something to eat, and talked a little to the woman, who I'm pretty sure was his mother. Soon after, he kissed the woman on the cheek and left again. This time he went to a nearby school, a college I think. He was hanging around talking to some other kids for a little bit before getting a soda and settling at a table outside to study."

"It sounds like he's taking some evening summer school classes before entering college in the fall," noted Phil.

"Sure does," Emma said. "That's pretty ambitious." She looked at Granny. "What about the money, Granny? Did you see it again?"

The ghost nodded. "He stashed the envelope in a box in his closet. A shoe box or something like that."

"What was the neighborhood like where Carlos lives?" Phil asked. "Could you tell?"

The ghost gave the question a lot of thought before answering. "It wasn't as grand as this one by a long shot," she said, describing what she remembered. "The houses were small and close together, but mostly tidy and well maintained. Lots of kids running around outside. Carlos waved to some folks when he drove up, so I'm guessing he grew up there or has lived there a long time."

Emma gave the report to the others. "Sounds like a typical blue-collar neighborhood." She looked at Granny again. "You didn't by any chance notice what city or area it was in, did you?"

The ghost shook her head. "That's a negative, Chief. And I'm not sure I could find it again. I was connected to Carlos, not the place. I do know we took the freeway to get there, but I'm not sure which one."

"That's okay, Granny," Emma told her. "You did great."

"Okay," said Phil. "We have this seemingly nice kid from a working-class family taking a lot of secret cash from a man in a suit. I don't think it was a drug exchange because it didn't look like Carlos gave the guy anything in return." Phil turned in Granny's direction. "You didn't see Carlos hand anything off to that man today, did you, Granny?"

"That's another negative," the ghost answered. Emma repeated her answer to Phil, this time word for word.

"We really need to identify that man in the photos," Emma said. "Phil, can you capture that frame where his face is the most clear and e-mail it to me? Maybe I can find out who he is."

"I can," Phil answered, "but I won't if you're going to flash it around."

"Why not?" she asked, a little annoyed.

"Because we don't know anything about this guy," Phil answered. "Use your head, Emma. If he has criminal connections, especially to any gangs, just showing his photo around could get you killed."

"Phil's right," Paul Miller agreed, taking his seat again.

Emma's mother picked up the near empty pitcher. "You two talk some sense into her hard head. I can't even listen to this." She went into the house through the back kitchen door, then stuck her head back out. "Are you two going to be here for dinner or going out?" she asked Phil and Emma. "Your father was going to grill swordfish tonight."

Emma and Phil looked at each other, then Emma said to Phil, "Would you be disappointed if we skipped that movie and stayed in?"

"Not at all," he answered with a smile. "We can all watch a movie here."

"Hot dog!" Granny said with excitement. "I love family movie nights."

"We'll join you, Mom," Emma said to Elizabeth. "Do you have enough?"

"Plenty," Elizabeth said with obvious pleasure at the thought of a family dinner at home. "Would you whip up that couscous salad to go with it?" Emma smiled and nodded. "And we'll also grill some eggplant and tomatoes," Elizabeth added. "How does that sound?"

"Better than any five-star restaurant, Elizabeth," Phil answered with a wide smile.

When Elizabeth went back into the house, Paul said to them, "What we need is a way to check on the identity of this guy without raising suspicion."

"We?" Emma said, snapping her eyes to her father.

"You know what I mean," Paul said. "Don't you have any connections you could ask for a favor, Phil?"

Phil laughed. "Tax attorneys do deal with criminals, Paul, but not usually this type." A silence fell over the table, then Phil added, "But I think I know of a contact Emma has and doesn't even realize it."

· CHAPTER TWELVE ·

"WHAT in the world are you talking about?" Emma asked Phil with surprise. "Or should I ask, who in the world are you talking about?"

Phil gave her a sly grin. "Who texted you just today?"

Emma gave the question quick thought, then asked, "Gino Costello?"

Paul Miller sat up with interest. "Isn't that Tanisha's father, the famous writer?"

"Yes," answered Phil. "And a few years ago he wrote a best-selling novel centered around Latino gangs in Los Angeles."

Granny move closer. "That doesn't mean he can finger the guy in the photos."

"I agree with Granny," said Emma. "She just said that doesn't mean Gino can identify the man with Carlos."

"I said *finger* him," the ghost said with emphasis. "If you're going to investigate crime, you have to learn the lingo." Emma didn't translate that.

"You don't know unless you ask," Phil said. "It's a great book. I remember seeing him on a lot of talk shows when it first came out. He'd done quite a bit of deep research for it, including being given direct access for interviews by the gangs themselves. Seems they were determined that he get it right in the book. He was even blindfolded and frisked for wires when he was taken to meet with them."

"I wished I'd been there," said an excited Granny.

"It wouldn't hurt to ask the man," offered Paul.

Emma fished her phone out of her purse, which she hadn't taken into the house yet. She put the phone on the table, where it remained quiet and still while she gave the idea thought. "He did text me to call him." She picked up the phone and started sending a message.

"You writing him now?" asked Paul.

"Yes, Dad. I'm going to ask him when is the best time to call tonight, if he's available. He lives in Chicago, which is two hours ahead of us, but he could be anywhere at the moment. I understand from Tanisha that he travels a lot."

Almost immediately, Emma got a text back. "Wow, that was fast!" She read it. "He says he's available for a call around nine tonight our time. He'll call me."

"Can I sit in on it?" asked an eager Phil.

"There he goes," said Granny, "going all fan-boy again."

Emma smiled at Granny, but said to Phil, "Sure and make sure you e-mail that photo to me so I can send it to him if he agrees to look at it. Meanwhile, I'm going to go make that cous-cous salad for dinner." She looked at the time on her phone as she got up from the table. "Today has flown by. Seems like we were just having lunch and now it's almost time for dinner."

"Don't you want to hear what else I found out?" asked Granny, her hands on her hips with impatience. "Or don't you care now that you have a fancy writer on board?"

Emma stared at the ghost. "You have more, Granny?"

"That's what I said, isn't it?" Granny tapped a foot on the patio floor.

"But I thought you said Carlos just went home then to school."

"He did," answered Granny. "But there was something else that happened at the restaurant that you haven't given me time to tell ya. You're not the only one who can do that fancy multitasking, ya know."

Emma took her seat, saying to the two men, "Granny said something else happened today at the restaurant." Once settled back at the table, she said to the ghost, "Okay, Granny, spill it."

"Well, not if you're going to get all snippy with me," the ghost said with a sniff.

"Really, Granny," Emma said, working to keep frustration out of her voice. Granny could be so touchy at times and sometimes needed to have information pulled from her. Emma attributed part of that to Granny being a ghost with a sketchy sense of time and the other part to Granny simply being ornery. "I want to hear what you found out. I'm all ears."

Even though the two men couldn't hear Granny, both leaned forward to show their eagerness for the report.

"After Carlos went back to work," Granny began, "it got kind of boring so I flitted around doing some hard-core surveillance." The ghost scrunched her hazy brow to show how serious she was taking her assignment. "The place was almost empty of customers. The chef was in the kitchen getting things ready for dinnertime. You know that pretty young hostess that was there before?"

"You mean Ana Gonzales? Hector's daughter?" asked Emma.

"Yeah," confirmed Granny. "Her. Well, she was on break and in the storeroom playing kissy face with one of the other waiters." Emma quickly told the men the report so far.

A muted chuckle came from deep in Phil's chest. "Good thing her father is off today." He'd gone back to researching on his laptop.

"Hector wasn't off today," Granny said, clearly confused.

"Yes, he was, Granny," Emma told the ghost. "Before you and Felix showed up today, Rikki told us that Hector takes Wednesdays off, including today."

"Well," Granny said with assurance, "working or not, he showed up and went straight upstairs and barged into Rikki's office. It looked more interesting than watching Carlos fold napkins and fill salt shakers so I followed him. Rikki was at her desk working and Hector started yelling at her."

"Hector and Rikki were fighting?" Emma asked with interest. She was looking at Granny but heard Phil's computer go silent next to her.

"Like cats and dogs," Granny confirmed. "He was growling and baring his teeth like a pit bull and she was hissing and fussing like an angry cornered feline."

"What about?" Emma asked. "Could you tell?"

Granny nodded. "At first it was difficult to understand. They were speaking in Spanish, but Hector was so wound up and talking so fast that I think Rikki was having trouble following him. He was pacing and gesturing like a windmill as he yelled." Granny herself paced while she tried to piece it all together. "I thought he was going to have a stroke."

"What is it?" asked Phil.

"Granny witnessed a big argument today between Hector and Rikki," Emma told the men. She turned back to Granny. "Go ahead, Granny. What else happened?"

"Rikki told Hector to calm down and to speak slower and in English. She got up and closed the door to her office and got him a bottle of water from one of them small ice-boxes she had by her desk. After she handed it to Hector, he plopped down on her sofa and drank some of it and collected himself a little, but he was still steaming mad. But at least I understood what he was saying after that."

Emma translated for Phil and Paul. "What else, Granny?" she asked when she was done.

Granny looked directly at Emma. "They were fighting about you, I think. At least part of the time."

Emma pointed at herself. "Me? Are you sure?"

The ghost nodded. "Hector was mad that Rikki had you come back. He said T.J. was right, that you were a fake and probably a plant by either Lucy or Fiesta Time. He demanded to know what you said to Rikki." Still surprised, Emma told the men.

"Wait a minute," said Phil. "Hector wasn't even there today when we were. I wonder who told him."

Granny shrugged. "Rikki asked him the same thing and he didn't answer."

"I'll bet it was his daughter who told him," Phil said even before Emma had a chance to translate Granny's response.

Emma shook her head. "But she wasn't there today when we were. At least I didn't see her."

"What about the other waiter we saw with Carlos?" Phil suggested. "Maybe that's her boyfriend and he told her and she told her dad."

"Granny," Emma said, returning her attention to the ghost, "what did the boy with Ana look like?"

The ghost gave it some thought. "He seemed about her age, maybe a little older, but not much. He wasn't as tall as Carlos, but not a little guy either. Oh, and he had a mustache, one of those scraggly ones that hardly seems worth the trouble."

Emma turned to Phil. "I think we found the source of Hector's information. From Granny's description, I think Ana's boyfriend is the same waiter we saw with Carlos when we arrived. It's a safe bet either he told Hector or he told Ana and she told her father." She looked back at Granny, who was now kneeling and cooing to Archie, who was on his back showing his belly to her. "What did Rikki tell Hector, Granny?"

"Sounded like the truth to me," Granny said. "She told him that Felix showed up and wanted her to sell the restaurant."

"That couldn't have gone over well," noted Emma.

"I've seen dynamite explosions with less bang," said Granny. The spirit stood up and came closer to Emma. "Hector got downright nasty after that. He called Rikki a fool if she listened to you and a fool to believe Felix could return from the dead." Granny furrowed her forehead and punched the air like a boxer. "I wanted to give him what's what for talking to that poor girl that way."

"What else did he say, Granny?" prodded Emma.

"Not much, but Rikki assured him that she has no intention of selling and he needs to be patient and to trust her."

"Did that calm him down any?" asked Emma.

"It did seem to mollify him a bit, at least until Rikki mentioned something about her father's death."

Emma sat up straighter. Quickly she brought the men up to speed on the conversation. "Did she ask Hector about it, Granny?"

"She sure did. She asked Hector if there was anyone who might have wanted to kill Felix. The question took him aback and he reminded her that the coroner called it an accident. Then Rikki said something like, but what if it wasn't? Hector was still for a moment, then exploded, calling Rikki a little fool again."

"What did Rikki do?" asked Emma.

"I half expected the child to dissolve into tears, and she seemed close to it, but then she changed."

"Changed how, Granny?" asked Emma, her senses pricked and sharp.

Granny floated back and forth as she remembered. "It was as if she became another person," reported Granny. "Just when I thought she was going to start sobbing, she straightened up in her chair with ramrod posture and glared at Hector. Then she reminded him that even if he was like family, in the end he wasn't. He was an employee and he needed to remember his place."

"Boy, that doesn't sound like Rikki at all," said Emma. She paused, then asked, "Granny, did you see any indication of Felix's spirit being present when this happened?"

"None," answered Granny with a shake of her head. "But I get what you're saying. It could be he was there but slipped in undetected and took her over, but I don't think so. I don't think Felix's spirit is that evolved. He can barely find his way down a hallway."

"What happened next?" asked Emma.

"Not much," Granny told her. "Hector seemed stunned by her turn of behavior. After a few seconds of silence, he got to his feet and left, but not before giving her one of them if-looks-could-kill stares."

When Emma finished giving a full report to Paul and Phil, Phil said, "Do you think Felix was there, or do you think Rikki had finally had enough badgering from Hector? Didn't you say he sometimes forgets she's in charge?"

Emma nodded. "That's what Rikki said. Maybe she finally did have enough. Everyone is telling her what to do, including the ghost of her father. Rikki needs to do what is right for Rikki, even if that means bucking Felix and Lucy or pushing back on the pressure from T.J. and Hector."

Emma got up from the table. "Nice work, Granny."

"Do you want me to keep tailing Carlos or keep looking for Felix?" the ghost asked.

"Neither," Emma answered. "Except for the call later with Gino Costello, let's all take the night off." Emma headed for the back door. "Meanwhile, I have a couscous salad to deal with, which is sounding like a whole lot more fun."

· CHAPTER THIRTEEN ·

"HI, Gino," Emma said into the speaker phone. "Nice to speak with you again." She and Phil were in the study using the speaker phone attached to the house's landline. Before Gino called, Emma had texted him the number, knowing the landline would give them a more consistent connection. Granny hovered close by. "I'm here with my friend Phil Bowers."

"Hello, Phil," called Gino through the phone in a hearty voice. "I've heard a lot about you both from my daughter. I hope we can all meet soon, which is why I'm calling."

"We have something to ask you about, too, Gino," Emma told him. "But first, are the girls okay?"

"I think so." Gino laughed. "Then again, we're just the parents, what do we know, right? Unless they deign to tell us or need our help."

"So true," added Phil. "I have two boys myself."

"But this isn't about Kelly and Tanisha," Gino continued.

"I have a favor to ask you, Emma. It's rather a big one, but I hope you'll consider it."

"Shoot," she said. "After the help you were to the girls last year, there is little I'd deny you."

"Aw, that was nothing," he said. "I'm just glad my contacts were still of use."

"This is actually about my work, Emma," Gino said, "and yours. I'm researching a new novel and want to add a bit of paranormal to it, specifically ghosts. I understand that's your forte."

"That's a real departure from your usual work, isn't it, Gino?" said Phil.

"Yes and no," said the noted author. "It will still be a crime novel, but I want to incorporate ghosts as part of the plotline."

"Real ghosts?" asked Emma with suspicion.

On the other end, they heard Gino Costello hem and haw, then he gave a nervous chuckle. "Listen, I know the girls believe in all that and I know, Emma, that you're greatly respected in your field, but I'm more of a science guy. As far as I'm concerned, what happened last fall with the girls was a fluke, something they stumbled upon due to two active imaginations. Even though they told me what happened, I have a hard time believing it at face value and was able to keep the ghost end out of the report to both the police and the media. For that, you should thank me."

Emma knew what Gino was saying was true. The media had focused mainly on Tanisha and Kelly being two friends who were also the daughters of famous people and who had stumbled upon a corpse, which eventually led to the capture of a killer. There had been nothing said about spirits, except for Kelly's mother being a host of a paranormal TV show.

In fact, Emma wasn't even mentioned much. Most of the celebrity focus had been absorbed by Grant Whitecastle and Gino himself, which Emma didn't mind one bit.

"So you didn't believe Kelly and Tanisha?" Phil asked, barely keeping the annoyance out of his voice.

"I believe that they believe what they saw and experienced," Gino answered carefully after a short hesitation. "But what the girls said back then planted a seed in my brain about incorporating ghosts into this new book I'm planning. Not for real, but maybe as a scapegoat for the real killer or killers."

"Scapegoat," groused Granny. "Ghosts are not scapegoats." She crossed her arms and scowled at the phone. "You tell him that, Emma."

Emma motioned for Granny to calm down and saw Phil glance in that direction. She made the same gesture to him, seeing him losing his fan-boy glow.

"Gino, if you don't believe in spirits," Emma said, aiming her voice at the speaker phone, "then why do you need my help? You're a novelist, why not just make the stuff up?"

"Good point," Gino answered, "but while I don't believe in ghosts and such myself, I'm sure many of my readers do and I always strive to give my work a ring of authenticity. If I just write it on the fly, it might sound too tongue in cheek."

Emma looked at Phil, but said into the phone, "So how can I help?"

"I would like you to be my guest at a farmhouse my wife and I are leasing this September in Massachusetts. You, too, Phil. I'll be setting up shop there while I research the history of the area and get a feel for the local people."

Emma ran the information around quickly in her head. "Phil has told me how thorough you are in your research," she said to Gino. "How do spirits come into play?"

"Much of the book takes place in a small New England farm community, and the locals believe that the spirits of a murdered family are responsible for a recent rash of deaths. Of course, they're not, but I want to build a real tension of possibility and fear of ghosts in the book before the reveal near the end."

"Is the farmhouse you're renting supposedly haunted?" she asked.

"Not to my knowledge," Gino answered with a deep laugh. "But I think you could provide the background to give the story that touch of realism." He paused, then added, "So what do you say? We can have the girls come down from Boston if they're available and make it a real family vacation, too."

Looking over at Phil, Emma could read the eagerness in his eyes. The fan-boy was back. She smiled at him and picked up her phone to check her calendar. "I don't know about Phil and the girls, but I could be there in September for a bit."

Phil also had his phone out. "I could move some things around and be there, too."

"Great," said Gino with enthusiasm.

Once again Granny folded her arms across her chest. "Does anyone care if I'm available?" When Emma raised her eyebrows at the ghost, Granny snapped, "I'll check my schedule and have my people call your people." Then she disappeared. Emma shook her head in amusement.

Phil looked at Emma, giving her a sign to go ahead and ask Gino for her favor.

"Book research is sort of what I wanted to ask you about, Gino," Emma said into the phone.

"You planning on getting into publishing?" he asked.

"No," Emma answered. "I'll leave that to my friend and mentor Milo Ravenscroft."

"Yes," Gino said, "I've heard of him. I haven't read any of his books, but I do know the name." He coughed, then they heard Gino take a drink of something and cough again. "Sorry," he said when he came back on. "I have a bit of a summer cold. So what's your question?"

"Remember the research you did on your book about LA gangs?" Phil asked.

"Of course I do," Gino answered. "It was some of the most interesting and dangerous research I've done to date."

"If Emma sent you a photo of a guy, would you be able to tell us, or do you know of anyone who could tell us, if he's involved in any LA-based gangs? It might even be someone you met in your research. We're concerned that if he is and we show the photo around, it could get dangerous."

"You're right about that." There was a long pause on Gino's end of the line and a couple of deep coughs. "But why do you need to know?" Before they could answer, Gino said, "Wait a minute, T told me that sometimes your ghost work gets you mixed up with cold case murders. Is that what this is about?"

"Actually," Emma answered, "a friend asked me to look into something and this man popped up unexpectedly. We want to know if he's dangerous or not before proceeding."

After another cough, Gino said, "I still have some contacts in LA. I could show it to some discreet folks and see, but if he is gang-related, you need to steer clear. Understand?"

"Yes," Emma agreed. "I'm sending the photo to you now." She sent a text to Gino and attached the photo of the man with Carlos.

Almost a full minute passed before Gino said, "Got it. I sure don't recognize him but let me see what I can do. I don't know how long it will take. I might have an answer tonight or not for a few days."

"We understand," Emma said. "Any help you can give would be great."

"And we're good for late September?" Gino asked. "Should be a good time for leaf peeping, too."

Both Phil and Emma confirmed that they would be there.

MIDMORNING THE NEXT day, Emma was running on the treadmill in her home office, which was housed in the guest house behind the garage of her parents' home. The guest house was originally set up as an exercise room by her parents with a treadmill, exercise bike, and various other workout equipment and mats, along with a DVR player for exercise videos. Her parents used it almost every day. Shortly after Emma moved back in, she commandeered half of the large studio apartment as her office, outfitting it with a desk and a love seat. Phil was at her desk. Having already put in his time on the treadmill, he was now handling his legal work, communicating with his office in San Diego and clients via e-mail. One wall of the room was a bank of sliding glass doors. The drapes were open, displaying flowers and shrubs and shaded sunshine from the Millers' backyard. In the background, soft classical music played.

"I could get used to this lifestyle," Phil said to Emma without looking up from his work. "It certainly beats getting dressed and going into the office every day."

She took a swig of water from a water bottle in a holder on the treadmill and laughed. "It is pretty sweet. I only go into my office at the studio for meetings and tapings. Everything else I do from here."

Emma's phone, which sat on the edge of the desk, rang. Phil looked at the display. "It's Gino," he informed her.

"Go ahead and answer it," she said as she slowed down and prepared to stop.

By the time she took another couple of drinks of water and mopped the sweat from her face, Gino Costello and Phil had exchanged pleasantries. "Emma's right here," Phil said into the phone. "Hang on. I'm putting you on speaker."

"I have information on the guy in the photo you sent me, but I don't think it's what you expected," Gino told them.

"So he's not part of a gang or anything?" Emma asked.

"Not that my source knows of," Gino said, "but he did recognize him. His name is Steve Bullock. His full name is Esteban Santiago Bullock," Gino reported. "He goes by Steve. His mother is Latina. His father a *gringo*."

"Santiago." Emma rolled the name around on her tongue, tasting it. "Where have I heard that name recently?"

"Fiesta Time," Phil said. "It's the name of the family that owns Fiesta Time. That's too much of a coincidence for there not to be a connection."

"Now you two are just stealing my thunder," said Gino. "That was my next bit of information. Steve Bullock is one of the VPs of a company called Fiesta Time, which is owned by his family. They manufacture and sell a line of Mexican food products."

"What about the kid in the second photo we sent you last night?" asked Emma. Before they went to bed, Emma had had an idea. She had Phil isolate a decent photo of Carlos from the ones Phil took and they sent that one to Gino, too.

"Nothing came from that," Gino told them. "He looks

like a million young men in LA, but nothing specific struck my sources. But don't be disappointed—that's a good thing. If he'd been in one of the gangs, they would have known him even if he was as young as ten or twelve."

Even though Emma felt relief at the news, she also felt sad at Gino's commentary. "Thanks, Gino," she told him. "We owe you."

"You owe me nothing," he said. "You and your family have become good friends to my daughter, and I intend to pick your brain and resources in September. Something tells me this is the start of a wonderful friendship."

They all laughed and were about to say good-bye when Gino remembered something. "By the way, I almost forgot. If you're interested in crossing paths again with ole Stevie Bullock, he lunches almost every day at his family's restaurant. It's called Santiago's and it's located in Alhambra."

Phil and Emma locked eyes in surprise. "Why would your contact know where Steve Bullock lunches?" Phil asked for the two of them.

"Steve Bullock might not be a gang member, but he is a person of interest to my source," Gino answered.

"Is that source law enforcement?" Emma asked.

"Can't say," Gino told them, "but I will tell you that he's thought to be a bit on the slimy side. Sort of a corporate fixer for his family. So be careful if you get close and call me if you need anything else."

Once they were off the phone, Emma said to Phil, "How do you feel about having lunch at Santiago's today?"

CHAPTER FOURTEEN

HOUSED in a stand-alone stucco building the color of a café latte with a dark red tile roof, Santiago's was located on a corner of a busy stretch of Garfield Boulevard. It also had ample parking. Emma and Phil arrived around twelve thirty and found the restaurant packed with patrons.

"Seems like a popular place," Phil noted after giving the hostess his name. The hostess was a thick-set middle-aged woman with a helmet of hair dyed the flat black of a dry Magic Marker. She was dressed in black slacks and a plain white blouse instead of a traditional costume like Ana at Roble. The waiters, both the men and the women, also wore black pants and white shirts but not *guayaberas*. Phil and Emma sat side by side on a wooden bench on the narrow patio in front of the building. Several other waiting customers were spread out on other benches.

"It sure does," said Emma. "If Steve's here, I hope we can spot him."

"So where are we now?" asked Granny as she popped up in front of them.

Emma immediately got out her phone, but instead of making a call, she pretended she was speaking into it so she could talk to Granny. "We're at a Mexican restaurant, Granny. Gino called this morning and said the man in the photos always eats lunch here."

"Did he find out who he was?" the ghost asked as she looked around at the other people nearby. "Is he some drug lord or maybe a hit man?" Granny asked with eagerness. "In those Italian mobster movies the mob bosses always hang out in restaurants. Maybe Mexican gangsters do the same."

"No," Emma said, glancing at Phil, who was trying to work out the conversation just from listening to Emma's side. "He works for Fiesta Time, the company that owns this place."

"You mean the company that's trying to buy Roble?" Granny asked.

"Yep, that's the one," Emma confirmed. She looked at Granny and had a thought. "Granny," she said in a quiet tone into the phone, "do you think you would recognize the man with Carlos if you saw him again?"

The ghost lit up with excitement. "Sure I would. I'm dead, not senile."

"Then how about you going inside and floating about? Let us know where he's sitting."

"You got it, Chief." Granny saluted and disappeared.

"Nice thinking," said Phil. "But where's your Bluetooth earpiece?"

"At home charging." Emma lowered her phone but didn't put it away. "This is a big place. We'd have a better chance of getting seated in his area if we know where he is."

Granny popped back out a few minutes later. "Señor Gorgeous is here. He's seated at a table in the bar."

Emma raised her phone up again. "Alone?"

"Looks that way, but it also looks like he might be expecting someone. There are two place settings at the table."

"Great job, Granny." Emma gave Phil a nod, then got up and went back inside to the hostess. Phil followed.

"Excuse me," Emma said to the woman at the podium. "We're on the list but I was wondering if there was any room in the bar. The name is Phil Bowers."

The hostess found Phil's name on the waiting list. "Your table just became available but it's not in the bar."

"Could we perhaps wait for one in the bar?" Emma asked.

"Most people prefer to sit in the dining room, but hold on a second." The woman left and returned a few seconds later. "There's a table almost ready back there. If you want to wait another minute or two, I can give you that one."

"Perfect," Emma said with a smile. The hostess returned the smile and called the next name on the list.

It wasn't long before they were following the hostess into the large bar area. As she walked through the room, Emma scanned it for any sign of Steve Bullock. She need not have worried about spotting him. Granny had gone on ahead and was perched by his table, waving her arms as if she were directing a 747 to a terminal. "He's over here," the ghost yelled to Emma.

"This place isn't as fancy as Roble," commented Phil as they walked behind the hostess. "It's more what I'm used to when I eat Mexican."

Phil was right. Santiago's had a more fun and traditional décor than the recently redecorated and modern Restaurante Roble. The chairs were painted a variety of bright colors with woven seats and backs. Instead of tablecloths, the tables were covered with green and teal tile squares with individual paper placemats in front of each chair. The booths were wood framed and upholstered with a colorful striped fabric. Above them, light fixtures of hammered metal lit the rooms. The walls were painted a muted orange and pink and decorated with sombreros, serapes, piñatas, and small shelves on which sat dozens of Mexican knickknacks. It looked to Emma as if the kiosks of Olvera Street had exploded inside the restaurant.

Without looking directly at Granny, Emma gave her a slight nod, letting her know that she'd seen her and Steve Bullock, who was seated in a corner booth poring over a tablet. When they reached their booth, Emma took the side facing Bullock's table. Phil slid into the booth opposite her and the hostess handed them their menus.

"You don't want to sit next to me today?" asked Emma with a laugh. "You usually do."

"Not when I'm trying to watch your back, I don't," Phil said from behind his menu, keeping his voice low. He pulled his reading glasses from a shirt pocket and put them on. "There's a guy at the bar checking you out, and I don't think it's just because you're a beautiful woman."

"Really?" Emma started to turn her head.

"Don't look at him," Phil snapped in a quick whisper. "Dang, even Granny knows better than that. Speaking of which, where is she?"

"Standing by the big semicircular booth in the corner," Emma whispered while studying her menu. "That's where Steve Bullock is seated." Unlike her, Phil did not turn around to look. "He's currently alone, but it looks like he might be expecting someone."

"Well, the fellow I'm talking about is staring in that direction, too. He's splitting his gaze between you and that corner." Without moving his head, Phil glanced toward the bar. "Do you think he can see Granny?"

It wasn't that common for people to be mediums, but there were enough out there to make Emma wary at Phil's words. She'd also learned that sometimes a person had the gift and chose not to let others know about it. "Could be," she said to Phil, "or maybe he recognizes me from my TV show."

"He doesn't exactly fit your usual demographic, Emma." Phil pretended to be pointing out something on the menu to her. "He looks like a retired cop to me. Or ex-military. Or maybe both. He has to be close to seventy, but in good condition and observant. He's nursing a beer and not paying much attention to the game on the TV over the bar."

"Talk about someone being observant," Emma quipped as she reached over and took Phil's hand. "Didn't Gino say that Steve Bullock was a person of interest to his source? Maybe that's a real cop pretending to be old and bored. And maybe he doesn't care for soccer."

Phil nodded. "Another good possibility." Phil lifted Emma's hand. Leaning forward, he kissed her knuckles before releasing it. He went back to reading his menu. "Or he's some old guy who can see Granny and your interaction with her."

"Seems you're stuck on that theory."

"Uh-huh. It's what my empty gut is telling me by the way he's watching you and that corner." Phil looked at Emma over the top of his reading glasses. "Tell you what. As careful as you can, get Granny to come over here. If the guy follows her with his eyes, we'll know he can see her."

"That's a great idea," Emma whispered back to him.

"Yep, that's why I get the big bucks," Phil said, seemingly absorbed in choosing his lunch.

Before Emma could take any action, a tiny waif of a

waitress popped up at their table, introduced herself as Brenda Ann, and plopped down a large basket of tortilla chips and a bowl of salsa. A busboy swung by and placed two glasses of water on the table and left. On Thursdays, Brenda Ann informed them with a bright smile, margaritas and Mexican beers were available at an all-day happy hour price.

"Feel like a margarita, my dear?" Phil asked Emma. She nodded. Phil turned to the waitress. "The lady will have a margarita, light salt on the rim. I'll take a Negra Modelo, no glass. And could you bring us some guacamole for the chips?"

"Sure," Brenda Ann said, her order pad held at the ready. "Our special today is grilled tilapia tacos with rice, beans, and corn cake. Our fajitas are the best, no matter which ones you get, and our *chiles rellenos* are legendary." She pointed the items out on Emma's menu, which was flat on the table.

"Legendary, huh?" asked Phil with a small wink.

"Yes, sir," said the spunky waitress with confidence.

Emma laughed. "Please give us a minute."

"Drinks and guacamole coming right up." The waitress left as quickly as she'd appeared. A few seconds later a bowl of guacamole was left on their table by the same speedy busboy.

"Well, the service is better here than at Roble," noted Emma. "But then Carlos was surly that day because he'd just been dressed down for showing his tattoos." She looked at the menu again. "The menus are similar except that Roble had a lot more healthier options."

"Roble caters to a tourist and executive lunch crowd," Phil said. "This place looks more like a local clientele." He picked up a chip and dipped it into the salsa. "And there are at least a half-dozen tiny places on Olvera Street that serve burritos and enchiladas. Rikki's plan to make Roble more upscale was a sound one. It separates it from the other places on the street."

Emma glanced over at Steve Bullock's table. Their booth was situated along a side wall between it and the end of the bar, where Phil said the watchful man was seated. Both were several yards away but in opposite directions. From their booth they could hear snippets of casual conversations in both English and Spanish spoken in normal tones mingling with each other from nearby tables and patrons seated along the bar. Emma could see Bullock but not directly, giving her a chance to observe without being too obvious, but doubted they'd be able to hear any of his conversations unless he raised his voice. He was still alone and Granny was still hovering around him, but she was watching the soccer game on the overhead bar TV instead of watching her target. Picking up her menu with one hand, Emma toyed with the diamond stud earring in her right ear—the ear facing in Granny's direction. As carefully as possible, she wiggled her index finger and gave a quick glance at the ghost. Granny still wasn't paying attention. She tried waving again, this time stretching as a ploy. No one noticed, including Granny. She didn't risk turning around to see if the man had seen her.

"Granny is watching the game on TV," Emma hissed at Phil.

"Where is she?" he asked.

"Still by the booth, but closer to that end of the bar now."

"Allow me," Phil said with a smile. Getting up from the table, he went over to the bar, inserting himself in a gap between two patrons who were eating lunch and watching the game. He asked the bartender, "Hey, son, can I have some lime slices for my lady's water?"

The bartender, a young fellow with thick jet-back hair and glasses, nodded. He placed several lime slices in a shot glass and held it out to Phil. "Is that enough, sir?"

"That's fine, thank you. I swear she's as bad as my *granny* when it comes to limes in her water." He took the glass with the limes, placed a buck tip on the bar, and returned to the table.

"I can't believe you did that," Emma said, giggling but keeping her voice low.

"The question is," Phil said as he plopped a lime slice into both his water glass and Emma's, "did it work?"

"Yep. She's no longer watching TV," Emma reported. "She's now glaring at us and tapping her foot." Emma took a drink of her water. "How about that guy?"

"He's watching Granny watch us," Phil said, cocking an eyebrow in Emma's direction. "And I'm guessing Granny's now here because so are his eyes."

"You guessed right, Phil," Emma confirmed. "So what do we do about this?"

"About what?" asked Granny.

Just then Brenda Ann returned with their drinks. She went right through Granny to place them on the table.

"Boy, I hate that," groused Granny, moving to the side.

"You ready to order now or do you still need a few minutes?" Brenda Ann asked Phil and Emma.

"I'll have the vegetable fajitas," Emma told Brenda Ann. Phil ordered the tilapia tacos.

"He can see and hear Granny," Phil said to Emma as soon as Brenda Ann left.

"Are you sure?" Emma asked.

Phil nodded. "When the waitress walked through Granny and Granny complained, he laughed. When I looked at him, he quickly turned away." Phil took a drink of his beer.

"What are you two talking about?" asked Granny. "Aren't we here to do surveillance on that Bullock guy?"

Emma picked up her margarita, which was served in a glass with a saguaro cactus stem. She took a drink. It was delicious so she took another, then answered carefully, "Yes, Granny, but there's a man at the bar who we think can see and hear you. He might also be watching Steve Bullock. We're not sure."

"It's the older guy with the very short gray hair," Phil said quietly right before taking a bite of chip and guacamole.

Granny turned around and studied the people at the bar. Most were men having a quick solo lunch. Before Emma could stop her, she took off, heading straight for the man in question.

"Uh-oh," Emma said.

"She's going over there, isn't she?" asked Phil. "I don't even have to see her to know it. It's typical of her. Not to mention, his eyes just got as big as the TV."

Emma got up and moved to Phil's side of the table, sliding in next to him. "Bullock will have to wait," she whispered to Phil. "I have to see this."

Phil leaned into her. "I can't tell you how jealous I am that you get to see it firsthand."

Emma patted his hand. "Don't worry, sweetheart, I'll give you a play-by-play."

As Granny reached the man at the bar, he turned away and took a sip of beer as if nothing were there.

"So," Granny said to him, "how's it hanging?" The man started coughing and wiped his mouth with the back of his hand, but did not make eye contact with the ghost.

Emma told Phil, who raised his beer and said into Emma's ear, "Now he knows what we go through. How soon do you think before he'll break and communicate with her?"

"Hard to say," Emma whispered back. "Depends on how long he's been doing this and how persistent she is."

"My money's on Granny," Phil told Emma with a grin. "Seasoned or not, she'll crack him like a soft-boiled egg and soon."

"My friends and I want to know," Granny continued, speaking loud enough for her voice to carry back to their table, "if you're just watching us or if you're watching that Bullock guy, too."

The man looked at Granny then through her at Phil and Emma, studying them a few seconds. They stared back. The man took a sip of his beer and moved his eyes toward Bullock's table, studying it with the same even deliberation. He took a bigger drink from his mug. Until now he'd been nursing his beer. Since Granny approached him, it was going down at a much faster pace. Holding his mug up to his lips, he said something.

"Did he just say something?" Emma asked Phil. "I could have sworn I saw his lips move right before he took his last drink.

"They did," Phil confirmed. "Too bad we can't wire Granny."

"He just asked me why we're so interested in Bullock," Granny called over to them. The spirit turned back to the man and jerked a hazy thumb back at Phil and Emma. "We're on a case," she told him. Back at the table, Emma groaned. "That's Emma Whitecastle, the world-famous medium, and her man, Phil, a world-famous tax attorney," Granny continued.

After Emma told Phil what Granny had said, both of them took long drinks of their own, after which Emma asked Phil, "Is there such a thing as a world-famous tax attorney?"

Phil wiped his mouth and mustache with a paper napkin. "I guess there is now."

Granny turned around to them. "He says he knows who you are, Emma. Sorry, Phil, but he doesn't seem to reckon you."

Without looking at Granny or them, the man drained his beer and ordered another. When it arrived, he slipped off his bar stool and headed their way, fresh frosty mug in hand. When he got to their table, he looked down at them, taking stock, holding his strong wiry body erect with disciplined posture. Before anything was said, their food arrived, served up by the busboy. Without waiting for an invitation, the man slipped into the side of the booth Emma had vacated.

"Sorry," Granny said after following him over. "He got away from me."

"Dig in, folks," he told them. "Don't let it get cold on my account." His voice was mostly even with a few rough patches, like speed bumps on his vocal chords.

"You have us at a disadvantage," Phil told him politely but with a firmness that promised they would not be easy prey. "You know who we are, but we don't have a clue about you except that you can see and hear ghosts. Oh, and by the way, the cheeky spirit with us is Ish Reynolds. Most call her Granny."

A slow smile oozed across his face before the man answered. Raising his beer mug to them in salute, he said, "Name's Jeremiah Jones. Most call me Jeremiah."

· CHAPTER FIFTEEN ·

JEREMIAH Jones was an African-American man with a well-worn face and salt-and-pepper stubble on both his head and his chin. He took stock of Emma and Phil through dark gray eyes. "Go on now, have your lunch. We can get to know each other while you eat."

Emma was the first to pick up her fork. She started assembling her grilled vegetables on a tortilla, along with salsa and guacamole, rolled it, and took a bite. She was into her second bite before Phil decided it was okay to let down his guard and tackle his fish tacos. Emma dabbed at her mouth with a napkin and said to Jeremiah, "So how long have you been a medium?"

"There'll be time enough to discuss that later," Jeremiah told her in a low voice. "What do you want with Steve Bullock?" He grabbed a chip from the basket, scooped up a liberal amount of guacamole with it, and popped it into his mouth whole.

Phil swallowed the bite he was working on before answering. "You on his payroll?"

Jeremiah leaned back against the booth and laughed. Just then Brenda Ann approached the table, "Everything good here?" she asked. Phil and Emma nodded. She turned to Jeremiah and gave him a quick peck on his cheek. "Good seeing you, Jeremiah. I saw you at the bar earlier but I've been too busy to even say hello. Are these nice people friends of yours?"

"Yeah, Brenda Ann, they are. This is Phil and Emma." He turned to them, "And this lovely lady is Brenda Ann Norris." Arching back, Jeremiah reached into a pocket of his jeans and pulled out some cash. Lifting up Brenda Ann's left hand, he discreetly stuffed some money into it. "If anyone asks about these two," he said, changing to a whisper, "you tell them they're friends of mine who came in to meet up with me. Got it?"

She started to protest, "You don't need to pay me to do that."

Jeremiah pressed the money on her more firmly, returning to a normal voice. "Then take those little girls of yours out for ice cream. And say hi to your mom and dad for me while you're at it. Oh, and could you bring me a couple of those fish tacos?" He pointed at Phil's plate. "They look great."

Brenda Ann nodded, sticking the money into her pants pocket as she left.

"I lived next door to her family about a hundred years ago," Jeremiah said by way of explanation. "Nice people."

"Do we need a reason to be here," asked Granny, "other than our real reason?" She was hovering next to Jeremiah, giving him a thorough examination.

"It's just a precaution," Jeremiah answered. He looked over at Phil. "Can you see this old woman here, or is it just Emma and me?"

"Old woman!" snapped Granny. "I'm younger than you, you old coot."

"Feisty little thing, aren't you?" Jeremiah said to the ghost. "He turned back to Emma and Phil. "She always like this?"

"Pretty much," answered Emma. "And to answer your question, no, Phil cannot see or hear spirits."

"The old—" Jeremiah began, then stopped and rechose his words. "This charming lady in the covered wagon outfit said you're working on a case." His voice had shifted back into a conspiratorial tone.

"Call me, Granny," snipped the ghost, crossing her arms in front of her.

Jeremiah smiled at the ghost. "You got it, Granny." He turned to Phil and Emma, catching them tossing glances at each other. "Seems you have some trust issues," he said to them. "Then how about I use the secret password?"

"Secret password?" asked Emma, looking at him with suspicion.

Brenda Ann showed up with Jeremiah's food. He fell upon it immediately, slathering salsa over everything, while Phil and Emma picked at their lunch and kept watch on him.

"Granny," Emma said to the ghost. "Let us know if something changes with that booth over there, like if someone joins him."

"You got it, Chief." Granny drifted back over to Bullock's booth.

Jeremiah chuckled through a mouthful of food. He swallowed. "I've never met any ghost with such an attitude, or with so much focus. They're usually kind of fuzzy."

"She's a pistol, even when you can't see or hear her," Phil told him.

When Jeremiah was almost done with his first taco, he said without looking up, "Read any good Gino Costello books lately?"

Phil nearly dropped his fork. Emma sloshed what was left of her margarita.

"Gino sent you?" asked Phil, recovering from the surprise.

"No, but he called me early this morning." Jeremiah scooped some rice and beans into his mouth, chewed slowly, and swallowed. "He said friends of his were looking to ID a guy in a grainy photo."

"So you're his gang contact?" Emma asked, leaning forward so she wouldn't be overheard.

"Used to be," Jeremiah admitted with a half smile. "I'm retired LAPD. Now I'm a part-time PI."

"I knew you had to be an ex-cop," Phil said with satisfaction. "So is Bullock under investigation?"

"I don't know of anything active," admitted Jeremiah. "He's thought to be kind of shady but nothing anyone can stick to him. I was really surprised to see his face on that photo Gino sent me. So I told Gino where his friends could find Bullock and came here to see who turned up."

"But what if we didn't?" asked Emma. She played with the stem of her glass, rolling it between her fingers as she ran a million questions around in her mind.

Jeremiah shrugged. "Then I'd have come back here tomorrow and the next day and all next week. I'm a semi-regular, which is why I knew where Bullock would be. No one would have suspected anything seeing my face here for lunch day after day. My gut told me that whoever Gino was helping would eventually show up." He laughed low. "My gut instincts are usually never wrong, but they were totally blindsided when a ghost showed up with Emma Whitecastle in tow." He paused. "How do you even know Gino? To my knowledge, he thinks paranormal activities are a bunch of BS."

"Our daughters are friends back in Boston," Emma explained. "Have you ever told Gino about your abilities?"

Jeremiah pursed his lips and looked off in the direction of Steve Bullock's table, where Granny was standing vigil. "Until now, no one else has ever known about this, not even my late wife."

"No one?" asked Phil with surprise.

"No one," emphasized Jeremiah. "It first started up when I was in the service in Nam. Just here and there, mostly dead buddies coming back. I thought at first it was just the stress of seeing all that death. Then it died out for many years and started up again after I was on the job for a while. Came in handy from time to time, though I never let on to anyone about it. But the spirits I met were not as communicative as your Granny there." He looked at Emma. "Is she really a relation or do you just call her that?"

"She's my great-great-great-grandmother," Emma told him. "On my mother's side."

Jeremiah looked again over toward Bullock's booth. "Someone like her would be a great advantage in police work." He looked at Emma and grinned. "Where in the world did she pick up the slang and street talk?"

"She watches a lot of TV, especially old crime dramas," Emma explained. Jeremiah shook his head and took a long pull from his mug.

"It looked to us like Bullock was expecting company," Phil said. "Or does he eat alone?"

"A bit of both. He seems to have a lady friend these days. At least he lunches here with her about twice a week. Pretty Latina. Big curvy girl always in a fancy suit like him."

"That sounds like Lucy Ricardo," Emma said to Phil. She looked to Jeremiah. "Do you know the Ricardo family? The ones who own Roble Foods?"

He shrugged. "I'd met Felix Ricardo a few times when a bunch of us got together for dinner on Olvera Street. I'd heard he died last year. Too bad. Seemed like a good guy—big on supporting his community and people in public service."

"Yes," Phil answered. "Supposedly he died from a heart attack."

Jeremiah's eyes bored into Phil's. "*Supposedly* is a loaded word in my world. It's like tacking on: *but I don't believe it.*"

Phil and Emma exchanged glances again.

"Would you like me to step out of the room while you two confer?" Jeremiah asked, his voice thick with sarcasm.

In response, Emma pulled out her phone and took a quick photo of Jeremiah, then started texting something.

"You sending that off to Gino?" Jeremiah chuckled.

"Yes," Emma answered. "I'm sorry if it's offensive, but we don't know you from a hole in the ground, even if you do know Gino." Done, Emma put the phone on the table between her and Phil.

"She has a point," added Phil. "Just because Gino asked you to identify someone doesn't mean we should trust you."

"Gino could be anywhere doing anything," Jeremiah pointed out. He glanced over to Bullock's booth. "Meanwhile it looks like Bullock's lunch date has arrived."

Almost as soon as he said it, Granny popped up next to the table. "Lucy's here," she announced. "You know, Rikki's crazy sister."

Emma scooted deeper into the booth closer to Phil to make sure Lucy didn't see her. She didn't want a scene and Lucy would be sure to make one. As she resettled, her phone vibrated. She read the message reply from Gino Costello, happy that it had arrived so quickly. She showed it to Phil. It read, *I'd trust Jeremiah Jones with my life but not with a jar of p-nut butter.—GC*

Phil looked across the table at Jeremiah. "You have a peanut butter problem? Aren't there twelve-step programs for that?"

Jeremiah laughed, showing large teeth the color of antique lace. "I'm horribly allergic to peanuts. Gino didn't know that and cooked something with peanut oil one night when I was visiting him in Chicago. We spent the rest of the night in the ER."

Next to the table, Granny fidgeted. "Are we gonna do something about that over there?"

"Hang on, Granny," Jeremiah told her. "Let the lady get settled, and Emma, get me up to speed."

Leaning forward and keeping her voice low, Emma quickly filled Jeremiah in on what had recently happened, including the encounter with the ghost of Felix Ricardo.

"Don't forget about the big fight I saw between Rikki and Hector," Granny added.

"Let me get this straight," Jeremiah said when Granny and Emma were finished. "The ghost of Felix wants them to sell and so does the woman over there with Bullock, but the younger daughter doesn't want to sell. And you don't think Felix died accidentally, as everyone else thinks, because of something he said to you?"

"Correct," said Phil. "He's told Emma several times that

if Rikki doesn't sell, she'll be in danger and might end up like him."

"Any other proof to believe he died by someone else's hand?" the ex-cop asked.

"No," answered Emma. "And Felix hasn't said that directly or pointed to anyone specifically. But I've found that sometimes spirits don't know exactly what happened to them."

Jeremiah rubbed his face, producing a scratchy sound. "Yeah, I've experienced the same thing. He also might not want to stir up any more trouble for his daughters by telling you who it is. It might be someone close to them. Close enough to hurt them." Jeremiah jerked his chin. "So how does Bullock play into this other than wanting to buy Roble?"

"The photos Gino showed you were taken while Steve Bullock was handing off a wad of cash to one of the waiters at Roble," Phil explained. "It was done behind a stand of trees away from the restaurant."

"That is suspicious, but not against the law unless the cash was for something illegal." Jeremiah took another sip of his beer and studied Emma. "So why don't you want that Lucy woman to see you?"

Emma took a deep breath. "The last time she saw me, she threw a fit because I was involved, and the last time her sister saw me, she ordered me to stay out of their lives."

Jeremiah put down his mug, smiled, and spread his hands. "Yet here you are. Why?"

"I was going to walk away and mind my own business," Emma told him.

"Yeah, right," quipped Granny. "You never do and you never will, Emma. You got nose trouble."

"I do not," Emma hissed back at the ghost.

Seeing Phil looking confused, Jeremiah explained, "Granny just called Emma nosy."

Phil grinned at the man across from him. "Actually, they both have nose trouble. I'm not sure who has it worse." Both Granny and Emma glared at Phil.

"I gotta tell you," Jeremiah said, shaking his head and laughing quietly, "you have certainly made my day. I'll have to send Gino a big bottle of peanut oil for this."

CHAPTER SIXTEEN

"I HAD decided to walk away," Emma explained, "but when we saw Steve Bullock giving cash to Carlos, we got concerned about Rikki's safety. We think Carlos also mentioned T.J. Mendoza during the exchange. That's the CFO at Roble and Rikki's boyfriend. Unfortunately, we couldn't make out what he said about him, so there's also concern that T.J. might be involved, too." Seeing her margarita glass empty, Emma picked up her water glass and took a drink. "I'm just very concerned about Rikki. If she gets hurt and I could have stopped it, I'd never forgive myself."

"And you want to get to the bottom of how Felix died, don't you?" Jeremiah asked with amusement. "That's really the scratch you need to itch—both you and Granny."

"Of course," Granny snapped. "If there's a murderer out there, he needs to be caught."

Jeremiah looked again over at Bullock's booth. "And you think Steve Bullock had something to do with it?"

Emma shrugged. "I really have no idea. I just find it odd that he's cozying up to Felix's daughter and paying off one of Roble's waiters while going after Roble Foods. Lucy is adamant that the company be sold to Fiesta Time."

"He could be romancing it out from under her?" suggested Phil.

Jeremiah stretched his neck, setting off a series of pops. Then he leaned forward, looking from Phil to Emma. "Over the years," he began in a very low voice, "several of Fiesta Time's smaller competitors have quietly disappeared or been hit with tragedies that have caused them to bail. In most cases, Fiesta Time picked up their business."

Emma's eyebrows rose. "So they've done this before?"

"There's never been any proof of wrongdoing," Jeremiah answered, "just suspicion. Bullock's uncle is Ramon Santiago. It started when he took over the company about ten to twelve years ago when his brother Miguel died suddenly."

Granny had disappeared and now popped up again. "I don't think Lucy and that Steve are boyfriend and girlfriend," she reported.

"No?" asked Emma.

The ghost shook her head. "They're friendly but not that kind of friendly. And they're talking business, not a word about mushy stuff."

"What are they talking about, Granny?" asked Jeremiah.

"Like I said," Granny answered, "business. Steve did say something about it will all be over soon." She paused and scratched her head. "I think he said something about the right family being in charge once and for all." The ghost jerked her head in confirmation. "Yeah, that's it. That's exactly what he said. And something about them making a great team."

"Oh yeah," said Jeremiah with a glance at Granny, "I could really see the advantages of having a ghost around."

Granny beamed. "Play your cards right, hot shot, and it could happen."

"Don't encourage her," Emma said with a roll of her eyes.

After Emma brought Phil up to speed, he said, "Lucy is telling her family that she wants to take time off to paint and find herself. This almost sounds like she's going to remain working for the company." He looked at each of the other people at the table, including in the direction he thought Granny was hovering. "You don't think she's stealing her own family's company out from under their noses, do you?"

"Do you know of any beef she might have with them?" asked Jeremiah.

"Lucy and Rikki don't seem to get along very well," Emma said. "T.J. Mendoza is an old college friend of Lucy's who is CFO of Roble Foods. He's currently dating Rikki. Maybe Lucy is jealous of that. He also mentioned to me that Lucy can be ruthless in the pursuit of what she wants."

"But ruthless enough to kill her own father, or at least to cause his death?" asked Phil.

"I've seen it happen," noted Jeremiah.

"I've gotten the feeling," Emma told them, "from being around both Lucy and Rikki that there's bad blood between Fiesta Time and Roble. So why would Lucy throw in with her family's enemy unless she was out to hurt her family?" She squeezed her eyes shut to force the information through her brain. When she opened them, she added, "Why would she want to do that? Unless, of course, she's in love with Steve."

"I'm telling ya," Granny said with conviction, "those two aren't kissy face with each other. Friends maybe, but not romantic friends."

Emma's phone vibrated. She glanced at it.

"Is that Gino again?" asked Jeremiah.

"No," said Emma with disbelief as she read the text. "It's from my mother."

"Everything okay?" asked Phil with concern.

She showed it to him. *At Roble. Come quick!!!*

"Roble?" asked Phil with surprise. "What in the world are your parents doing there?"

"Who knows?" Emma pushed her plate away and slung her purse over her shoulder. "Let's pay the bill and get out of here."

While Phil flagged down Brenda Ann for the check, Emma said to Granny, "Try to find Mother, Granny. See what's going on."

"Got it," said the ghost and disappeared.

Emma looked at Jeremiah. "Sorry, Jeremiah, but my parents just asked us to meet them at Roble. It sounds urgent." She dug a business card out of her purse. "Please e-mail me your contact information, so we can talk more about this."

"No need," he said, pulling out a card of his own and handing it to Emma. "You folks go. I'll take care of the check." When Phil started to protest, he cut him off, "I said to go."

As Emma and Phil scooted out of the booth, Lucy Ricardo spotted them. "Hey, what are you doing here?" she called to Emma. "Are you spying on me?" With surprising agility, she slipped out of her own booth and grabbed Emma's arm just before she left the bar. "I asked you a question, you fraud."

Emma yanked her arm from Lucy's clutches. "We were here having lunch with a friend, if it's any of your business," she snapped. "Now we have to go."

Lucy made a grab for Emma again, but before she could connect, Phil got between the two women. "Back off," he said to Lucy, his voice low but menacing.

Lucy was about to say something when Jeremiah quickly joined them. "Look," he said and pointed at the TV. On the television set above the bar a breaking news report had replaced the soccer game. The sound was off but a banner below a live picture of police cars and milling people read: *Shooting on Olvera Street.*

Emma ran from the restaurant with Phil fast on her heels. Behind them was Jeremiah. After tucking Emma into her vehicle with Phil behind the wheel, he said to them, "I'll meet you there."

· CHAPTER SEVENTEEN ·

FEAR and anxiety coursed through Emma's veins, replacing her blood with a high-voltage current. Alhambra was less than ten miles from downtown Los Angeles and Olvera Street, but with the weekday traffic on the 10 Freeway, it seemed like hundreds of miles in bad weather. On the way, Emma kept up contact with her mother. They were fine, Elizabeth's texts confirmed. The police were taking statements and contact information from all of the customers at Roble for questioning later. They were still waiting their turn. Her mother didn't know who had been shot, only that it was a man. They didn't see it happen.

Phil circled the area around Olvera Street and the Plaza trying to find parking. The police had blocked off the section of Main Street that fed into the parking lot they'd used the day before. Other street closures, including a section of Cesar Chavez, only made the usual traffic snarl ghastlier.

"Get out here," Phil said to Emma. "I'll find parking somewhere and meet up with you."

She didn't argue and had her seat belt off and the door of the Lexus open before he'd come to a full stop. Once on the street, Emma looked around to get her bearings. She was on Los Angeles Street, close to the Chinese American Museum she and Phil had visited just twenty-four hours earlier. She turned around, spotted the Plaza, and took off at a run. Olvera Street, she knew, was just on the other side of it.

The entrance to the small touristy street was packed with lookie-loos, barely restrained by the temporary barricades set up by the police. There was no gnashing of teeth or hysteria but rather the low rumble of people asking what was going on followed by people passing along information, true or not—the hum of a shocked and angry hive of bees. Roble was down the other end, closer to Cesar Chavez, but Emma knew it would be impossible to slip in that way since most of the police cars were congregated there. Even though her parents assured her they were fine, it didn't stem her urge to reach them as soon as possible.

"They're okay, Emma." Emma turned to see Granny begin to materialize next to her. "I told Elizabeth that you and Phil were on your way." The ghost looked concerned, but not upset. "She and Paul are shaken up a bit but doing good." Granny looked around. "Where's Phil?"

"Thanks for the update, Granny," Emma said with relief. "Phil's trying to find parking. He'll catch up. Jeremiah's on his way, too." She kept her voice low but didn't take her usual precaution. At the moment she didn't care if anyone overheard her talking to thin air.

"Jeremiah just arrived on a motorcycle," Granny told her. "He's talking to some cop friends of his."

"I'm going to try to work my way down there somehow." Emma paused, then asked, "Who was shot?"

The ghost shrugged. "I don't know, but I don't think it was fatal, because when I got here, an ambulance was racing off with its siren blaring. The dead don't need sirens."

"Only one victim?"

"Looks that way," answered Granny.

"Rikki? Did you see her?"

Granny nodded. "Last I saw, she was up in her office surrounded by police. She was sobbing and in shock. Felix was with her but didn't say anything to me. Hector and Lupe, you know, the chef, were in Hector's office with other police. They were also very upset. The waiters and cooks are being kept together in the kitchen while the cops do their thing. Customers are being kept in the main dining room. Some are slowly being let go."

"Could Felix tell you anything?" Emma danced from foot to foot with anxiety. "Like maybe what happened? Who was shot? Who did the shooting? Anything?"

Granny shook her head. "Like I said, he wasn't talking so I don't know what he saw, if anything. And I couldn't tell from what I saw what happened except that someone was shot." She watched Emma's body twitch with worry. "Calm down," the ghost told her. "You look like a child who needs the outhouse."

"Go back and stay with Mother and Dad," Emma told her. "Tell Mother I'll be there soon."

"How are you gonna get past this?" asked Granny, indicating the barriers.

"I'll think of something," Emma said. The ghost gave her a thumbs-up and disappeared.

Emma scanned the barriers and the police officers keeping watch. Civilians on the other side of the blockade looked like merchants who owned businesses or worked on the street. They were gathered here and there. Some kept to themselves, straightening their wares or sweeping their already clean steps. It was busywork done by people with foreheads furrowed with worry about lost business and possible bad press for the street in general. Emma, with her blond hair and blue eyes, knew passing for one of them would almost be impossible.

She worked her way through the sweating, milling crowd until she reached the end of the street entrance where it met the wall of the first solid building. She watched the handful of officers as they paced and chatted with people, or clustered together in pairs. She squinted against the sun to see better. She'd left her sunglasses in the SUV and was now missing them. One of the merchants came out of his store with cold drinks for the police to provide relief against the heat. He was passing them out and the officers were gladly taking them. Now was the time for Emma to make a move. Slipping by the edge of one barrier, she moved evenly, not too fast or too slow, so as not to attract attention. She forced her body to relax, to adopt the air that she belonged there and it was just an ordinary day.

"Hey, where do you think you're going?" a male voice shouted at her. It was one of the patrol cops. He was young and clean shaven, with the wide shoulders of a gym rat. His eyes were hidden behind sunglasses. Under his arms dark sweat rings soiled his short-sleeved blue uniform. He moved toward her, transferring his half-empty bottle of Jarritos soda from his right hand to his left, freeing his gun hand just in case.

Lying didn't come easy to Emma, but this was an emergency. Taking control of her jumpy nerves, she looked at the officer and said, "I was at Roble having lunch and left my car keys."

"Roble is off limits. There's been an incident," the cop told her as he came a few steps closer. He had a ruddy complexion and hair somewhere between red and brown on the color spectrum.

"I know," she told him, looking sad and tragic, which was something she didn't have to fake. She wiped the sweat from her forehead with the back of a hand. The run from Los Angeles Street had trashed any freshness she had left. "I was there when the shooting happened. The police took my information and let me go but I left my keys on my table. I really need to get home."

He took off his sunglasses and studied her a long moment, taking in her canvas slip-on shoes, capris, and cheerful summer blouse. He even eyed her purse, which was small and slung cross-body. Without his shades, Emma saw the beginning of lines around his eyes. He wasn't as young as she first thought and might not be as gullible as a rookie. Now she was glad she looked like a summer visitor. "Okay," he said with some reluctance. "But make it quick and come right back. If anyone stops you, tell them Hanover said it was okay." He put his sunglasses back on and took a long drink from his soda, dismissing her.

She scurried down the street. The customers were gone. The mariachi music was silent. Uncertainty hung over the usually buoyant street like a low-hanging storm cloud. When she got to Restaurante Roble, another uniformed cop stopped her. "You can't be here, ma'am," said the officer standing at the entrance to the patio, where the hostess podium had stood just a couple days before. The podium was near the entrance, moved out of the way. His name tag identified him simply as *Adams*. He wasn't wearing sunglasses and this one did look young to Emma. She did a quick double take, thinking he didn't even look old enough to be out of high school.

"Over here, Emma," Granny shouted from the closed door to the restaurant. "They're just inside the door."

"I left my car keys on the table," Emma said to Adams. "Officer Hanover said I could come back to get them." For emphasis, she pointed in the direction from which she'd come.

"Do you remember which table?" he asked her.

"Yes, I do. It was just inside the doorway, to the right."

For a minute Emma thought he might go look for the keys himself, but instead he waved her past him. "Be quick about it."

She crossed though the patio and yanked open the big double door. Just inside, where Granny said they'd be, she saw her parents. They were talking to another officer, a young Asian woman dressed in an LAPD uniform with shorts—a cop from the bicycle unit. At a nearby table, a male officer with light brown hair and also wearing shorts was taking down information from two men in business suits. "She's getting their phone number and stuff like that," explained Granny.

Emma threw her arms around her mother, interrupting the exchange of information. Then she squeezed her father's neck. "What in the world were you two doing here?" she asked, releasing herself from Paul. Relieved to see them, now her tone was accusatory, like a parent to naughty children.

"After you raved about the food here, we decided to try

it for ourselves," Paul Miller explained. Elizabeth remained silent, looking down at her hands. Emma knew immediately that her father wasn't giving her the whole story, but she let it slide since the officer was watching.

"How did you get in here?" the officer asked Emma. Her name tag said *Rush*. In her hand was a pen poised over a small notebook.

Without answering the question directly, Emma said truthfully, "My mother texted me to come. On the way I heard about the shooting."

"She's with me, Officer," said a familiar voice. They all turned to see Jeremiah standing with a middle-aged Latino, who wore a suit with a badge fastened at his belt line. Jeremiah introduced him as Detective Aaron Espinoza.

"How's it coming, Officer Rush?" the detective asked the bike cop.

"Just finished," she reported. "There's one more set of customers over there to interview, then we're done with those." She indicated the other side of the restaurant.

For the first time, Emma noticed the state of the restaurant. Some tables were set for new customers but most contained remnants of meals in various stages. Some had plates that looked untouched; others held dirty dishes and glassware of meals in progress or finished. On her parents' table was a basket of chips with salsa and fresh utensils. It looked like they had just arrived.

"Good," Espinoza said to the officer. "Why don't you get their information, then go? The other officers can finish up with the staff." Officer Rush started to leave when Detective Espinoza tacked on, "And thanks for your help, both you and your partner." Officer Rush nodded to him and went off to do her job.

"The bike cops were the first on the scene," Detective Espinoza explained to Jeremiah. "They were having lunch right across the way at a taco stand when the call about the shooting came through." He turned to Emma. "I understand you have some information that could have a bearing on this case."

Emma looked from Espinoza to Jeremiah, unsure of where she stood or how much Jeremiah had told the detective.

"Did he snitch on us?" asked an indignant Granny. Hearing her words, Jeremiah looked straight at the ghost, who was next to Emma, and explained to everyone, "Aaron is my old partner. The one I had right before I retired. He works homicide now and needs to know what you know." He moved close to Emma and whispered, "I told him what you shared with me at the restaurant about the handoff with the waiter and the animosity about the sale." Their eyes locked and Emma knew without hearing it that Jeremiah had left out the part about Felix and Granny. "T.J. Mendoza was shot," he added, his words quick and unembellished. "Upstairs in Rikki Ricardo's office."

Emma gasped and plopped herself down in the chair Officer Rush had vacated. "Is he . . ."

"No," answered Jeremiah, instinctively knowing her question. "He's at the hospital, but he's in bad shape." He looked around. "Where's Phil?" Without waiting for an answer, Jeremiah moved over a few steps, closer to the detective. "He's the one who took the photos."

"He dropped me off while he searched for parking," Emma answered. She pulled out her phone and called Phil. "Where are you? T.J. Mendoza has been shot and the police want to talk to us." She listened, then said to Jeremiah. "Phil is at the barricade near the Plaza."

"What's this guy's name again?" Detective Espinoza asked.

"Phil Bowers," Paul Miller answered. He was still sitting at the table, holding Elizabeth's hand to comfort her. "Bald guy in his fifties with a mustache."

Espinoza opened the door and called to the young cop standing guard outside. He gave him instructions. Adams set off down Olvera Street to fetch Phil while Emma told Phil by phone to look for the officer. With the phone still to her ear, Emma made eye contact with Granny and whispered to the ghost, hoping Espinoza didn't hear, "Stick with Felix. Find out everything you can."

It was clear that Granny was torn about what to do. "I'd rather stay here," she said to Emma, "but I know that's important." When Granny disappeared, Emma lowered her phone and turned to find Jeremiah watching her. His face was stern, lips a straight line, but he gave her a tiny wink.

Officer Adams had barely left to get Phil when there was a commotion outside in the patio area followed a woman's screeching demands. Even before the door opened, Emma knew it was Lucy Ricardo on the other side. Her voice was raised in indignation, not tragedy, and Emma wondered if the volatile CEO of Roble Foods even knew yet about T.J.

"Let go of me, blondie," Lucy snapped as she fought her way into the restaurant and out of the grip of a female officer.

Lucy took a few steps into the restaurant and stopped, letting her eyes and mind absorb the people in front of her, clearly taking stock of the situation. Detective Espinoza waved off the officer still trying to detain Lucy without the use of a club. "Can I help you?" he asked Lucy.

"I'm Lucinda Ricardo," Lucy said, pulling on the hem

of her suit jacket to straighten it. "I own this place. Who are you?" She held her head high and straight, well aware that all eyes were on her. Her face glistened with perspiration.

"I'm Detective Aaron Espinoza of the LAPD. I'm in charge of this matter."

"This matter?" Lucy paused and took a deep breath. "I heard on the news that there was a shooting on Olvera Street, so I came right over. Was it near here?"

"I'm sorry to tell you, Ms. Ricardo," Espinoza told her in a calm, matter-of-fact voice, "that it happened here in the restaurant."

Lucy took another deep breath and held it. "Where's Rikki? Where's my sister?" Her voice didn't hold concern, but anger. "I told her not to hire thugs. This is going to ruin everything."

Unable to contain herself, Emma snapped to her feet. "Aren't you the least bit concerned about your sister's safety? Or even about who got shot?"

Lucy swung around to face the speaker. Emma and her parents had been sitting behind her and she hadn't seen them yet. "You! What are you doing here? First at lunch and now here." She pointed at Emma and spoke to Detective Espinoza. "Arrest this woman," she demanded. "She's stalking my family. She might even be behind this." Lucy noticed Jeremiah and narrowed her eyes at him. "You were there today, too, with her." Lucy pointed again at Emma and back at the detective. "This is a conspiracy to ruin my company, plain and simple."

"Calm down, Ms. Ricardo," Espinoza told her. "There is no need to be making wild accusations. We're talking to everyone, including your sister, who is shaken but safe, in case you're interested." The sarcasm in Espinoza's voice wasn't lost on anyone, including Lucy, who took a deep breath, biting back her next words. She managed to hold her tongue but continued to split her glare between Emma and Jeremiah.

"Here's Mr. Bowers," announced Adams, coming through the door with Phil in tow.

"Oh great!" said Lucy, getting a good look at Phil. "He was at lunch today, too. In fact, he manhandled me."

"Actually," said Phil, standing beside Emma, "you were grabbing at Emma as she left the restaurant and I simply got between the two of you to stop it."

"Lucy!" cried a voice from the hallway. A few seconds later Rikki Ricardo flung herself into Lucy's surprised arms and held her tight. "I thought I heard your voice. It was so awful." Rikki's face was red and swollen from crying. "T.J.," she choked out, then started crying again.

Lucy pried her sister from her. It was then Emma noticed the dried blood smeared down the front of Rikki's white embroidered shirt. Phil nudged Emma and she knew he'd seen it, too.

"What about T.J.?" This time there wasn't outrage in Lucy's voice, but panic. She held her younger sister by her shoulders and shook her, demanding, "What about T.J.?" She shook her again.

Jeremiah pulled Rikki out of Lucy's grasp. "That's enough now. Can't you see this woman's beside herself?" He guided Rikki to a chair and gently got her seated.

Lucy looked at the detective. "What about Tomas Mendoza?"

Detective Espinoza looked at the remaining customers being interviewed and said to the two bike cops, "Finish your interviews outside."

Without a word, the two officers shepherded their witnesses outside to the patio to complete their work, closing the door behind them. "He was the victim, Ms. Ricardo," Detective Espinoza told Lucy once they were gone. "Mr. Mendoza was shot upstairs in your sister's office."

Lucy staggered a bit. Jeremiah reached out to steady her, but she yanked away without looking at him. "Is he . . ." she asked Espinoza. The question went unfinished out of fear, much as Emma's had when she'd asked the same thing.

"Dead?" Espinoza said, finishing her question. "Not that I know of, but he's in very critical condition. He's at the hospital right now."

Lucy turned to leave, but Espinoza stopped her. "I need to ask you some questions."

"Not now," Lucy snapped. "I need to get to the hospital."

"Your sister was heading there in a few minutes," Espinoza told her. Everyone else wisely kept out of Lucy's way.

Lucy shot an icy glare at Rikki, who was focusing on collecting herself. Emma wasn't sure if any comfort she offered would be accepted or spurned, but she tried anyway. Stepping closer to Rikki, she put a hand on the younger woman's shoulder but said nothing. Rikki looked up, noticing for the first time that Emma was present. Instead of shaking off the hand, Rikki put one of her own over it and said in a small raw voice, "You were right, Emma. I should have listened."

"Listen to that fraud?" Lucy snapped. "Grow up, Rikki." Lucy turned to Espinoza. "No, my sister will not be going to the hospital. I'll be going. It's my place. T.J. is an officer in my company."

Rikki popped out of the chair with the speed of a jack-in-the-box. "You mean *our* company, don't you, sis?"

Lucy waved her off as she would a servant. "Whatever. But T.J. works for me. I'll go to the hospital. You'll only screw it up."

"Ms. Ricardo," Espinoza said, speaking to Lucy. "I don't know squat about your family dynamics or your company, but I have an attempted homicide on my hands that might move into murder if Mr. Mendoza doesn't survive."

Rikki let out a low mewl of anguish, but cut it short and squared her shoulders. It was obvious to Emma she was trying to stand her ground with Lucy in spite of her personal pain.

"We have questions to ask you," Espinoza said to Lucy. "Besides, she's his fiancée. It's really her place to be by Mr. Mendoza's side, don't you think?"

Lucy turned on Rikki. "That's right, I got your hearts and flowers e-mail announcement this morning. How touching."

In response, Rikki held up her left hand, displaying an impressive engagement ring. "He asked me last night over dinner. I had hoped you'd be happy for us, Lucy. Mom was."

"You conniving little bitch," Lucy hissed to her sister. "You'll do anything to stop this sale, won't you?"

"Our engagement has nothing to do with your attempt to sell everything," Rikki bit back.

Lucy did not back down. "Did you shoot T.J. thinking it would buy you time?"

Before the last words were out of Lucy's mouth, Rikki's right hand shot out and slapped Lucy hard. "How dare you even suggest that?" she screamed. "I'm the one who found him. I thought he was dead." She indicated her clothing. "This is T.J.'s blood on me, Lucy. His blood!"

Lucy raised herself up straight, towering over her more petite sister. "How convenient. Aren't you the one who found Dad, too?"

Despite her size, Rikki ploughed into Lucy headfirst with a ferocity that surprised everyone, including her target. Lucy's fancy-suited body hit the floor with a sound thud, and the two women rolled around and around on the floor like a couple of wild animals, screeching and hollering in both English and Spanish. Thrashing, they knocked into chairs and tables but didn't stop. It was clearly a fight to the death.

The commotion brought spectators from the kitchen, both staff and police. The hired help, murmuring in Spanish among themselves, spilled into the hallway to watch the spectacle of their bosses beating on each other. Emma saw both Hector and Lupe make their way through to the front of the crowd. Off to the side was Ana, Hector's daughter, looking upset, and the waiter who'd been working with Carlos the day before. He had an arm around Ana's shoulders, comforting her. Emma didn't notice Carlos in the crowd.

Hector yelled at the Ricardo sisters in Spanish, while Lupe tried to control the staff. Both Phil and Jeremiah started to step in, but were beaten to it by two uniform cops, who made several attempts to grab the sisters and break them apart before being successful. The blond officer tackled the smaller Rikki while a burly cop grabbed the heftier Lucy. Another man in a suit with a badge at his waist approached wearing an amused quarter moon of a smile. He was Asian and slightly younger and trimmer than Espinoza. "Everything okay here, Aaron?" he asked Detective Espinoza.

"It's getting there," Espinoza told him with the weariness of someone who'd seen too much family drama while trying to do his job.

The two cops holding the Ricardos continued to hold on tight, pinning their arms to their sides. Lucy kicked backward at the officer holding her but he deftly avoided the attack. She spit blood at Rikki's feet. "It should have been you who was shot," she said to her sister. "That would have solved all my problems."

"Enough!" yelled Hector, coming closer. He said something to the two of them in Spanish that sounded like a serious scolding, but it had no effect on the women.

"Glad I didn't miss the catfight," said Granny, popping up next to Emma, who turned in surprise. "Don't worry," Granny said, noticing Emma's displeasure, "Felix took off. He was really weak and fading, but he did tell me that he'd find us later, and I think he meant it." Granny pointed to the Ricardo sisters. "Glad he didn't see this. It would have broken his heart." Emma nodded in agreement, but said nothing.

"Mr. Gonzales is right," said Espinoza, turning back to the Ricardos. "This behavior is shameful. If we let you go, will you both behave?"

It looked doubtful, but finally Rikki nodded. After getting the nod from Espinoza, the cop holding her let her go. Rikki's blouse was ripped at the neckline, exposing a pale pink bra beneath it. A large bruise was starting to blossom on her left cheek and her nose was bleeding. She swiped at the dripping blood with the back of her hand. "Ms. Ricardo," Espinoza said to Rikki, "finish up with Detective Wu here, then go on to the hospital. We'll be in touch again soon. I'm sure we can get any other information we need about your staff from Mr. Gonzales."

Espinoza turned to Lucy, who was still in the grasp of the big cop. "We'd like to ask you those questions now, Ms. Ricardo," he said to her.

"Now is inconvenient," Lucy told him, her chin tilted up. Rikki's handprint was still evident on her cheek, matching the angry split of her lower lip. Drops of blood spotted the front of her suit. Unable to use her hands, she blew a lock of hair out of her eyes.

"It's now and here," Espinoza told her, "or we can take you to the police station in the back of a squad car. Your choice."

Lucy turned, giving everyone in the room a look of disdain, especially Rikki, who watched, her face a boiling stew of anger and concern. When Lucy's eyes came to rest again on Detective Espinoza, she said, "I'll stay, but I'm not saying a word without my lawyer."

The detective met her icy look with his own frigid stare before spreading his arms and hands outward in a frustrated gesture. "Fine, then call and get him or her down here." Espinoza signaled to the cop holding Lucy. "Let her go so she can make the call."

Free of her bonds, Lucy shook out her arms before bending down for her purse, which she'd dropped when Rikki charged her. The two detectives had their heads together, discussing something. Emma was telling her parents to go home and she and Phil would be along soon. Rikki was giving instructions to Hector and Lupe and speaking with the gathered staff. Jeremiah was checking his phone. The uniforms had stepped back, waiting for further orders.

Granny floated over to Lucy and watched as she rummaged in her purse for her phone. Then the ghost shouted, "She's got a gun!"

Emma, Jeremiah, and Elizabeth Miller snapped their heads in Granny's direction simultaneously, but they were the only ones who'd heard the warning. Just as Lucy pulled the weapon free and fired, Jeremiah made a dive for her. Elizabeth screamed and slipped out of her chair to the floor, yanking her husband down with her. Emma shouted the warning, "Gun!" She threw herself over her parents and Phil threw himself over her.

The cops jumped into action, helping Jeremiah subdue Lucy Ricardo and disarm her while chaos ruled. Other police had come through the door with their guns drawn. Spanish shouts and curses crowded the air along with English counterparts. Several of the kitchen and waitstaff stampeded for cover in the kitchen. Then a scream split the air. It was Ana Gonzales. The young woman let out a wail that cut the air thin and exact like a scalpel. At her feet lay Chef Lupe Lopez, a red stain spreading across her white chef's coat like spilled sangria.

CHAPTER EIGHTEEN

DETECTIVE Wu called for an ambulance while Paul Miller bent over the still figure of the talented chef and administered medical aid. Kneeling next to Lupe was Rikki. She was crying and holding Lupe's hand.

"I think she's going to make it," announced Paul with caution, "if she gets to the hospital quickly."

"Ambulance on its way," announced Detective Wu.

Rikki dropped Lupe's hand, got up, and charged again at her sister. This time, she didn't make the connection. Lucy had been knocked to the ground again, this time by Jeremiah. Now she was on her feet with her hands cuffed behind her and guarded by the cops, one on either side of her like bookends. Before the enraged Rikki could reach her sister, Jeremiah grabbed her around her waist and held her back.

"Calm down," he ordered as she flailed in rage.

Rikki fought him, but she couldn't break his hold. Across the few feet that separated them, Rikki screamed at Lucy,

"You want me dead so bad you'd risk killing an innocent woman by mistake?"

Lucy said nothing.

"We're sisters, Lucy," Rikki continued. "Sisters with the same blood in our veins. The blood of a proud and decent people who built all this from nothing, yet you're willing to kill to destroy it." She was crying hard, gasping for breath. "If the sale of Roble is making you this insane, then sell the damn thing. Sell all of it! I can't be a part of it. Not like this."

"That Lucy is going to be selling nothing if she's in prison," noted Granny, who was hovering close to Emma and Elizabeth. Elizabeth was back in her chair.

"You've got a point there, Granny," whispered Elizabeth in a shaky voice while she watched the drama unfolding in front of them along with everyone else.

Lucy let out a shrill cackle. "You still don't know, do you?" she asked Rikki. When Rikki didn't answer, Lucy continued, "We're not sisters, Rikki. Not full sisters. That's why we don't look alike. Ever wonder about that? Ever wonder why you and Dad were so close but he always found fault with me? Mom was screwing around on Dad when she got pregnant with me, and Dad, being the public saint he was, raised me as his own."

"I don't believe you." Rikki stared at Lucy.

"Go ahead, Rikki, ask Mom," Lucy sneered at her sister. "I found out shortly before Dad died."

Rikki went silent, followed by a shake of her head in disbelief. The violence drained out of her—air escaping a pierced tire. Carefully, Jeremiah loosened his grip on her. "That's why you want to destroy Roble?" Rikki asked Lucy, still not comprehending the reasoning behind her sister's actions. "Because you're not the daughter of Felix Ricardo?"

She paused, then said slowly, "But Lucy, you're still Mom's. You're still the daughter of Elena Ricardo. We're still sisters. You're still a part of all this."

Lucy flashed a wide maniacal grin. "Why have a part when I can have it all?"

Rikki shook her head and said with sadness, "And now you have none."

"Don't be so sure of that, *sis*," Lucy shot back, putting extra venom on the last word.

Sirens could be heard outside. A nearby officer holstered his gun and went out to meet the ambulance. In short order, paramedics entered and assessed the situation while getting an update from Paul on the injury. Soon they had Lupe Lopez on a stretcher and on her way to the hospital. It had been the second time in a very short time a gunshot victim had been wheeled out of the restaurant. Shortly after, Lucy was read her rights and taken away by the police.

Granny leaned toward Emma, who was watching Jeremiah. "Wow! Talk about a soap opera. What do you want me to do next?"

Emma turned to Phil but said to the ghost in a whisper, "I'm not sure, Granny. Phil and I might be tied up here for a bit. Why don't you go recharge and find us later." Emma glanced back over at Jeremiah, wanting to know what he was saying to the detectives. "But first why don't you float on over to Jeremiah and see if you can pick up some information."

Phil shook his head. "Won't it be rather difficult for her to sneak up on him if he can see and hear her?"

"True," agreed Emma. "But worth a try."

"Why Jeremiah?" asked Granny.

"I just want to know what's going on, Granny, and I'm sure the police won't tell us what they're telling him."

"Just go over there and be your ornery nosy self, Granny," Phil said, picking up on the gist of the conversation. "He won't suspect a thing."

"The cowboy's getting kind of cheeky, isn't he?" Granny pursed her lips.

"I take it my last comment didn't go over very well," Phil said to Emma.

"You've got that right," Emma told him with a discreet grin. She tilted her chin toward Granny. "If Jeremiah says anything, Granny, tell him you want to know how to be a PI, but don't go right over there from here. Kind of float around or pop in and out so it doesn't look like we sent you."

Phil chuckled softly and said under his breath, "Yeah, like he'll fall for that."

"You got it, Chief," Granny said. Ignoring Phil, she started to disappear. "I'll be like one of those fancy surveillance drones I saw on the news the other night."

Emma and Phil were talking to the Millers and Detective Espinoza, making sure Emma's parents were free to go. The detective said they were, but he still wanted to speak with Emma and Phil, so he asked them to stay. Emma had just sent her parents on their way with a promise to keep them informed if something new occurred, when Rikki approached them. She was wearing a different blouse and had washed up, leaving her face makeup-free. A purse was slung over her shoulder. The bruise on her cheek was starting to turn ugly and would get worse before it got better. For the first time, Emma noticed scratches near her eyes.

"Emma," she began, but stopped, squeezing her eyes shut to gather strength.

"Rikki," Emma said, taking her hands. Like before, Rikki didn't pull away. She gave them a warm squeeze before releasing them. "I'm so sorry about T.J. Any updates?"

"I know you are," Rikki said after a long pause. "In spite of the things he said about you, I know you didn't wish him any harm." She took a deep breath. "He's in surgery but it's too soon to tell how it will go. He was shot twice, once in the chest and another in his left shoulder. His family is at the hospital now and I'm finally heading over there."

"Are you okay to drive?" Phil asked, giving her an encouraging smile. "You've had several big shocks. I'm sure Detective Espinoza will let us slip away for a bit to help you out."

Rikki shook her head and said in a tired voice, "No, I'm okay to drive, but thank you."

"I'm also very sorry about Lucy," Emma said. "I'm sure that took you by surprise."

Tears began to well in Rikki's eyes, glistening around the edges but not spilling over. "We've never gotten along, but I had no idea her resentment was this deep or dangerous. It also makes me wonder if she's in love with T.J. even though they stopped dating years ago." She picked up a linen napkin from a nearby table—a table that wouldn't be seeing any customers at least for the rest of the day, if not longer—and wiped her eyes.

"Why would Lucy have a gun in her purse unless she was up to no good?" asked Phil. "I worry that she came here to kill you."

"As I told the police, Lucy's been carrying a handgun for about six or seven months now," Rikki explained. "She started after several people were mugged near the Roble corporate offices. She often works late and was worried about her safety." She started to tear up again. "The gun was no surprise. Lucy aiming it at me was. I had no idea she felt such hatred for me."

"She really went off the rails there," added Phil. "I'm

sure her attorney is going to suggest a psych evaluation and claim temporary insanity caused by stress over the sale and T.J.'s shooting."

Rikki gave up an exhausted half shrug. "There's another problem," she told them. "I just called my mother to tell her what happened and to ask her about what Lucy claimed. Her cleaning lady told me Mom is gone."

"Gone?" Emma asked. "You mean out for the day shopping or something?"

Rikki shook her head. "No. The housekeeper said my mother didn't say anything about going anywhere, but she saw her slipping into the garage with a suitcase, then taking off in the car. Maria said it was around lunchtime."

"About the time T.J. was shot?" Phil asked.

Rikki nodded. "T.J. and I stopped by her house this morning to tell her about the engagement and to show her my ring, and she didn't say anything about leaving town. The three of us had breakfast together, and Mom seemed her usual self and was happy about T.J. and me. She even gushed about planning a big wedding. Then I went to the restaurant and T.J. went to his place to clean up for work. We were both running late because we'd stopped at Mom's."

"Did you tell the police about your mother's disappearance?" Emma asked.

"Yes, I did. Just now." Rikki looked scared. "I hope she had nothing to do with this or even knew about it, but she's been flip-flopping between both sides on this sale issue, so who knows." A pained expression crossed her face. "I felt like a traitor telling the police about Mom."

"You did the right thing, Rikki," Phil told her. "Maybe your mother received some sort of threat or even felt she'd had enough of being caught between you and Lucy."

"Maybe. Mom and Lucy may look alike, but they're nothing alike in personality. Mom will almost always back down from a confrontation." Rikki looked around, then moved closer and said to them, "I know I told you to stay away from me and my family, but now I'm begging for your help. Please find out who did this to T.J."

"The police don't have any suspects?" Phil asked.

"None that I know of, except that I'm probably somewhere on the list." She tightened her lips. "They took my blouse and did something to my hands. That's to check for gunshot residue, isn't it?"

Phil nodded. "Most likely, but it's also to rule out possible suspects as much as pinpoint them. I'm sure they're checking the hands of everyone in the restaurant at the time of the shooting."

"Why was T.J. even here?" Emma asked.

"He showed up and said it was urgent that he speak with me right away," she told them. "He seemed agitated. I thought it might have something to do with the sale of Roble. We were very busy and shorthanded, so I told him to go up to my office and wait, and as soon as I had a chance, I'd come up. About twenty minutes later, I went to my office. The door was closed. When I opened it, I found him on the floor, shot." She put a hand over her heart and gasped for breath a few times. "It was like finding my father all over again." Emma put a reassuring hand on Rikki's arm and she calmed down.

"No one heard gunshots?" Phil asked.

Rikki shook her head. "We were busy and the AC was on. I heard one of the detectives say something about possibly a silencer being used."

Phil fingered his mustache. "And no one saw anyone go upstairs around that time?"

Again Rikki shook her head. "We were very busy and it was all hands on deck. A tour bus had come in unexpectedly and we had a full house. Even Hector and I were taking orders and bussing tables. Lupe and her people couldn't get the food out fast enough."

Emma glanced around the dining room. "I didn't see Carlos here today."

"He called in sick," Rikki said. "It was one of the reasons we were shorthanded. We tried to call in a waiter who had the day off but couldn't reach him."

Rikki leaned in closer to Emma. She smelled of soap—commercial soap, strong with a sharp-edge clean. "I know you have special . . . um . . . help that the police don't. Please find out who tried to kill T.J.," she pleaded again. She looked into Emma's eyes. "I don't care about the company or the restaurant right now. I just want to know who did this and why."

"We'll do what we can, Rikki," Emma told her.

Rikki started to leave, but turned back. "Were the people sitting at that table in the corner really your parents? And is your father really a doctor?"

"Yes, those were my folks," confirmed Emma. "And my father is a retired heart surgeon, but I did not send them here to spy on you, I swear."

Rikki shook her head and Emma half expected her to call her a liar. Instead, Rikki said in a voice dull as cardboard, "Your parents are giving me more support than my own mother is giving me. Tell them thank you, especially your father. He may have saved Lupe's life."

CHAPTER NINETEEN

"SO what do you think Jeremiah's real story is?" Phil asked. He was back behind the wheel of Emma's SUV and they were finally heading home.

The detectives had questioned them extensively, mostly separately. Detective Espinoza had taken Emma, and Detective Wu had interviewed Phil. They had wanted to take Phil's phone, but since he was an attorney and his smart phone also contained access to confidential client matters, Phil suggested he send them all the photos he'd taken the day before. The detectives agreed and Phil did it on the spot. As soon as he and Emma returned to their vehicle, they compared notes of their questionings. Between them they had told Wu and Espinoza everything they knew. Emma had even told Espinoza about Felix Ricardo's spirit hinting that his death might not have been accidental. He didn't appear to be either skeptical or accepting of the information, but said they would look into it.

"Hmm," Emma said, looking out the windshield as they drove along the 110 Freeway toward Pasadena. It was familiar scenery but she wasn't paying attention to it. Instead she was running through her head what she knew of the shooting. She stopped the turbine in her brain and considered Phil's question. "So you picked up on that, too?"

Phil glanced over at her. "I think in some way he's connected to this, and not just because he's good friends with Espinoza."

"Yes, it's been nagging at me off and on today," she told him as she dug through her brain to fit together the odds and ends she'd picked up on Jeremiah in all the chaos. "First of all, why did he want to go to Olvera Street with us in the first place? And did you see how easily he moved around the crime scene without anyone challenging him?" She turned away from the windshield and toward Phil. Her seat belt cut across her neck as she twisted and she took a second to fix it. "Maybe he's not a retired cop at all but an active one and working undercover."

Phil turned on his blinker and made ready to merge into the lane on their left. "I had that thought myself, but I think he may be too old to still be with the department. I believe they have a mandatory retirement age, but I'm not sure."

"Good point." Emma pointed a finger at Phil to emphasize her thoughts as she verbalized them. "He told us he went to Santiago's out of curiosity just to see if the people who asked Gino about Steve Bullock showed up. But I'm not so sure he hasn't been staking out the place long before that."

"Didn't he say that he was a regular at Santiago's or did we assume it because he knew the waitress?" Phil asked, with a cock of his head, as if changing its direction would help him remember.

"He told us he was a regular," Emma answered. "I'm sure of it. But he still could have been watching Bullock." She paused, then said, "Okay, so he is a private investigator, as he said, but I'll bet someone hired him to watch Bullock." She drew out the words slowly as the idea formed for the first time in her mind.

"But he left his surveillance post the minute he heard about the shooting," Phil pointed out. "I'm thinking he already knew there was a connection between Roble and Bullock and I'm also thinking he knew darn well who Bullock had been lunching with before we told him."

"Argh," Emma snapped in frustration. "I think you're right. We've been played."

"More like used to further his investigation, whatever that is."

They drove along, starting and stopping with the usual rush hour traffic heading out of Los Angeles toward Pasadena. "Seems like all we've done today is fight traffic," Phil noted. "Physically and intellectually."

Emma nodded in agreement, but her mind was still going over all the things she could remember about Jeremiah Jones and his interest in Steve Bullock and the Ricardos.

"Emma," Phil began. When Emma didn't respond, he said, "Earth to Emma."

"Huh? Oh, sorry, Phil. I'm still trying to piece it all together."

"I wanted to discuss something else with you before we get home."

"My parents?" she guessed.

"Yes," he confirmed.

"That's also heavy on my mind," she told him. "What in the world were they thinking, Phil? Especially after my mother's lecture about danger and how worried she is about me." She let out a big puff of air. "I could have strangled them. And I will when we get home."

"And that's exactly why we need to have this conversation now." He glanced over at her. "Leave it be, Emma."

"What?" she stared at him with surprise.

"You heard me, honey. Leave it be, unless they bring it up. They've been through enough today and having you come through the door huffing and puffing and ready to blow the house down isn't going to change anything. It will only make them defensive."

Emma pursed her lips in annoyance. "I deserve an explanation."

Phil chuckled, his eyes back on the road. "No, you don't. They are two grown people. They can do as they like just like you and me. Maybe they went there out of curiosity, maybe for the food, maybe to help you. Who knows? I'm just saying you shouldn't come down on them for it. Let them come to you."

"And what if they don't?"

"Then they don't," he told her, glancing at her again. "There's no denying it will be a big fat elephant in the room when we get home, but that doesn't mean you need to go poking at the elephant with a stick. Elizabeth and Paul are very reasonable people, and they love you more than anything in the world. Something tells me in time, maybe not right away, but I'm betting sometime tonight or tomorrow they will bring it up. Let them make that first move. I think they will appreciate it."

Emma ran both of her hands through her short hair and rubbed roughly. Phil laughed. "The idea of sitting on your hands about this must really be bothering you," he said to her with a grin. "You only do a two-fisted head scratch when you're about to explode from frustration."

"He's right," said Granny, popping up in the backseat.

Emma dropped her hands into her lap as if caught stealing. She shot both Phil and Granny a look of annoyance, her brows deep with furrows, her eyes narrowed.

"Want your face to freeze like that?" asked Granny.

"Never mind that, Granny," Emma said to the spirit. "Did you learn anything?"

"Nothing we didn't already know," reported Granny. "Problem is Jeremiah can see me. Every time I came close, he'd clam up or give me the stink eye."

"The stink eye, Granny?" Emma asked with disbelief. "Jeremiah gave you the stink eye?" Next to her, Phil laughed but said nothing.

"He'd just look at me and slightly shake his head as if warning me to mind my own business," the ghost said. She leaned forward. "Something's up with him."

"We were just discussing that," Emma told her. She gave Phil an update.

"Couldn't you go invisible, Granny?" Phil asked. "I thought ghosts were only seen when they wanted to be or when they were caught off guard."

"I tried that," Granny replied, "but he always knew when I was around. The Force is strong with him, Obi Wan."

Emma was drinking from a water bottle stored in the console and started coughing. The *Star Wars* reference was new for Granny. It took her a few seconds before Emma could relay the comment to Phil, who nearly choked with laughter upon hearing it.

"What do you know about Obi Wan, Granny?" Phil asked. "Not that calling me that isn't flattering."

"Kelly and some of her friends were watching the movie last week," the ghost answered. "She told me there are a whole bunch of movies just like it. Do we have them at home?" The ghost leaned forward with childlike eagerness. "Can we watch them sometime?"

"I'm going to kill Kelly," Emma said quietly as she stared out the window at the traffic ahead of them. "Right after I kill my parents."

Fortunately, Emma didn't have to hold her tongue for long. When she and Phil got back to the Miller house, they found Emma's parents where they'd found them the day before—on the back patio enjoying chilly gin and tonics. Without waiting for them to ask, Elizabeth poured one for her and Phil.

"Seems this family might have a problem with the drink," quipped Granny. "I never partook, so you must have gotten that from Jacob's side."

"We just started, Granny," Elizabeth told the ghost, nearly snapping at her. "So don't be so quick to judge."

Phil and Emma exchanged glances. It wasn't like Elizabeth to be so testy. Emma stuck her nose in her glass and took a long drink. It tasted wonderful and refreshing and kept her from saying something she might regret.

Emma was halfway through her drink, determined not to say anything, when her mother trotted out the elephant. "You don't have anything to say about today, Emma? About our being at the restaurant?"

Emma put her glass down on the patio table with a fair to medium thud. Phil shot her a look of warning. She played with the glass a few seconds before answering. "Yes, I do, Mother, plenty, but I'm not going to say a word. You and Dad are free to go wherever you like. You're not children."

"No, we're not," added Paul. "But we're sorry we gave you

a scare. We really did want to try the restaurant, and we thought maybe we would notice something while there."

"It didn't look to me like you got anything to eat," Emma said.

Both her parents shook their heads. "We'd only been at our table a few minutes when the commotion started," Elizabeth told them. "There was a bus of tourists ahead of us so we had to wait to be seated." Elizabeth took a drink from her glass. "I made us a nice chicken salad when we got home. We weren't very hungry after what happened."

Emma paused, started to take another drink, but took a few deep breaths instead. "Rikki wanted me to thank you both for caring. And Dad, your being there may have saved Lupe Lopez's life."

"That woman was very lucky," Paul said. "Too bad we didn't know what had happened upstairs. I might have been able to help him before the ambulance arrived."

"So you didn't know about the shooting upstairs?" Granny asked. Elizabeth repeated the question for Phil and Paul.

Archie was nudging Granny so the ghost went off to play with him. "Don't worry," she told everyone. "I'll still be able to hear ya."

Emma snorted. "She has ears like satellite dishes."

"I heard that!" the ghost yelled from the back of the yard. "And I'm taking it as a compliment."

Both Paul and Elizabeth shook their heads at Granny's question. Paul answered, "No, Granny, we didn't. The first we knew of any problem was when those officers wearing shorts came flying through the door."

"I was told the bike cops were just across the street

having lunch when the call came through," Emma said. "That's why they showed up so quickly."

"There was a scream first, Paul," Elizabeth said. "Remember?"

Paul nodded slightly. "That's right. There was a scream and a woman yelling for help. It was coming from elsewhere in the building. It was difficult to tell. Everyone in the dining room stopped what they were doing and just looked at each other. The one waiter, the middle-aged man with the ponytail?"

"That would have been Hector," Emma noted. "He manages the place with Rikki."

"Well, he took off toward the back at a run and disappeared down the hallway."

Emma nodded, taking in the sequence of events. This was information the police hadn't given her. "There's a staircase in the back leading upstairs to the offices," she told them.

"Very soon after, the bike cops showed up, then the paramedics, along with other police, and we were all told we couldn't leave," added Paul. "Then they wheeled that poor man out on a stretcher." He shook his head. "I wish I'd known earlier."

"But you didn't, Dad," Emma told him, giving him a weak smile. "T.J. was still in surgery when we left. Rikki and his family are at the hospital."

"So you didn't actually see T.J. Mendoza arrive or speak to Rikki?" Phil asked.

The Millers looked at each other, then shook their heads. "Not that we know of," Paul answered for them both. "We got seated near the end of that huge rush of tourists, then not more than ten minutes later all the panic started."

Elizabeth left the table and went into the house. She came out a few minutes later with a snack platter of hummus, vegetables, and crackers and placed them on the table along with napkins. The men fell on the food immediately.

"I could have gotten that for you, Mother," Emma protested before her mother could sit down.

"Nonsense, it was leftover from last night. All I had to do was open a box of crackers." Elizabeth started to return to her chair then stopped and came back to Emma. She threw her arms around her daughter and gave her a tight hug. "I'm sorry if we worried you. Thank you for coming to the restaurant so quickly."

"Oh, Mother," Emma said, hugging her back. "I'm sorry, too. Today I got a real taste of the worry you go through with some of my activities."

After Elizabeth sat down, she said, "Actually it was quite exciting. I'm not sure if I'd want to be in the middle of another shooting, but solving the puzzle of it all is fun."

Paul put an arm around his wife and pulled her close. "That's us, the geriatric Nick and Nora Charles."

"So who does that make us?" Phil asked Emma.

She gave it some thought before answering. "Maybe those two Day of the Dead dolls I bought you a couple of days ago?"

"Emma!" Elizabeth said, her voice tight and cracking. "Please don't say such a thing. Not even in jest. Not after today."

"Yeah," called Granny while Archie ran around her. "One ghost in the family is enough. I don't need the competition." The table hushed at the thought.

"Who was that man, the tall black man, talking with the police?" asked Paul, breaking the silence and changing the subject. "He seemed to know you two quite well."

"That's Jeremiah," Granny said, heading back to the table. "We just met him today. He can see and hear me."

"Really, Granny?" asked Elizabeth with surprise. "He can hear *and* see you?"

"Every bit as well as Emma," the ghost told her.

"It's true, Mother. Jeremiah Jones is a medium just like me except that he claims until he met me and Phil today, he's never told anyone."

"He was the person Gino Costello contacted to identify the man in that photograph I took," Phil told them. "He's a former detective with the LAPD."

"So how did you cross his path?" Paul asked. "Did Gino give you his number?"

Phil laughed. "It's quite a story." He got up and kissed Emma on the forehead. "You tell them, honey. I need to go inside for a minute."

While Phil was gone, Emma and Granny brought the Millers up to speed on Jeremiah Jones and what happened at Santiago's. At the end, Paul asked, "So you think he has something to do with this?"

"We don't think he's involved with the crime," Emma said after chewing and swallowing a carrot stick with hummus, "but he knows a lot more than he's telling us. Of that we're pretty sure."

"Why not send Granny in to spy on him?" Paul suggested.

"They did," Granny answered, "but Jeremiah was onto me and was cagey. That's the problem when they can see ya." Elizabeth relayed the comment to her husband.

When Phil came out of the house, he was carrying the Day of the Dead bride and groom dolls. He placed them in front of Emma, who looked at them, then up at him with surprise.

"Phil," Elizabeth admonished, "those are really ghoulish."

"I think so, too, Elizabeth," Granny said, "but Emma likes them."

"I do like them, Granny," Emma said. "That's why I bought them and gave them to Phil."

"And that's why I'm giving them back to you," Phil told her.

Emma looked even more surprised. "But I thought you liked them."

"I do," he assured her. "That's why I gussied them up a bit more. Take a closer look."

Emma first picked up the male figure but saw nothing out of place. Then she picked up the female figure and gave it close review. "Oh my!" She slapped a hand over her mouth and looked up at Phil, who was still standing next to her chair.

"What is it, Emma?" Paul asked.

Without answering, she plucked something from the bride's bouquet and held it up for everyone to see.

"Well, it's about time!" groused Granny, but the ghost had a wide smile on her face.

"Oh, Emma," said Elizabeth, choking back tears.

Phil took the diamond ring from Emma's hand. "I bought this right after we got back from Las Vegas and have been carting it around with me every time I see you, just waiting for the right moment. When you gave me those dolls, I thought maybe the time had arrived."

Granny hopped up and down. Around her, the dog barked and danced thinking she was playing with him. The Millers, showing more restraint, beamed with happiness.

"Welcome to the family, son," Paul said. He stood up and reached out to shake Phil's hand.

"Hold your horses," Phil said, "the lady hasn't said yes yet." Groaning, Phil got down on one knee. "Emma, will you marry this old broken-down cowboy?"

She threw her arms around his neck. *"Sí!"*

CHAPTER TWENTY

"So what's on the agenda today, Chief?" Granny Apples was in the bathroom with Emma, watching her put on her makeup. Emma had recently finished a good morning workout and taken her shower. Phil had done the same.

"Phil and I were thinking of contacting Jeremiah," Emma told Granny, "and grilling him on his activities. We want to let him know we're onto him."

"You won't need to do that," Granny said. "I checked in with him early this morning and told him he needs to fess up."

Emma stopped running a bulky soft brush across her face and stared at the ghost, who was perched on the edge of the big tub. "You did?"

"Yep. I told him we're not greenhorns and know he's up to something." Granny got up and drifted in and out between the bathroom and Emma's bedroom. "Where's Phil?"

"Downstairs in the kitchen." Emma put down the brush. "And what about Jeremiah? What did he say?"

Granny came back close to Emma. "He said I was right. He also said to tell you to put on a fresh pot of coffee."

"Why's that?" Emma eyed the ghost with suspicion.

"Because he's on his way here right now." Granny put her hands on her hips. "Do I have to spell everything out for you?"

Emma put her hands up to her face in frustration. She'd never had a sister to fuss and argue with but often Granny felt like that to her. When Granny died, she was only in her early forties, just a few years younger than Emma was now, adding to the feeling that they were siblings and not separated by both generations and death.

"Careful," Granny cautioned, "you might mess up that goo you put on your face."

"Emma," Phil called to her. Emma could hear him coming up the back stairs from the kitchen. She met him just as he came into the bedroom. "Jeremiah just called. He wants to talk to us, said the sooner the better. He said he'd be here in about ten to fifteen minutes if that's okay by us. I said sure."

Emma turned and stared at Granny. "Told ya," the ghost said with a sniff.

When Jeremiah arrived, they all went out to the back patio. Already on the table was a carafe of coffee, mugs, sugar, and cream. It was just past nine o'clock and already shaping up to be a hot day. Before sitting down, Jeremiah looked at the large white house and pristine property, taking it all in. "When I was growing up," he said as he took his seat at the large glass patio table, "I used to pass by these grand Pasadena houses and wonder what they looked like inside. Same with the mansions in Beverly Hills. This is beautiful. Grand but homey." He pointed to the single-story building close to the house. "Is that a guest house?"

"Yes," Emma answered, "although now it serves as a workout room and my home office."

"So you grew up here in Southern California?" Phil asked.

Jeremiah nodded. "Yep. Spent almost all my life in and around Inglewood until I went off to Nam. How about you?"

"Raised in Julian down by San Diego," Phil told him.

"I know where Julian is," Jeremiah said. "Love to go there every now and then. Peaceful place. Love the apple pie."

"There's a ghost in Julian," Phil told him, "by the name of Albert Robinson. He hangs out mostly at the Julian Hotel. He's African-American and the original owner of the hotel."

"Really? I didn't know that," Jeremiah said with interest.

"Next time you go down there, look him up," Phil said. "You might even find him in the graveyard by his headstone. Tell him Emma sent you. They're pals."

Emma nodded and smiled. "That we are. I often go up to the old Pioneer Cemetery and visit with Albert when I'm in Julian."

Jeremiah grinned. "I should be surprised, but I'm not."

"Emma grew up here," Phil continued. "She shares the house with her parents, but she also has a home in Julian, which is where Granny is from. Emma built her home on Granny's old homestead."

At the mention of Granny, Jeremiah smiled. "That old ghost is quite a character."

"You don't know the half of it," Phil told him with a shake of his head.

Emma got up. "Phil, why don't you pour the man some coffee while I get the other stuff." She went into the house and came out a few minutes later with a basket of hot blueberry muffins, along with jam and butter, plates, and knives.

"Jeremiah," she said to their guest after putting the muffins on the table, "we ate breakfast much earlier but I'd be happy to whip you up something more substantial like eggs."

"No, Emma, but thanks. Had my breakfast hours ago, too. I'm an early riser. Looks like you two are also."

"All my life," Phil said with a laugh. "Grew up on a ranch. Never could understand how my boys could sleep in until noon. Now Emma has me on the treadmill at the crack of dawn instead of feeding horses." He reached over and gave Emma's arm an affectionate squeeze.

Jeremiah gave them both a sly grin over the rim of his coffee mug. "I understand congratulations are in order." He pointed at her engagement ring.

"Very observant of you," Emma said with a bright smile.

"Nah," Jeremiah said after taking another sip of his coffee. "Granny told me this morning. She's very happy about it. Kept saying it was about time. Hopefully your engagement will be happier than Rikki Ricardo's." He looked around again. "By the way, where is Granny?"

"She'll be back," Emma told him. "I think she's recharging. I don't know how much you know about spirits, Jeremiah, but they can't materialize for long periods of time without needing to reenergize. It's like putting your phone on a charger. Granny has learned how to maintain her presence longer than any other spirit I've met, but still needs to rest. She wanted to be fresh for this meeting."

"And where are Dr. and Mrs. Miller?" Jeremiah asked. "Dr. Miller did some fine work stabilizing Chef Lopez yesterday. We're very glad he was there. I'd like to thank him."

"Emma's parents got up very early this morning and headed down to Julian for the weekend. They are good friends with my aunt and uncle, who live across from Emma's home."

Emma laughed and shook her head. "I think Mother and Phil's aunt Susan are already planning our wedding. You'd think we were a couple of kids fresh out of college."

Silence, not uncomfortable, but peaceful and as easy as a pair of old slippers, fell over the table while they drank their coffee. The air was still and dry with only the occasional buzz of insects as background music.

Jeremiah broke the silence. "In Granny's words, seems you're onto me about some things."

Phil and Emma exchanged looks. "More like we think there is more to you than meets the eye," Phil said to him.

"Like my business card says, I'm a private investigator. You already know that I'm an ex-cop and used to partner with Aaron Espinoza." Jeremiah leaned back in his chair and crossed one long leg over the other. Like the day before, he was dressed in jeans and a T-shirt. "What else do you want to know?"

"Wait for me?" called a disembodied voice. "I want to hear this, too."

"Don't worry, Granny," Jeremiah said with a chuckle. "I'll wait for you."

The ghost popped in and looked around. She floated here and there. "Where's Archie?"

"Who's Archie?" asked Jeremiah, looking at Phil and Emma with curiosity.

"That's our Scottish terrier," Emma explained, "and Granny's best bud." Emma turned to Granny. "Mother and Dad took Archie to Julian with them, Granny. You can visit him down there."

Satisfied, Granny turned to Jeremiah, hands on hips. "So spill it, gumshoe, or we'll make you talk."

Jeremiah leaned his head back and roared with rich,

throaty laughter. "Where do you come up with this stuff, Granny? You're a real pistol."

"Too much TV," Emma said. "That's where she gets it." Granny made a face at her, causing Jeremiah to laugh again.

"So," Phil said, getting the conversation back on track. "What's your connection to the Ricardos and/or to Steve Bullock?"

"Spoken like a true lawyer, Phil. Getting right to the meat of the matter." Jeremiah drank more coffee and reached for a muffin. "You and Emma are right, there is more to it. It's true I am a semi-regular at Santiago's and have been for years, but that just made my surveillance easier. I've been hired to keep track of Steve Bullock."

"And you knew that he was lunching regularly with Lucy Ricardo, didn't you?" Emma asked.

"Yes, I did," Jeremiah admitted. "I knew about the sale and how it was causing a rift in the Ricardo family. I also knew that Bullock had been linked to some shady business dealings in the past, though nothing was ever proved. So did my client. I was hired to see if he was doing anything underhanded in his pursuit of Roble Foods. Bullock's uncle is the majority owner of Fiesta Time, but Ramon Santiago is ill and Steve is positioned to take over the company when his uncle retires or dies. Ramon and his wife never had any children of their own."

"What about his relationship with Lucy?" Emma asked. "Granny doesn't think they are romantically connected. Do you?

"Trust me, they aren't," said Granny. "They never once touched each other or gave each other so much as a peck on the cheek."

"Granny's right," Jeremiah said. "They aren't a couple, but they are working together in the takeover of Roble Foods by Fiesta Time. Of that I'm sure. Other than that, I couldn't find so much as a shared milkshake."

"What about that bombshell yesterday about Rikki and Lucy having different fathers?" asked Emma. "Lucy said she found out about that around the time Felix died. Do you think that's why she's determined to break up Felix's company?"

"Yes, that was a shocker yesterday," admitted Phil, grabbing a muffin for himself, "even if not for the attempted murder of Rikki Ricardo. Did you know about Lucy's paternity?"

Jeremiah shook his head, drained his coffee mug, and reached for the carafe. Emma started to pour for him, but he waved her off. "I can get it myself, Emma. Just keep it coming. I live off the stuff even though my doc tells me to cut back." Once he poured his coffee, Jeremiah answered, "The father thing was news to me, too. But I do know she's a very vindictive woman. Her hatred of her sister was evident in everything I've heard and seen. She's hell-bent on destroying everything the Ricardo family built. Although she sabotaged her own plans by getting arrested. The push for the sale might have survived T.J.'s shooting, and might even have helped it through by distracting Rikki, but Lucy's arrest will probably bring the process to a halt." He bit into his muffin. "Mmmm, these are outstanding, just like my wife used to make. She was quite a cook and baker."

"Phil made them," Emma said with pride. "One of his specialties." Jeremiah lifted the half-eaten muffin toward Phil in appreciation.

"It's my aunt's recipe. They were already in the oven when you called," Phil said after swallowing a big bite of his own muffin. He eyed Jeremiah with suspicion while he wiped his mouth with a napkin. "So you just happened to overhear Lucy Ricardo and Steven Bullock talking on several occasions? All the way from the far end of the bar?"

"No flies on you, eh, Phil?" Jeremiah gave him a sly glance.

"Only when I step in horseshit," Phil said. He hesitated, then asked, "Where's the bug? Under the table? Somewhere in the booth? Or is it back at Lucy's office?"

Jeremiah leaned back in his chair, relaxed and unconcerned. "That would be illegal, Phil. As an attorney you should know that." He polished off his muffin and dusted crumbs from the front of his shirt.

"I do," Phil responded, "but that doesn't mean you didn't do it."

"Tell me, Counselor," Jeremiah said, leaning forward again, "is tapping a conversation any different from sending a ghost to eavesdrop on someone? It's still a violation of privacy, wouldn't you say? After all, in each case the parties have no idea they're being listened to."

"I was doing surveillance," Granny snapped. "We were on a case."

"I was on a case, too, Granny, and I'm a licensed private detective." Jeremiah smiled at the ghost. "Where are your credentials?"

"We were looking into this because Rikki had asked me for help," Emma told him, leaving out the part where Rikki had earlier told her to keep out of it. "We're not professional investigators like yourself, Jeremiah. We're just friends helping friends." She picked at the muffin on her plate with telltale nervous fingers, Jeremiah noticed.

"Uh-huh," the PI said with a smile and buried his nose in his coffee mug. He was starting to annoy Emma, and it was clear to all that he was enjoying it.

"When did you start tailing Lucy?" Phil asked.

"I didn't say I was," Jeremiah said, looking right at him. "Bullock was my target."

Jeremiah reached into his pocket and pulled out his phone. He scrolled through it until he found what he was looking for, and passed it along to Phil. "These look familiar?"

Phil looked at the photo, then flipped to the next and then to a few others. He showed them to Emma, then said to Jeremiah, "You were snapping photos of me photographing Steve and Carlos?" He glanced down. One of the photos was of Emma driving the SUV right before Phil hopped into it.

"I was already there taking shots from farther away with a zoom lens when along comes some bald guy slipping in and out between cars to take his own pics." Jeremiah picked up his mug and took another long drink of his coffee. "You guys were a big surprise, both then and in the restaurant. Add a ghost to the mix and you can bet I was curious."

Granny got very close to Jeremiah, "So cough it up: Who's your client?"

"You're in my space, Granny," Jeremiah said to the ghost in a calm voice.

"Granny's just asking the question on all of our minds," Emma noted. "Who's your client?"

Jeremiah stared at Granny, waiting. When the ghost backed up a few feet, he said, "T.J. Mendoza hired me. He met me when I was working gangs while with the LAPD."

"T.J. was in a gang?" asked Emma with surprise.

Jeremiah shook his head. "No, but his older brother was and was killed in a gun battle years ago." He paused while the sad irony sank into everyone's mind. "Frankly, I don't think T.J. cared if the company got sold or not. He's a very bright guy. He would have landed on his feet no matter what. He wasn't invested in the company like the Ricardos, but he did care a lot about Rikki."

"That's exactly the feeling I got from T.J. when I spoke to him," Emma said. "So that's why you took off for Roble when we did, isn't it?"

Jeremiah shrugged. "At the time, none of us knew it was T.J. who'd been shot, but I had a very bad feeling in my gut and it wasn't the fish tacos. I also had a feeling Lucy would be right behind us and Steve would scatter like a roach, so no sense sticking around Santiago's."

They sat quietly for a few minutes, each with their own thoughts, even Granny. "What's been bothering me," Emma finally said, "is why was T.J. there or, more importantly, who knew he was there? Rikki said he dashed in unexpectedly and said he needed to talk to her. She made him wait until the lunch rush was over, then found him near death when she finally went to talk to him."

"That's not sitting right with me either," Jeremiah said. "If T.J. wasn't supposed to be there, did the shooter track him into Roble or was the shooter already in the restaurant and decided on the spot to kill T.J. when he saw him arrive?"

"Hold on," Phil said. He went into Emma's guest house office and came out with a large pad of paper and a pen. When he returned to the table, he said, "Okay, let's brainstorm in an orderly manner." Flipping the pad horizontally, at the top in capital letters he wrote: *T.J.* He put a *1* in the left margin and wrote: *Killer tracked T.J. into Roble?* He followed up by listing a *2* under that on the left side and writing: *Killer already in Roble?*

"That's a good start," noted Emma. "Next make a list each for Steve Bullock and Lucy." Phil wrote both of their names at the top and drew lines between them to make columns.

"We know that Lucy didn't shoot T.J.," Jeremiah said, "because she was at Santiago's with us. Same with Bullock."

"True," Phil said, "but what about having someone else do the shooting? We know Bullock gave Carlos money for something, and I definitely overhead Carlos say something about T.J. during the exchange." Under both Steve and Lucy's names he wrote: *Hired shooter?* Under Lucy's name he also added: *Felix not father.*

"But Carlos wasn't at Roble yesterday," Emma pointed out. "Rikki told me he called in sick."

"That doesn't mean he didn't have anything to do with it," noted Jeremiah. "He could have arranged for the shooter to come in."

Phil made another column and wrote: *Carlos Fuentes* at the top. "Fuentes was his last name, correct?" he asked the others.

"Yes," Granny answered. "I remember that." The ghost came behind Phil and looked over his shoulder.

"You can read, Granny?" asked Jeremiah.

Granny scowled. "Why are people always surprised at that?"

"Sorry." Jeremiah held his hands up in a defensive gesture. "I meant no offense."

"Granny already knew how to read some," Emma said, giving the ghost an encouraging smile. "Now she's working with my mother to improve it."

"Yeah," said the ghost with a jerk of her set chin. "Turns out you can teach an old ghost new tricks."

While Jeremiah shook his head in amusement at the ghost, Phil kept writing, adding new information to each list as he remembered it. "Okay," he said. "We know that Carlos was out yesterday and that Steve paid him for something that might have to do with T.J. We also know that Lucy wasn't at the restaurant yesterday, but could have had a part in hiring a shooter. We also know that Felix wasn't her father but we have no clue who is."

"One of the things I overhead discussed between Lucy and Steve," Jeremiah said, "was what her role would be at Fiesta Time after the sale."

Emma pushed away her plate with the half-eaten muffin and looked at Jeremiah with surprise. "Both Rikki and T.J. were under the impression that after the sale Lucy wanted to leave the area and go off and paint and live a simpler lifestyle."

"No way was that her plan," Jeremiah said with conviction. "That might be what she told them, but the truth was that Ramon Santiago would retire after the sale closed and Lucy would become president of Fiesta Time with Bullock as CEO and chairman of the board. I also heard her say she hoped T.J. would join them."

"Interesting," noted Phil. "But do you think T.J. would go with them after they sandbagged Rikki? He was going to marry her after all. Might cause some pretty tense family holidays."

"That could be why T.J. hired me," Jeremiah said, refilling his coffee mug again. "He wanted to make sure if the sale went through, it was on the up-and-up. If he found out about any dirty dealings, I don't think he would have gone along with them, and I think he would have joined forces with Rikki to stop them. From what I've seen, T.J. Mendoza is the opposite of Steve Bullock. T.J. believes business is a game of strategy played fairly and with integrity. He's helped

Rikki implement a lot of changes at the restaurant that have increased business and their public brand. Bullock also believes it's a game, but no holds barred. It's like Olympic boxing versus street fighting."

"What about the girls' mother?" asked Emma. "Did you know that Elena Ricardo took off about the time of the shooting?" Phil made a column for Elena Ricardo and under it wrote: *Whereabouts?* Followed by *Involved?*

Jeremiah nodded. "Yeah. I heard Rikki tell Espinoza that. That poor girl's family is breaking apart all around her."

"Rikki said her mother was going back and forth about the sale, depending on which daughter talked to her last," Emma said. "But the last I knew, Elena Ricardo had sided with Lucy on selling the company. Rikki also said her mother seemed fine when she and T.J. stopped by there yesterday to tell her about the engagement."

"We need to find that woman," said Phil.

"They did, sort of," Jeremiah told them. "I spoke to Aaron already this morning. He's also an early riser, though I doubt he got much sleep last night to begin with." Jeremiah got up from the table and stretched his legs. "The mom slipped across the border into Tijuana yesterday afternoon. Who knows where she is now?"

"Can't they track her vehicle?" asked Emma.

"They can and did," Jeremiah said. "The car was left in one of the U.S.-side parking lots. She walked across the border and melted into the crowd, taking public transportation or even a taxi to wherever she was heading. They're checking her phone records now, both landline and cell, but if she's smart, she's discarded the cell and got herself a burner phone."

"She probably planned to take off," said Emma with

disgust. "She was all hearts and flowers with Rikki that morning knowing she was going to leave. What kind of mother does that?"

"Another possibility," noted Jeremiah, "is that Elena heard about the shooting on TV and took off, knowing the shit was going to hit the fan. She could have easily thrown clothes together and made it to the border by the time everything got sorted out and people started looking for her. Aaron is going to contact the authorities in the town her family is from and a few others in the area to see if she shows up, but Mexican *policia* are not known for being cooperative with American cops, especially if those cops want information about a Mexican, American-born or not. Hopefully, through some miracle, Aaron will learn something. I doubt the mother shot anyone, but I'll bet she could be a big help in sorting some of this out."

"Do you think Detective Espinoza will tell you if he learns anything?" asked Phil.

"He'll tell me as much as he can about what he can," Jeremiah answered. "I've told him everything I know, including about the cash handoff. It won't be the first time I've helped him out. He owes me and knows it." Granny floated back and forth behind Emma and Phil as if on a track. Jeremiah noticed. "Careful, Granny, or you're going to wear a hole in that air." Granny ignored him.

"She's a pacer when she thinks," Emma explained.

Finally, Granny stopped and returned to hover behind Phil again. "Did any of you geniuses think that maybe T.J. wasn't the target yesterday?"

CHAPTER TWENTY-ONE

EMMA repeated Granny's comment for Phil, then he, Jeremiah, and Emma went still, their eyes darting from one to the other as they considered the possibility.

"Good theory, Granny," Jeremiah said. "And one Aaron floated by me briefly yesterday. It could be that the target was Rikki and the shooter found T.J. in her office. Both were surprised and the shooter tried to take T.J. out." On his note pad, Phil wrote under T.J.'s name: *Wrong victim?* He also made a column for Rikki and wrote: *Target?*

"Granny makes a great point," agreed Emma. "T.J. made a surprise visit to Roble, so unless the shooter was following him, he wouldn't have known he was there. And if the shooter was someone working at the restaurant, he would have been surprised, too."

Jeremiah leaned against the low brick wall that bordered a section of the patio. "Aaron's people searched the entire restaurant from top to bottom, including personal lockers, cupboards, drawers, even the sacks of flour and other food items, looking for the gun. Nothing. He also said everyone was accounted for. People vouched for each other. No one working could remember anyone leaving their post for even a few minutes from the time T.J. arrived until Rikki found him. Several saw T.J. go upstairs, but said it was way too busy for anyone to take even a bathroom break."

"That rules out Carlos as the shooter," Emma noted. "If he had called in sick and then showed up, he would have been recognized and remembered."

"Very true," Phil agreed, "but that still doesn't mean he didn't assist in it. We really need to find out more about that money and what it was for." Phil turned to where he thought Granny was hovering. He was wrong but Granny moved into his sightline. "Granny, do you think you could zero in on Carlos Fuentes and see where he is?"

"I could try," said the ghost.

"And if you can't," added Emma, "how about trying to locate Felix again? Didn't you say he was up there at the time of the shooting?"

"I think he was, or at least he was there when Rikki found T.J.," Granny said.

"We have to get Felix to talk," said Emma. "He might have seen everything." With a salute, Granny was gone.

The remaining three all gave the situation more thought. Jeremiah returned to the table, and both he and Phil each reached for another muffin. It was getting warmer but still not hot. Emma went into the house and returned with a pitcher of cold water and glasses, along with her cell phone. "I received a text from Rikki," she said after putting the water down. "I texted her this morning to see how T.J. is doing." She looked down at the message. "The surgery went well but he's in very critical condition and not out of the woods yet. She also says the police haven't been able to question him because he's too weak and drugged up." She read further. "She also said that Chef Lupe's surgery went well."

"That's good news," said Phil. Jeremiah, his mouth full of muffin, agreed with a nod.

Emma poured herself a glass of water. While she was drinking, she pieced together another theory. "One thing everyone agrees on is that the place was busier than usual because of that tour bus, right?"

Phil nodded. "Didn't Rikki say they weren't expecting it?"

"Yes, she did," Emma said. "Rikki said they were surprised by it showing up. I don't think it's unusual for tour buses to come and go at Olvera Street, but I would think most of those would be scheduled stops by the same companies, not something spontaneous. A good tour company would want to make sure there was enough seating and service for everyone."

Jeremiah put down his muffin. "That's a very good point. I wonder if anyone caught the name of the tour bus." He picked up his phone and started texting. "I'm sure Aaron's people would have asked about it. Let's see if they got any information he's willing to share. In the meantime, I need to get off my butt and start talking to people."

Phil ripped off another sheet of paper and started writing, making a list of names. "Why don't we make a list and divvy up the names. It will go faster."

"Normally," Jeremiah said, "I'd put my foot down on civilians being involved, but we need to work fast on this." He looked from Emma to Phil and back to Emma. "And my research showed some interesting facts about you two, especially you, Emma."

Phil stopped writing. Emma put down her water glass. The two of them looked at each other, then at Jeremiah, but said nothing.

Jeremiah laughed. "Don't play coy with me. Besides what I turned up, Aaron confirmed that you've been involved on the solving end of a couple of crimes in the past few years, most recently in Las Vegas, and before that the mess with Max Naiman's family. I'll bet Granny was involved in those, too."

"I was just helping friends out, Jeremiah," Emma told him firmly. "That's all it was."

"I have no doubt." Jeremiah looked at her a long while, then pointed at Phil's list. "What do you have there so far, Phil?"

Phil looked down at his list of names. "We need to talk to Hector Gonzales. He might remember something since he was at the restaurant and could be directly impacted by the sale."

"And his daughter, Ana," Emma added. "She might have seen something, especially the tour bus or the name of the company. She stands right outside the entrance all day."

"Restaurante Roble will be closed today," Jeremiah noted. "It won't open again until the police release the crime scene, so we'll have to run down their addresses. Same thing with any of the waiters or cooks we might want to talk to. That information the police will not be sharing."

"Obviously we need to speak to Carlos Fuentes when we locate him," Phil said, reading the next name. He put a star by Carlos's name. "He's perhaps the most important one."

"Granny has been to his home," Emma said, "but she might not be able to give us an address. She's not good with geographic locations and distances, but she did say he went to a college that seemed not far from his home, and from her description, he lives in well-maintained blue-collar neighborhood with small houses."

"Well, that leaves out UCLA," Jeremiah said, making a sarcastic remark about the famous university plopped down in the middle of some of the area's most expensive homes. "I'm betting Carlos is getting a jump on his education at LA City College. They have an extensive summer program. As for his neighborhood, from the description that could be one of hundreds in that area. He could even have disappeared by now like Elena."

"You mean run for Mexico?" asked Emma.

Jeremiah shook his head. "It would be easy for a Latino kid like him to melt into any crowd in LA."

Phil looked at his list and added another. "If we find the tour company, we need to speak to whoever the guide was yesterday." He pointed his pen to a name at the top of the list. "And we definitely need to pin down Steve Bullock and talk to him."

"He's at his office already this morning," Jeremiah told them.

"How do you know that?" asked Emma. "The day has barely started and you're here."

Jeremiah smiled. "I have an associate who's keeping watch on him today."

Emma studied Jeremiah, then said, "I'd like to go to Roble Foods. Rikki told me in her text that since T.J. is stable, she's going into the corporate offices today to calm down their employees."

"Damage control is not a bad idea," Phil said, "the sooner the better, especially since both the CFO and CEO are out of commission and she's now the only board member available."

Jeremiah scratched his chin. Today he was clean shaven.

"Does this give her full power now over Roble?" He aimed the question at Phil.

"Yes and no," Phil answered. "She is the only available director and shareholder so people will naturally look to her for guidance in this emergency situation, but she can't take over the board on a dime unless they have some special clause in the bylaws for such emergencies, which I doubt."

"But Lucy is in jail for attempted murder," Emma pointed out.

"Yes," agreed Phil, "and in California, directors can be removed for a felonious act, but only if convicted, not simply charged. The shareholders could remove Lucy as a director, but Lucy and Elena are both shareholders equal to Rikki. To remove Lucy and/or Elena from the board in other ways would take time."

Emma mulled that over, then said, "I'd also like to talk to Isabel."

"Who's Isabel?" asked Jeremiah.

"The executive secretary at Roble Foods," Emma answered. "From what I can tell, she's been privy to a lot of heated arguments between T.J. and Lucy. She even gave T.J. a heads-up when Lucy charged over to the restaurant in a rage on Tuesday, so she might not be that loyal to Lucy."

"How about you and Phil take both Rikki and Isabel today," Jeremiah said. "It'll be one-stop shopping. I'll talk to Elena's maid and to Carlos if we locate him, and I'll check in with my associate on Bullock. I'm riding my motorcycle again today so I'll be able to cover more miles faster than you folks."

"What about me?" asked Granny, who popped up.

"Did you find Carlos?" Emma asked.

"Yes and no," the ghost answered. "I made a connection,

but it wasn't very strong. First he was on that motorbike of his. Then I lost him. When I connected again, he was at a fast-food place getting something to eat and drink. That's where he is now. Just sitting outside eating as calmly as you please, but I couldn't tell where he was, just what he was doing." Emma gave Phil the report.

"A fast-food place," repeated Jeremiah. "Another needle in a haystack."

"I did my best," snapped Granny.

"I wasn't criticizing you, Granny," Jeremiah said. "I'm just frustrated. Don't be so sensitive."

"Welcome to my world," Emma told him.

"Why don't you also try to find out more from Detective Espinoza," Emma said to Jeremiah. "And if we find out the name of the tour company, we'll tackle that."

"Sounds good," Jeremiah said, looking at his watch. "It's about ten thirty now. Let's get a move on and check in with each other around one."

A phone vibrated. Jeremiah and Emma both looked at theirs. "It's mine," Jeremiah said. He looked at it. "Talk about timely. It's Aaron. He says the name of the tour company is Quickie LA. That's all he said."

Phil wrote it down on the list of people. "Don't worry, we'll find it."

· CHAPTER TWENTY-TWO ·

THE offices of Quickie LA were located on Central Avenue in the industrial section of downtown Los Angeles. It was an area that housed garment manufacturers and produce companies along with trucking firms. The office wasn't much, just a small building painted robin's egg blue with a sloped roof. It was attached to the backside of another business facing in the opposite direction like a lean-to or cheerful growth. The front door of the business faced a small parking lot. On the side of the building facing the street a plain sign announced, *Quickie LA—big city, little time.* Emma and Phil pulled Emma's SUV into the parking lot and into a vacant spot next to a white tour van sporting the same name and logo.

Phil opened the door to the office and held it for Emma to enter. A pencil-thin older woman with a fake tan and sandy-colored wig in a chin-length blunt cut with bangs looked up from behind the counter and peered at them over the top of half glasses. "Is this Quickie LA?" Emma asked as she stood on the threshold. From a small side window, an air-conditioning unit was making a heroic effort against the day's heat.

"It is, but don't stand there letting all the AC out. We can't afford to cool the parking lot." The woman stood up as Emma and Phil came in and closed the door behind them. "What can I do for you?"

"We'd like to ask you a couple of questions, if you don't mind," Emma began. "It's about what happened yesterday at Restaurante Roble."

"You mean that Mexican place on Olvera Street?" the woman asked.

"Yes," answered Emma. "We understand one of your vans stopped there yesterday about the time of the shooting."

The woman looked them over closely, squinting over the glasses. "You're not cops," she observed. "Besides they were here early this morning as soon as we opened asking all kinds of questions."

"You're right, we're not the police," Phil said. "This is Emma Whitecastle and I'm Phil Bowers. We're friends of Rikki Ricardo, one of the owners of the restaurant. She wanted us to look into some things for her."

The woman leaned over the counter and squinted again, this time specifically at Emma. The action left creases in her thick green eye shadow. "Aren't you on TV?" Emma nodded but said nothing. "Yeah, I know who you are," the woman continued with satisfaction. "You're the lady that looks into all that spooky stuff on that cable show. I saw it a few times when I stayed at my sister's place when she was recuperating from hip surgery. She's a big fan of all that crap." The woman waved a dismissive hand in the air. "Me, not so much."

"I'm not here about my show, Mrs. . . . ." Emma said, leading the woman into giving up her name.

"Bradford. Mrs. Nancy Bradford," the woman offered up. "Call me Nancy."

Emma smiled at the woman. "And you can call me Emma and that's Phil."

"Yeah, caught your names the first time around," Nancy told her. "I'm old, not senile. Now what do you want to know? I'm busy."

From the look of the tiny business, Nancy was anything but busy, but Emma proceeded. "I understand one of your vans took a group of tourists over to Restaurante Roble yesterday. Is that a regular stop for your tour busses?"

"No, first time for us. Our specialty is quick tours of LA. You know, for people just spending a day in the area and don't want to take one of those Starline tours or hop on and off tour buses all day. We load them up and drive them around town, pointing out sights. Mostly, though, we handle private groups in town for conferences. You know, shuttle them around to events or dinners together so they don't all have to find their own way. We also hire out for special things like bachelor parties." She rummaged around below the counter until she found what she was looking for. She put a couple of brochures on the counter and handed one to Emma. The brochure was not fancy and glossy, but budget quality and simple. "Sorry, but we almost never have walk-ins. Our brochures are mostly in hotels or we advertise online. Most of our business comes from referrals."

Phil stepped up to the counter next to Emma. "Did someone on your tour yesterday ask to stop by Roble?"

"No, that was a promotion from the restaurant," Nancy told them. She caught Emma and Phil exchanging glances and looked at them with the slyness of a fox. "Tell me again what's in this for me if I tell you what I told the police?" Another glance passed between Phil and Emma, followed by Phil reaching into his pocket and pulling out a money clip. He peeled off two twenty-dollar bills and placed them on the counter without saying a word. Nancy put a knobby hand sporting several gaudy costume jewelry rings on the money, then said, "And an autograph from her," she said, pointing at Emma, "to my sister Helen."

Emma took another of the brochures from the small pile on the counter, and grabbing a nearby cheap pen, she scrawled across a section with the least amount of printing: *To Helen, Happy ghost hunting. Best, Emma Whitecastle.* She pushed the signed brochure across the counter to Nancy. "Done."

"And a photo," Nancy said, upping her price.

"I don't have any PR photos with me," Emma told her, struggling to maintain her cool.

Nancy produced a cell phone and handed it to Phil. "He can take it." She came from behind the counter and stood with Emma. She was a tiny thing, like a garden gnome robed in polyester. Standing next to the tallish Emma, her head barely cleared Emma's shoulder. Phil took the photo. "Take another just in case," Nancy directed him. He took another. Nancy took the camera back from him and checked the photos. "Good." She looked up at them. "Now what was that question again?"

After taking a deep breath, Phil asked, "So why did the tour van stop by Restaurante Roble yesterday? You said something about a restaurant promotion."

"Yes," answered Nancy after putting away both the cash and the autograph as if the offer ran the risk of being revoked. "And it was rather a weird one, too. I mean, we sometimes get promos from restaurants or attractions for our customers, but this one was very different."

"How so?" asked Emma.

"Well," Nancy began, "the restaurant offered us cash up front to stop by, not the usual discount on food and drink for our customers."

Emma frowned. "You mean they gave you a kick-back?"

• "More like a kick-front," answered Nancy. "We got cash up front to stop at Roble."

"Do you know who offered you that? Was it the owner or the manager of the restaurant? Can you describe the person?" asked Phil. He smiled at Nancy, turning on his charm. She smiled back and nearly blushed.

"You'd have to ask my grandson Peter that. He owns this business and that parking lot outside. The property was left to him by his grandfather on his other side. My side doesn't own so much as a blade of grass in this city. Besides the tour business, he leases out monthly parking spaces to people who work in the area. Easy money."

"So he gives the tours?" Emma asked.

"Yes, and when we have more than a van full, one of his friends drives the other van. But it was Peter who took the group to that restaurant."

Phil glanced outside then turned back around. "There's one van parked outside. Where's the other today?"

Nancy looked up at a big round clock fastened to the wall. "I'd say just pulling into San Diego. The group from yesterday wanted to go down there for the day. They all fly home this weekend. It was some sort of group from a company in Kansas City."

Phil smiled again at Nancy. "So you have no idea who gave Peter the money?"

"None, just that Peter peeled off a couple of hundreds and gave them to me saying it was a bonus." She smiled again, showing off dentures behind apricot lipstick. "He's good to me. I do his books and man this booth a couple times a week and he pays me under the table." She leaned forward and whispered, "But I didn't tell the police that part."

"Did you tell them about the cash *kick-front*?" Emma asked with a slight wink.

"Nope, just told them that the stop was a last-minute change on the tour." She winked back at Emma. "I don't like nosy cops. I told them only what they asked about. Not a thing more."

"Do you know if they talked to Peter yet?" Phil asked.

Nancy shrugged. "Not sure, but I don't think so. I told them he was with a tour and they might have called his cell. I didn't give the number to them, but I'm sure they have their ways of finding it."

Emma and Phil thanked Nancy and started to leave when Emma turned back around. Phil had opened the door and now closed it to corral the struggling cool air. "Nancy," Emma began, "do you know if the person from the restaurant specified any particular day for the drop-in at Roble for the promotion?"

"You mean did it have to be yesterday?" Nancy asked.

"Yes," Emma said. "Or was it to be anytime you had a tour in the area?"

Nancy sat back down in her desk chair to think. Emma and Phil had to look over the counter to see her. On the other side of the counter was a computer with Facebook on the screen and a small TV. A talk show was on the TV with the sound off.

"You know," Nancy began, "I believe it could be anytime.

Peter just said we had to give them a heads-up ahead of time so they would be ready for us." Emma felt her eyebrows rise at the information. Next to her, Phil nudged her hip with his.

"So did you call the restaurant and let them know the van would be coming yesterday?" Emma asked.

Nancy shook her head back and forth, dislodging her wig a quarter of an inch to the left. "Peter said he called them, so I didn't have to do a thing."

"Thank you for your valuable time," Phil said to Nancy, "but one last question and we'll be on our way. Do you remember when Peter received the money for the promotional stop?"

"Not exactly," she answered, "but he gave me my bonus last week. Wednesday, I think. We didn't have this group booked until this Monday. Fortunately for them, we had a van available. Summertime is a lot busier."

Phil took one of the brochures and pushed it across the counter at Nancy. He pulled out two more twenties and laid them on top. "Peter's cell number would be very helpful," he told Nancy with a devilish wink.

Back in their SUV, Phil turned on the vehicle and said, "The snippiness of that woman reminded me a bit of Granny."

Emma chuckled. "Especially the comment about not being senile." She buckled up. "That last bit of information was worth the payoff, don't you think?"

"Yes, but I'm a bit hurt that she didn't ask for *my* autograph," Phil said with a fake pout. "After all, I am a world-famous tax attorney." He put the SUV in gear. "Where to now?"

"Roble Foods. I don't think it's far from here." Emma looked at the address she'd jotted down from the Roble Foods website before they left and plugged it into the vehicle's GPS. "It's over off of Main, not too far from Dodger Stadium."

"Which means not too far from the restaurant."

"Yes," Emma agreed. "No wonder Lucy and T.J. dropped in so easily."

Once they were on their way, Emma started talking out the pieces of the puzzle harvested from Nancy Bradford. "Rikki said they were blindsided by the tour van's arrival, so it's safe to say whoever set up the van's visit might have done it as a distraction but they had to wait until Quickie LA had a busload of tourists to bring by the restaurant."

Phil nodded in agreement as he maneuvered his way through the maze of downtown city streets. "And it could have been someone from inside the restaurant or someone from the outside, so no help with that." He glanced over at Emma. "Nancy said she received the extra money from her grandson last Wednesday, so it couldn't have come from the cash Steve handed Carlos just a few days ago."

"That still doesn't mean that Carlos didn't set it up," Emma said. Before leaving the house she'd grabbed Phil's notes and was updating them so she wouldn't forget what they'd learned. "Maybe he paid Peter and was reimbursed by Steve."

"Maybe," Phil said, "but a kid going off to college and waiting tables usually doesn't have a lot of loose cash to pay for things up front."

They rode along in silence. When they stopped at a red light, Phil said, "Maybe the tour was more than a distraction to keep people busy while the shooter went after his target."

Emma turned toward him. "How so?"

"Maybe the shooter slipped in with the tour group, did his business, then slipped out with them," he suggested.

"Vans like the ones Quickie LA uses hold around thirty people. That would mean about seven extra tables to wait on during a busy lunch rush. It could have been chaotic with people waiting to be seated and the kitchen and waitstaff on fast forward—an easy time for someone to slip in and out without being noticed."

"So someone paid Quickie LA to be their cover and waited for the right moment?"

"It's a possibility," Phil said.

Emma started texting. "I'm going to update Jeremiah now about this."

"Good thinking," Phil agreed. "Maybe it will encourage him to keep us updated. I'm still not sure he's telling us everything he knows."

· CHAPTER TWENTY-THREE ·

THE corporate offices and manufacturing plant of Roble Foods were not close to Dodger Stadium, but definitely in the vicinity. Located in another downtown industrial area, the office was off Main Street on a side street that dead ended at its gated entrance. The buildings sprawled across acres of real estate like a small brick and concrete city.

"Here's a good reason to buy Roble," Phil noted after giving their names to the guard at the gate and the purpose of their visit. "I'll bet the Ricardo family bought this property for a song decades ago compared to what it's worth today." After clearing them, the guard waved them through and directed them to a building and parking lot just off to the right of the guard shack. It was a two-story concrete building and the only building with a lot of windows.

A receptionist greeted them when they entered. She was in her forties with a trim figure dressed in nice dress slacks in gun metal gray and a crisp light blue blouse with short sleeves. She was stationed at a white counter in front of a curved staircase. The simple name plaque on her desk identified her as *Christina*. Adorning the walls in the reception area and along the wall going up the staircase were colorful posters of Roble's various commercial food products. The receptionist greeted them with warmth but no smile. Her attractive face was splotchy. "Ms. Whitecastle and Mr. Bowers?" When they nodded, she said, "Rikki is expecting you. Isabel will be down shortly to get you. Please have a seat." She indicated some cushioned chairs near the front entrance with a shaky hand.

They had barely taken their seats when Emma received a text from Jeremiah. All it said was: *VERY interesting!* She texted back: *At Roble Foods right now.* She showed the text to Phil.

"Ms. Whitecastle? Mr. Bowers?" asked a woman coming down the open staircase. She was long and lithe and dressed in a summer dress that showed plenty of leg. She looked a lot like Ana Gonzales with large luminous eyes and long thick black hair, just older and without the full face of youth.

"I'm Isabel," she said when she reached them. Isabel smiled, but her eyes did not. They were underscored by dark crescents of worry or lack of sleep or both. "Please follow me and I'll take you upstairs to the executive offices."

When they reach the top of the stairs, Isabel guided them down a short corridor past an open workspace. Several employees, both men and women, sat in cubes working, but there was no chitchat or laughter from anyone. A thick molasses of sorrow covered the atmosphere, leaving it with a sticky film you could almost touch, interrupted only by the sound of ringing phones and the tapping on computer keyboards. Occasionally a worker would raise their head to see who was with Isabel.

They passed several offices with doors hanging open displaying paper-laden desks but no occupants in sight. One door was closed. The name plate on the door read: *Tomas Mendoza*. The next office door was open. It was a spacious corner office and the name plate indicated it was the office of Lucinda Ricardo. It was into this office that Isabel directed them. "Rikki is in a meeting right now with the leadership team, but should be free soon. Please have a seat." With a graceful hand, she indicated a sitting area against a bank of windows. "Can I get you coffee or something else to drink?" When they both declined, Isabel said with another sad smile, "My desk is right outside. Please don't hesitate to ask if there's something I can do for you."

"Thank you, Isabel," Emma said. "I'm sorry about what happened yesterday with both T.J. and Lucy. I'm sure you're all in shock about it."

Her eyes turned down and she sucked her bottom lip into her mouth, her top lip leaving a smudge of lipstick behind. "Yes. We're all pulling for T.J."

Fighting back tears, Isabel left. Emma turned to Phil. "Not a single word about Lucy. Interesting."

"Knowing Lucy's volatile personality," Phil said, "are you really surprised?"

"I suppose not." Emma sat down and put her handbag down on the table in front of the sofa.

Phil remained standing and scanned the paintings on the wall. "Who knows, the employees might even have broken into a chorus of 'Ding Dong! The Witch Is Dead.'" He walked over to one painting and studied it up close. "I think Lucy painted these. At least this one."

"Really?" Emma got up and went to the painting. It was a primitive landscape. "That's quite good." Together they moved to inspect the rest of the paintings on the wall. "All of these are hers," said Emma, "except the one on the end. T.J. told me she was talented. What a shame that her story about wanting to go away and just paint was a ruse."

Emma moved on to inspect some photos on the credenza behind the desk. "There are several photos here of Lucy with different people, but none of Lucy with her father or sister." She turned to Phil. "Do you think she got rid of those when she found out that Felix wasn't her father?"

"Maybe," answered Phil, still inspecting the paintings.

"There you guys are," said Granny, slowly coming into view. "Where are we?"

"Hi, Granny," Emma said, sidling up near the ghost.

Phil turned and looked in the direction Emma was speaking. "Do you have anything for us, Granny?"

The ghost shook her head. "That Carlos is sticking like glue to the spot he's at. He even pulled out a schoolbook and started studying."

Emma shook her head in Phil's direction. "That hardly seems like something someone in hiding would do," Emma said. "I wonder what's going on."

"Granny," Phil said, "you still don't have an idea where Carlos is?"

"Nope. He's at the same fast-food joint that I can see."

"You couldn't read the food wrappers or cups or anything like that?" Emma asked. "Most places have their name plastered on everything."

"That's the thing," answered Granny. "It's not one of them big places that's on every corner. There are no arches or clowns or anything like that. It's very small."

Emma shook her head at Phil. "It doesn't sound like a

big chain. More likely it's a mom-and-pop place. Emma then said to Granny, "What about Felix?"

"He's disappeared," Granny said. "Can't find him anywhere."

"Emma. Phil. Thanks for coming here," said Rikki, coming through the door. Instead of the clothing she usually wore at the restaurant, Rikki was dressed in a skirt and blouse with stylish high heels on her feet. The outfit made her look more mature and businesslike, and Emma wondered if it was to help portray the image that she was now in charge in light of the two tragedies and in spite of the large and very ugly bruise on the left side of her face. Like Isabel's, Rikki's eyes were ringed with dark circles and her shoulders sagged as if carrying heavy weights. She didn't look like a person in charge. Rikki Ricardo looked like a woman who needed a couple of days in bed. She closed the door to the office and approached them.

"How are T.J. and Chef Lopez doing?" Emma asked.

"Pretty much the same as this morning," Rikki answered in a voice laced with exhaustion. "I'm going back to the hospital once I finish up here." She indicated the sofa. "Let's sit over here. I can't quite bring myself to sit behind Lucy's desk. It's like it has bad karma or something."

"The poor child looks about to drop," noted Granny.

Phil and Emma took seats on the sofa, and Rikki took a seat on the matching chair. The arrangement was much like in her office at the restaurant only larger and much more plush. Once they were seated, Phil asked, "How is everyone here handling what has happened?"

Rikki shrugged. "As well as can be expected. I had a meeting with our outside counsel first thing this morning about how to proceed, followed by a very long meeting with the executives. Together we redistributed the workload. I will be the interim CEO until this mess is sorted out, and T.J.'s vice president of finance will be the interim CFO until T.J.'s return." Rikki paused to swallow hard after mentioning T.J. "I've asked Hector Gonzales to step into my current spot as director of restaurant affairs and as manager of the restaurant."

"How is Hector doing?" Emma asked. "He and his daughter Ana seemed very fond of T.J."

"They are," Rikki answered, "as well as Isabel, Hector's other daughter. Their two families are very close. T.J., Isabel, and Ana even refer to themselves as cousins though they aren't related. Both girls had big crushes on T.J. when they were little. This has hit them very hard. Hector just left. He was going to go to the hospital to visit T.J. and Lupe over his lunch break but I told him to take the rest of the day off." She sighed deeply and her eyes squeezed together. "T.J. is very well respected and liked by everyone." She played with the engagement ring on her left hand, turning it as if screwing off her finger.

"I thought Isabel looked like Ana," said Emma. "So they are sisters?"

Rikki nodded. "Yes. They've been very loyal to my family. I hope when the dust settles that I'm able to reward Hector in a way my father neglected."

"You want to make him a shareholder?" Phil asked.

"Yes, I do, providing the company still isn't sold out from under me." She got up and went to the window. "That's one of our factories on the other side of this building. We have another out near San Bernardino. I'm going to do my best to hold on to everything, even if I'm the last one standing."

"But didn't Lucy's arrest stop the sale?" asked Phil.

"You'd think so, wouldn't you?" Rikki whipped around. "But Steve Bullock of Fiesta Time was on the phone to me bright and early like a vulture scouting a carcass. Spouting well wishes for T.J. with one side of his mouth and upping the offer out the other side." She crossed her arms and hugged herself as if chilled.

"Some people have no decency," snapped Granny, going to stand beside Rikki.

"I told him that it would be impossible to move forward since there can be no vote at this time. At least Lucy's arrest and my mother's disappearance resulted in some good."

Emma got up and went to the window to stand beside Rikki, she and Granny flanking the young woman like bodyguards. "Have the police told you where your mother is?"

Rikki nodded. "Yes, she fled to Mexico."

"And you've heard nothing from her at all?" Emma asked.

"Not a word, the little coward." Rikki spit the words out. "I'm beginning to think she had something to do with this. I know the police are thinking that." Rikki sagged against the window ledge. "But why? What did she have against T.J. or me? I know I was Dad's favorite and Lucy was hers, but it still doesn't make sense. Especially since she was so happy for me yesterday morning about my engagement."

Emma placed an encouraging hand on Rikki's shoulder. "I'm sure she'll turn up and explain herself." But even as the words came out of her mouth, Emma only half believed them. "Have you talked at all with Lucy since the shooting?"

"No." Another word spit on the ground like bad food. "I don't want to talk to her, at least not right now. I have other people, people who love me and who are struggling to comprehend what has happened, that I need to worry about."

Emma walked back over to the sofa and sat. "Rikki, there's something we learned today that we want to talk to you about."

Rikki returned to her chair and sat, waiting with expectation. "Is it about my father? Have you been in contact with him again?"

"No," Emma said, "but I believe he might have been there when T.J. was shot. I'm trying to reach him to see if I can learn anything from him."

"We were looking into that tour bus that came in yesterday," Phil said.

Rikki's eyes widened with surprise. "The tour bus? But why?"

"You said it showed up unexpectedly, right?" asked Emma.

Rikki nodded. "Out of the blue."

Emma looked at Phil, encouraging him to continue. "Rikki," he began, "did you offer Quickie LA a special promotional offer to drop by yesterday with a busload of people?"

"No," Rikki responded immediately. "We never do promos in the summer. We don't have to. We're always busy. We only do them during the off-season."

"Quickie LA claims they were given a special promotion to send that tour van and its occupants to your restaurant yesterday," Phil explained.

"We believe the tour bus customers were used as a diversion during the shooting," Emma added. "By filling up the restaurant, everyone was too busy to notice anyone who should not have been there."

"Are you kidding me?" Rikki's mouth fell open, causing

her to flinch in pain and lift her hand to her left cheek. "So it was someone from the restaurant?"

"Not necessarily," Phil answered on the heels of her question. "T.J.'s attacker could have been someone who slipped in with the tour and left just as easily in all the hubbub."

"Do the police know this?" Rikki asked, still incredulous.

Emma nodded. "We're pretty sure they do. They were at the tour company asking questions before us this morning."

"There's more," Phil told her.

Rikki turned to him, the undamaged side of her face pale but steady and serious, ready to take the next onslaught of information like a slap meant to even out her face.

"We saw Steve Bullock hand off an envelope of cash to Carlos Fuentes on Wednesday," he told her. "Do you know of any reason why he might do that?"

Rikki stood up, her face changing from pale to dark with anger, the bruise coming alive. Emma wondered if she was going to throw them out again. "Carlos? You think Carlos Fuentes might have something to do with all this?" Arms curled around herself again, she paced. "Is that why he called in sick yesterday, because he knew something was going down?"

"We don't know that for sure," Phil answered. "But he is someone the police are interested in."

Rikki turned and looked at Phil. "So the police know about the payoff or whatever it was?"

"Yes, they do, and we weren't the only ones who witnessed it," he told her, not offering any more information on the matter.

Rikki stamped her foot. "And after everything we've done for him!" She pointed a finger at Phil. "Did you know that T.J. helped him wrangle a scholarship? And Roble Foods gave him one, too." Rikki was incensed and building steam in spite of her exhaustion.

"Do something," Granny said to Emma. "The child is going to give herself a stroke."

"Calm down, Rikki," Emma said to her. "We don't know for sure that Carlos was behind this, or what that money was for. It's just a possibility."

"Do you think Carlos was the one who set up the tour bus?" Rikki asked, after taking several deep breaths.

"One thing we do know," Emma said, "is that the promotion . . ." Emma paused, being careful not to label it a payoff. "The promotion," she continued, "was given to Quickie LA before the cash handoff to Carlos, so they might not have had anything to do with each other."

"And," added Phil, "we know that Carlos wasn't the one who shot T.J. If it had been him, people would have seen him at the restaurant. He's a tall, good-looking kid, not easy to miss."

Rikki shook her head. "Maybe Lucy was right about him being a *cholo.*"

"No," said Granny, even though only Emma could hear her. "I don't believe that for a minute." The ghost looked at Emma. "If Carlos is involved, I don't think it was to hurt T.J. Just something about the kid and how he handles himself is telling me that."

Emma carefully nodded at the ghost, letting her know her opinion was heard and being considered. "Don't be so hasty, Rikki. Until the police talk to Carlos, we won't know what the deal was between him and Steve Bullock."

There was a knock on the door. Isabel poked her head in. "Your attorney is on the phone," she told Rikki.

Phil got to his feet. "We should leave you be to take that," he said to Rikki.

"No, please stay," Rikki said, holding up a hand to stop him. "At least a little bit longer." She turned to Isabel. "I'll take it in T.J.'s office." Isabel left. Rikki turned to them. "There's a minifridge behind one of the doors in the credenza. Please help yourself to something cool to drink. If you'd like coffee, just ask Isabel."

When she left, Phil went over to the credenza and touched a couple of the lower doors until one popped open to reveal a minifridge stocked with sodas, teas, and water. "There's even beer in here," he said to Emma. "Do you want a bottle of iced tea?" He held one up in question.

"Sure," Emma said, leaning back on the sofa.

Phil brought over two and handed one to her. They opened them and took a couple of sips in silence.

"Hold down the fort," Emma said, "I'm going to find the ladies' room." She put her tea down on one of the coasters set on the table and picked up her bag. "And I want to speak with Isabel."

"I could use the facilities myself," Phil said.

CHAPTER TWENTY-FOUR

OUTSIDE Lucy's office there was no sign of Isabel. Emma stopped another woman and asked for directions to the restrooms. Granny followed her as she often did. "Something's not right here about Carlos," Granny said.

Emma stopped to listen a few seconds to make sure no one else was in the restroom with them. It was a large bathroom with several stalls. "I heard you in the office back there," she told Granny in a hushed whisper just in case.

"So what are you going to do about it?" Granny persisted.

Emma started to roll her eyes, then stopped mid-circle. She hated when Kelly and Granny did that to her and tried not to do it herself, even when Granny earned the gesture. "Right now I'm trying to pee and this is a very small stall."

"I'm a ghost. I don't take up much room."

"I'd still like some privacy," Emma said, giving her an eye roll anyway.

Granny disappeared. "I'm out here when you're ready to talk about it," she called to Emma.

Emma was almost done when she heard the bathroom door open and a couple of women walk in. Emma was about to open the door to her stall when one of them said, "Can you believe Isabel? The way she's carrying on, you'd think T.J. was her fiancé instead of Rikki's."

"I know," said the other, who had a more mature voice. "She's almost as bad as Queen Lucy when it comes to being bat-crap crazy."

"And did you hear," said the younger voice, "that Lucy was actually aiming at Rikki when she fired the gun?"

"I'm not surprised," responded the second one, her voice more somber and halting like she wasn't sure she wanted to continue the conversation. "She probably flipped out when she found out about the engagement, just like Isabel."

Emma couldn't wait any longer. She had to let her presence be known or it would look like she was spying, which she was. She flushed, opened the door, and proceeded to the sink to wash her hands. There were two women—one was about her daughter's age; the other was Christina, the haggard receptionist. Both gave her a plastic smile and clammed up. Emma took her time reapplying lipstick, but the two weren't talking in front of her. Christina went into a stall and the other fussed with her hair.

"Don't worry," said Granny to Emma, "when you leave, I'll stick around."

When Emma returned to Lucy's office, Isabel was back at her desk. She didn't look at Emma but turned away, whispering something into her phone. Emma paused at her desk until it became clear Isabel had no intention of acknowledging her.

"More drama," Emma said to Phil after she entered the office and closed the door.

"Another shooting?" Phil asked without looking up. He'd returned before her and was reading e-mails on his smart phone.

"Thankfully not," Emma said, taking her seat again. "A couple of employees were gabbing in the ladies' room, gossiping about Isabel and Lucy."

Phil raised his eyebrows. "About them together or individually?"

"If these two are to be believed, it seems both Lucy and Isabel were carrying a torch for T.J. Mendoza, a big Olympic-size torch." Emma took a sip of her tea. "Granny's still there trying to get more information."

"Jeremiah's right," Phil said with a grin, "we do use Granny as our own personal bugging device. It's scary to think if that kind of power got into the wrong hands."

"Shh," Emma said. "Don't give Granny any ideas or she'll be off looking for work with the FBI or CIA." She picked up her tea and took a drink. "I tried to speak to Isabel but she was absorbed in a private phone call."

Phil chuckled, leaned against the back of the sofa, and looked up at the ceiling. "I'm really liking the theory that Rikki was the intended target and not T.J. Maybe Lucy set up the diversion and sent someone to kill her sister. Then when Lucy showed up at Roble after the shooting and saw Rikki still alive and T.J. the victim, she lost it?"

"I'm liking that theory more and more myself," Emma told him. "Lucy could certainly have set up the fake promotion and she'd have an alibi by having lunch with Steve Bullock. She and Bullock could have been in this together. That money could have been paid to Carlos to find a hit man.

If he has any ties to gangs, as Lucy thinks, he'd be able to find someone." Emma stopped to consider something. "Although Granny's gut is telling her that Carlos isn't part of this."

"Granny's gut, huh?" Phil snorted. "And when was the last time her gut digested anything?"

"I heard that!" Granny materialized and glared at Phil.

"Granny heard that and is pretty angry with you right now," Emma told him.

"Sorry, Granny," Phil apologized, aiming his words to where Emma pointed. "Just cracking a joke."

"He's getting as disrespectful as you," Granny said to Emma. "When he starts giving me the stink eye, too, I'm outta here."

"No one is giving anyone the stink eye, Granny," Emma told the touchy ghost. "So did you hear anything else in the ladies' room?"

"Those two were pretty chatty after you left," Granny said with satisfaction. "At least the young one was. The older one grunted and nodded mostly. The younger one, the one with the long hair, was complaining about how Isabel disappears sometimes for long lunches and fake doctor's appointments. She even suggested that Isabel and T.J. were seeing each other on the sly, but the one with the short hair, the older one, shut her down on that, saying there was no way T.J. would do that to Rikki." Emma gave Granny's report to Phil.

"And the plot thickens," said Phil with amusement. "Sex, money, and power, the three reasons people kill and this has them all."

"Anything else, Granny," Emma asked, "or was that it?"

Granny screwed up her face in concentration. "Oh yeah, the girl who thought Isabel was tramping around with T.J., the younger one, said something about Isabel wanting to trade up from some loser named Peter."

Emma straightened. "Are you sure that's what she said?"

She paused and reconsidered her words. "Yep, I'm pretty sure that's what she said."

Emma repeated Granny's report for Phil. "Peter?" he asked when she'd finished. "Isn't that the name of the guy who owns the tour company?"

"Yes," she confirmed. She pulled the brochure out of her purse and studied the number Nancy had scrawled across it. Pulling her phone out of her purse, she called the number but it went straight to voice mail. The message informed her that she had reached Peter Bradford of Quickie LA tours. She ended the call without leaving a message. "I'd like to talk to this guy."

"Just say when," Phil said with enthusiasm. "But I'll need to stop at an ATM first, just in case he needs to be encouraged like his grandmother."

Emma stared at her phone. "I missed a text from Jeremiah. He says Elena Ricardo is in Mexico with Ramon Santiago." She stared a long time at the text, hardly believing it.

"Isn't that the guy who owns Fiesta Time?" asked Phil.

"He took the question right out of my mouth," added Granny.

"It sure is," Emma answered, reading another text from Jeremiah. She looked from Phil to Granny. "Are you two thinking what I'm thinking?"

Phil shrugged, too stunned to speak.

"I'll bet he's Lucy's daddy," Granny said. "That would explain a lot."

"Yes, Granny," Emma agreed. "Ramon being Lucy's

father would explain a lot. Rikki told me that there was bad blood between Fiesta Time and her father but never said why. Maybe this was it and maybe Rikki thought it was just business competition."

"If Lucy found out after all those years that her father was Ramon Santiago and not Felix," said Phil, finding his voice, "she might have been angry enough to push the sale and take down Roble Foods, especially if she had a vindictive personally already."

"Didn't Lucy say she found out Felix wasn't her father about the time Felix died?" asked Granny. "Maybe she's the one who killed Felix."

"No," came a voice out of the blue. The ghost of Felix materialized but didn't fully form.

Emma squinted at a cloud forming near the window. It didn't look like much more than a convention of dust mites. "Felix, is that you?" she asked the shimmery cluster.

"It's him," confirmed Granny.

"Please, Felix," coaxed Emma. "We need you to answer some questions. The future of your daughters depends on it."

"My daughters," said the ghost with heavy sadness as his image began to take sharper form. "I loved Lucinda like my own," he explained. "She wanted for nothing, but it was never enough."

"She said she didn't know about her father until last year, shortly before you died," Emma said.

Felix nodded. "That's true. Elena and I were having troubles shortly after we married. She was complaining about the hours I kept at the restaurant. She couldn't understand that my father and I were building a business to last for many generations. She found comfort in the arms of another man."

"Ramon Santiago?" Granny asked.

Felix nodded. "At first I thought it was Hector. He wasn't married yet, and he and Elena got along quite well. I confronted him when I found out that Elena was pregnant. I was so hurt because Hector was like a brother to me. We actually came to blows. But he said it wasn't him and my father confirmed that, saying he'd seen Elena out with Ramon Santiago, a man of questionable ethics, both personally and in business. When I questioned Elena, she didn't deny it and said she was going leave me for Ramon, who had told her he was going to leave his wife for her and the baby. Before that happened, Ramon dumped her and Elena came to me begging for mercy. My father and Hector both told me to throw her out into the street, but I couldn't. I loved Elena. She was so beautiful and lively, I fell in love the first time I laid eyes on her. I was surprised when she seemed to love me back, but she didn't really. She was drawn to our family's wealth and position."

It was the most Emma had ever heard the ghost of Felix Ricardo speak. In spite of his sadness, his words were clear and spoken with a determination to do the right thing.

"So you took her back," Emma said, "stayed together, and raised Lucy as your own."

He nodded. "I love Lucinda very much, but I did a very bad thing all those years ago and now my bad deeds are coming back to ruin my family."

"What did you do?" asked Granny with great interest.

Felix drifted back and forth then said, "Ramon wanted children badly and he had every intention of starting over with Elena and their child, but I paid him off." As he spoke, Felix came more into focus. "When Ramon and Elena were seeing each other, his company was small and not well established. They had one really good restaurant and were trying to break into the commercial food business, as we had done, but didn't have the capital. I made a deal with Ramon that if he ended it with Elena and relinquished all rights to the child, I would give him the money to expand his business. I took a gamble that Ramon Santiago wanted power more than he wanted a family, and I won. After that he became one of our biggest rivals in the food business, especially here in California, but I didn't mind. I had Elena and my girls."

"So it didn't surprise you that Lucy threw in with Steve Bullock after she found out about her paternity?" Phil asked.

"No, it didn't. Not one bit," Felix said with a sad shake of his head. "I'm sure as soon as the cat was out of the bag, they courted her support and won her over easily. Lucinda is not a forgiving woman. She has the same cutthroat drive as her real father."

Emma got up and went to Felix, looking him straight in the eye. "Did Lucy find out about Ramon and kill you?"

The ghost shook his head, this time with energy. "No one killed me, not directly. I did have a heart attack and crack my head on my desk, just as everyone believes. That day, the day I died, Elena called and said she had to speak with me immediately. I took the call in my office. She told me that she was going away with Ramon and I would not be able to stop her this time. She said Ramon had cancer and was going to go to Mexico to live out the rest of his days and he wanted her with him." He looked away. "She told me that she was going to tell Lucinda the truth. I begged her not to tell Lucinda. I told her to go, that I wouldn't stop her, but not to tell Lucinda the truth. We got into a huge fight."

"Is that when you had the heart attack and fell?" asked Granny.

"No. After I hung up with Elena, I called Ramon and told him if he or Elena told Lucinda the truth that I would bury him. You see, I didn't exactly give him the money. It was set up as a loan that I could call in on demand at any time with interest, and the payback also included stock in his company. He was to keep his distance from Elena and Lucinda or I'd demand payment. With years of interest, that loan and those stock options would be worth a bundle today."

"But I thought Fiesta Time approached you to sell Roble Foods to them?" asked Phil, leaning in the same direction Emma was looking.

"No," said Felix. "Only Crown had approached us at that time. Fiesta Time didn't make an official bid for Roble until after I was dead and Lucinda knew the truth."

"So it was the call with Ramon that triggered the heart attack?" Emma asked, looking for clarification.

Felix nodded. "Ramon told me he didn't care about our agreement. He said he was taking my wife and his daughter, and if I exposed that agreement, he would take my daughter from me as I had taken his from him. I knew that he meant he would harm or even kill Ricarda. It was then I felt this horrible pain in my chest. I called out for help, but fell when I tried to move. I'd not been feeling well the few days before and I guess the stress was too much." He dusted his hands together to put a finish on his words and his life.

Emma went back to the sofa and quickly filled in Phil. "Where is that loan document, Felix?" Phil asked. "You must have put that in writing to have been so confident in it all those years."

"It's back at the restaurant," the ghost answered. "Hidden in my office." Emma passed along the information.

"Wow," said Granny. "Talk about your family intrigue. This is better than watching the daytime soaps."

"I'm so sorry about all this, Felix," Emma said. "It must have been difficult watching the fighting between Lucy and Rikki without being able to do something about it."

"I had no hope," the ghost said, "until you came into the restaurant. Then Ricarda wouldn't listen to you and I became frustrated all over again."

"Did you see who shot T.J.?" Granny asked.

Felix shook his head. "No. I came in just after Ricarda found him. She was screaming, and the screams pulled me to her."

Once Phil was back up to speed, he asked, "And where in your office is that loan document?"

"In the closet," the ghost answered. "There is a safe there, but it's not in the safe. It's behind a fake wall panel opposite the safe." Emma relayed Felix's response.

"And who knew about the loan and its real purpose?" Phil asked.

"Me, Ramon, and my attorney, but my attorney passed away shortly before I did," Felix answered.

"Not even Hector knew?" Emma asked.

The ghost shook his head. "Not even my own father knew. Elena might have known, but only if Ramon told her. I used money from a personal account."

"Why in the office and not in a safe-deposit box?" asked Phil.

The ghost shrugged. "I couldn't leave it at home in case Elena stumbled across it, and I was worried that if I died, someone in my family would find it when they went through my things, including a safe-deposit box. If I died, the agreement would die with me. That's not in the agreement, but it's what I wanted."

Something was tugging as Emma's brain. "If you died a year ago, why did Elena wait all this time to go off with Ramon Santiago? Why not go away with him after she was widowed?"

"As far as I could tell, that was Lucinda's idea. Once, when I was visiting our home, I overhead Lucinda tell her mother it would be best to wait until the sale went through to go off with Ramon. Even Ramon convinced Elena it would be best to wait until all was settled." The ghost shook her head. "Poor Elena was trapped between her love for the two girls, but Lucinda always had a stronger influence over her. It did not surprise me to learn she'd disappeared after the shooting. I think she would have gone even if Ramon did not, just to avoid the mess and scandal."

Felix was starting to fade and his voice was trailing. "Now if you will pardon me, I'd like to leave. This is just too much and I feel so tired." As the ghost departed, he made one more request. "Please help Ricarda. She's all I have left."

After Felix disappeared, Emma told Phil his response. Phil walked to the window and looked out. Through his shirt Emma could see his muscles bunched and knew he was in deep thought. She came up to him and put a hand on his shoulder. His muscles relaxed. "What are you thinking, Phil?"

"That document," Phil said. "I'm not sure about its enforceability after all these years, especially considering Lucy is no longer a minor, but it could still cause a lot of trouble if someone tried to enforce it on Fiesta Time."

"And it could probably stop a disputed sale in its tracks," added Emma, "or at least slow it down."

Phil nodded. "It's a darn good motive for shooting

someone. Maybe it wasn't jealousy or the sale itself that caused T.J. to get shot."

"And maybe," said Emma as she formed another thought, "Steve Bullock was paying Carlos to find and steal that document."

"They could even be two separate things," noted Granny, joining them at the window.

"Granny's right," Emma said. "Carlos could have been paid to steal the loan document. I'll bet Ramon told his nephew about that document and the threat it contained. He might have done it when he told Steve about Lucy's parentage."

"That's why they were so chummy," Phil said as he ran a hand over his bald head. "They weren't lovers; they were cousins plotting the takedown of Roble."

"I told you those two weren't all kissy face with each other," said Granny with satisfaction.

Emma's phone vibrated. She picked it up. "It's Jeremiah. He said he just learned that Elena Ricardo is in Mexico with Ramon Santiago."

"He's a little late to the party," Granny quipped.

"He also says that Steve Bullock is staying put today. He didn't even lunch at Santiago's."

"What do you want to bet," said Granny with narrowed eyes, "that the waitress, that Brenda Ann, is Jeremiah's operative?"

After Emma repeated Granny's comment, Phil added, "I wouldn't be surprised if she's one of them, Granny. A good PI would need eyes and ears everywhere. I don't think she'd be the one watching Bullock today, but no doubt she alerted Jeremiah that Bullock didn't show up at the restaurant."

"He wants to meet us for an update," Emma told them.

She texted Jeremiah back letting him know they had found a connection between Roble Foods and the tour company and another motive for the shooting. Another text came in. It made Emma smile. "He says we've been more productive than he has." She texted back. "I'm telling him that Hector's daughter Isabel might be involved and could be the link to the tour bus." Almost immediately a text came back and she responded. "Jeremiah said he's going to track down Hector. I'll let him know to try the hospital first."

"We really need to find Carlos and talk to him," Phil said.

"That's my cue." With a salute to both Phil and Emma, Granny left.

"You're coming up in the world," Emma said to Phil. "Granny just saluted you, too."

CHAPTER TWENTY-FIVE

THE door to the office opened and Rikki came in. "I'm so sorry I took so long," she apologized. "Seems my mother's disappearance was also good for something else."

Emma glanced at Phil, wondering if Rikki knew about and would mention Ramon Santiago.

Without waiting for them to say anything, Rikki said, "My attorney filed a restraining order against Lucy this morning preventing her from coming anywhere near me, this office, or the restaurant, but that might not have been necessary. She was denied bail. My attorney said the prosecution claimed Lucy was a flight risk, especially in light of our mother disappearing into Mexico about the time T.J. was shot. The judge agreed, so she's staying in jail." Rikki got herself a bottle of water from the minifridge and sat down across from them again. "That's a relief. At least I don't have to worry about her waiting somewhere to gun me down."

Phil and Emma waited, but no mention of Ramon

Santiago came. Emma looked at Phil, questioning if she should say something. He gave her a slight nod.

"Rikki," Emma began, leaning slightly toward her, "we received some rather startling information just now that involves your mother."

Rikki put down her water and waited, not taking her eyes off Emma while bracing herself for the next unexpected blow.

"It seems," Emma continued, "that she's in Mexico with Ramon Santiago."

Slowly Rikki moved her head back and forth. "That can't be. Ramon owns Fiesta Time. They barely know each other."

"Felix was just here," Phil told her. "What he told us shed a lot of light on the situation."

"My father was just here?" Rikki asked, looking around.

"Yes," answered Emma, "but he's gone, at least for the time being. While talking to us, he disclosed, among other things, that Ramon Santiago is Lucy's father."

"Ramon?"

Emma nodded. "Yes. He and your mother had an affair early on in your parents' marriage, and Lucy was conceived during that time."

Rikki sat still as a post for a long time, then finally said in a low, tired voice, "Now it makes sense why she's hell-bent on selling Roble to Fiesta Time."

"You know Jeremiah Jones, the man who was with the police yesterday?" asked Phil. Rikki nodded. "Well," Phil continued, "he was hired by T.J. to look into Fiesta Time, specifically Steve Bullock, to make sure if there was a sale, it was on the up-and-up. Jeremiah learned that Lucy had no intention of taking the money and going off to paint. Ramon is ill and retiring and Steve will be taking over the company. Lucy was going to run it with him."

"And that's why T.J. was shot?" Rikki asked.

"We don't know exactly," admitted Emma. "There seem to be several motives. One is jealousy of you, but another is that someone may have been trying to find a secret document laying out an agreement between Felix and Ramon that could seriously hurt Fiesta Time and nix the sale."

Rikki sat straight in her chair and absorbed everything she was being told. She didn't look at them, but at a point on the wall behind them. Finally, she said, "And what does this have to do with Carlos and that tour bus company?"

"We're not sure yet. It could be two unrelated things," Phil explained. "Carlos could have been paid to search for that document when no one was around. No one would think twice if he was upstairs at the restaurant. That's where the staff stashed their belongings and sometimes changed."

"What's the jealousy angle?" Rikki asked.

"Did Isabel have a thing for T.J. that you knew of?" Emma asked.

"As I told you before, she did when they were kids, but not now, I'm sure. I remember T.J. telling me that she recently hooked up with a new boyfriend."

"Did he mention that boyfriend's name?" Emma prodded.

Rikki thought about it, then said, "I want to say Paul or Peter or something like that. I remember T.J. also saying he wasn't Latino, and when Hector found out, he wouldn't be happy."

"How about Peter Bradshaw?" Phil asked. "Does that ring a bell?"

"Maybe," Rikki answered, "but T.J. only mentioned it once that I can recall. Why?"

"Peter Bradshaw is the owner-operator of Quickie LA," Emma told her. "There might be a connection."

Rikki looked stunned, then she jumped to her feet and yanked open the door, going out to the office cube area. A minute later she returned and shut the door again. "Apparently, Isabel has left for the day. Something about cramps." Rikki's mouth became a tight straight line. "So you think either Isabel or this Peter guy shot T.J.?"

"We're still not sure," Phil said. "There are so many possibilities at this point. Why don't you have a seat and let us tell you more about that document."

Instead of sitting down, Rikki went to the credenza. She popped open one of the cabinets, a different one from the one hiding the minifridge, and plucked something from it. She came back to the sofa and plopped a bottle of tequila down on the table along with three glasses. "You folks joining me?"

Emma and Phil shook their heads. As soon as Rikki was settled, they told her everything they knew so far.

When they were done, Rikki sat in her chair and stared again at a spot behind Emma and Phil. She took one more sip of her tequila, then put the glass down on the coffee table with resolve. "I need to get to the restaurant and hunt for that loan document."

"I'm sure the police still have it blocked off," noted Phil.

Emma was also lost in thought but came out of it to agree. "Phil's right," she said after putting the pieces together in her head. "I propose you sit tight and let us work with Jeremiah on getting to the bottom of this. Jeremiah also has a link to the detective working the case."

"And what about Isabel?" Rikki asked, standing up and walking back and forth in front of Lucy's desk. "She's running around out there, doing who knows what." She stopped in her tracks. "This might even mean that Hector is involved." She perched on the arm of her chair and covered her face with her hands. "Argh! I can't trust anyone anymore!"

"You can trust us, Rikki," Emma told her. "We don't have a stake in this. And you can trust Jeremiah. T.J. trusted him enough to hire him, didn't he?"

"T.J.," Rikki said in a soft voice. She lowered her hands. She looked stricken. "I can't lose him, Emma. I can't."

"For now why don't you go about the business of holding this company together," Phil suggested, "and taking care of T.J. You can't do anything about the restaurant until the police release it. We'll let you know if anything more develops. If Isabel returns, just act normal, and if you can't, then just avoid her." He got to his feet. "We really don't know how much she's involved, if at all. These are all theories that still need solid proof to be real. And if she is involved, you wouldn't want to spook her."

"That's good advice," Emma said, standing and picking up her purse. "We're off to meet Jeremiah now. You have my cell number in case you need to reach me. Text or call anytime."

Rikki got up and hugged them both. "Thank you for being here for me." There were tears in her eyes. "My family may be in pieces, but I have good friends like you and T.J.'s family to support me." She let loose with a sad little laugh. "Although by the time this is over, the Mendozas may change their minds about wanting me in the family."

On the way out to the SUV, Emma's cell phone rang. She looked at the display with surprise. "It's Grant," she said to Phil. "I hope nothing's wrong with Kelly."

"Wouldn't she call you first?" Phil asked as he opened the passenger's side door for Emma.

"Usually, yes," she told him. "But the only thing he and I ever talk about is her. Otherwise we have no contact." She stopped mid-breath. "Unless something has happened to Celeste, his mother." Right before the call went to voice mail, she answered it. "Grant, is everything okay?" She listened as she climbed into the SUV. "Thank you," she said with surprise. "It's very gracious of you to call." Phil gave her raised eyebrows as he closed her door and went to the driver's side. "No, we haven't discussed when yet," she said into the phone. "It just happened yesterday." She looked out the windshield as she listened and Phil started the vehicle and got the AC moving. "Okay," she said to Grant, "I will and thanks again for calling."

When the call ended, she turned to Phil. "He called to congratulate us on our engagement. Kelly called him this morning and mentioned it."

Phil smiled. "Mentioned it or to rub it in?"

"Could be," Emma said, laughing. "I wouldn't put it past Kelly. As much as she loves you, she's still harboring a lot of resentment toward her father for dumping me for Carolyn. And I've heard that his marriage is kind of rocky, so it could be Kelly was giving her father a big ole raspberry, stuck out tongue and all."

"It was still nice of him to call with best wishes."

"Yes," Emma said with a frown. "And so unlike him. I'm wondering if Kelly shamed him into it."

Phil leaned over. Placing one hand behind her neck, he pulled Emma close for a kiss. "His loss. My gain." He kissed her quick again. "Now where to? I hope it's somewhere we can grab some lunch. It's well after one."

"There are some protein bars in the glove compartment," Emma told him as she plugged the address Jeremiah had given her in a text into the GPS.

"Thanks," Phil said, making a face, "but I'm going to

hold out for a better offer. It's not like I'll starve to death in the meantime."

Emma's phone rang. She looked at it, half expecting it to be Grant calling back with his real reason for the contact. But it was Jeremiah. She put him on speaker. "Hey, Jeremiah," she said. "We were just on our way to meet you."

"Something's come up," Jeremiah told her. "We need to postpone our meeting for a bit. Maybe an hour or two. I'll have to call and let you know." Emma glanced at Phil, who was mouthing the word *lunch*.

"What's going on?" Emma asked. "Did you find out anything useful? We already knew about Elena being in Mexico with Ramon Santiago. Ramon is Lucy's real father."

"Yeah, heard all that from the police," Jeremiah said. They could hear traffic noise in the background. "How did you find out?"

"Felix paid us a visit and finally decided to talk," Emma explained. "Unfortunately, he didn't see who shot T.J." She looked over at Phil and saw him watching her closely.

"That's too bad," Jeremiah agreed. "It could have been a big help." He paused. "Why don't you folks go home and relax and wait for my call."

When the call ended, Phil didn't pull the SUV out of the parking spot. Instead he looked at Emma and asked, "Why didn't you tell him about the hidden document?"

Emma sat still, looking straight ahead. "I think Jeremiah is withholding information from us. So I did a bit of the same, at least for the time being."

"Do you think he's involved in this, too?" Phil turned in his seat to look Emma square in the face.

"I don't think so, Phil, but I don't think he's sharing everything he knows. Maybe it's to protect us. Maybe to protect his informants. Maybe he really is working for the cops. But I have a feeling that we've just been patted on the head and sent home. We're going to explore this on our own."

Phil sighed. "Something tells me I might just be eating a protein bar for lunch."

Shaking her head with amusement, Emma dug out the tour bus brochure again and called the number on it—not the cell number Nancy sold them, but the office line. She put the phone on speaker. "Nancy," she said when a woman answered. "It's Emma Whitecastle. I was in your office a short while ago."

"Yeah. Yeah. The ghost lady," Nancy said. "You forget something?"

"Yes, I did," Emma told her. "I wanted to ask you, does your grandson have a girlfriend?"

"What does that have to do with the price of tea in China?"

Emma smiled. The woman was a bit batty but far from dull. "It's just that you seem so nice and your grandson seems like quite a go-getter and entrepreneur, something I appreciate. I have a daughter that is probably around his age and was wondering if maybe we should at least try to get them together."

"Don't tell me," Nancy said. "Your girl didn't inherit your good looks. That's why she needs help, right?"

"She has a great personality," Emma added.

"Sorry, but Peter has a girlfriend. Some Latina named Isabel. She came here once, just last week, and treated me like crap while she waited for my grandson. She's beautiful but a real piece of work. I tried to tell Peter she'd just make him miserable in the end, but would he listen?"

"Oh well," Emma said, infusing her voice with defeat. "Can't say I didn't try."

"Don't worry, honey," Nancy said, trying to be encouraging. "I'm sure your girl will find someone just as nice as my Peter, especially with such a concerned mother supporting her."

When Emma ended the call, Phil said to her with a dead-pan face, "You're going straight to hell for that stunt."

"Does that mean I'll be going alone?"

He laughed and kissed her. "Not on your life."

"Here I am working my backside off and you two are spooning." Granny popped up in the back. Instead of answering, Emma kissed Phil back. "If neither of you are interested in my big breakthrough," groused the ghost, "then I guess I'll have to find Jeremiah."

Emma laughed and turned to Granny. "I just learned that the Peter you heard was Isabel's boyfriend is the same Peter who owns the tour bus company."

"I can top that," replied Granny with a gleam in her eye. "I know where Carlos is hanging out."

Emma turned back to Phil. "She says she knows where Carlos is."

Phil looked in the back. "Great job, Granny. So where is he?"

"Wherever that Fiesta company is," the ghost answered proudly.

"You mean the offices of Fiesta Time?" asked Emma with surprise. "That's where Carlos is right now?"

"Are you sure, Granny?" asked Phil.

"The boy isn't quite inside the company," the ghost explained. "He's still sitting at the fast-food place, but I got curious about why he's doing that. It's looking a lot like a stake-out to me, especially since he keeps looking over at something."

Emma passed along the information to Phil, then asked Granny, "Could you tell what he was watching?"

"That's the thing," Granny answered. "It looked like just a parking lot to me. There's a chain link fence between it and the food place and Carlos is right next to the fence keeping an eye on something. One of the cars, I think. So I wandered over there to see what I could see." She paused.

"And?" prodded Emma.

"I still didn't get it," said Granny, scratching her head, "then I saw the sign on the building. It said, *Fiesta Time*."

Once Phil was brought up to speed, he asked, "Did anyone come out and meet with Carlos?"

"Not while I was there," answered Granny. "Of course, I wasn't there the entire time. Sometimes I was with you or looking for Felix, but you'd think if Carlos had already had his meeting, he still wouldn't be there, wouldn't you?"

"Good point, Granny," Emma said before relaying the comment on to Phil.

Phil studied Emma, then said. "I guess our next stop is Montebello."

"Is that where Fiesta Time is?" Emma asked.

Phil started backing the SUV out of the space. "As I recall. Why don't you look up the exact address on your phone?"

"Should I go tell Jeremiah?" asked Granny.

Emma went to work searching on her smart phone for the address of Fiesta Time. She glanced back at Granny. "No, Granny, don't tell Jeremiah just yet. He's busy on a hot lead. We can handle this. Besides, I have a feeling Jeremiah already knows where he can find Carlos."

"You do?" asked Granny.

"You know how Jeremiah said he has an associate watching Steve Bullock today? I think Carlos Fuentes is that watchdog."

• CHAPTER TWENTY-SIX •

LIKE Roble Foods, Fiesta Time was housed in a beige concrete office building with manufacturing and warehouse facilities in the back. The only difference was it was on a smaller scale and didn't have a guard at a gate. The entrance to its parking lot was secured by an automated gate.

"There's the food place," Emma said, pointing to a small structure next to the fence that secured Fiesta Time's property. As they suspected, it wasn't a chain fast-food restaurant but a small mom-and-pop take-out place painted dark red with all of its seating outside at tables and benches. The sign above it said, *Maria's Place.* As they passed by, Emma could see Carlos, his head down, seated at a table next to the fence just as Granny had said.

"Looks like you might get lunch after all," Emma said to Phil.

"Sounds good to me," he said with a grin. "Usually, these small places have the best and most authentic food."

"I said 'might,'" she reminded him. "Depends on whether Carlos takes off or not when he sees us." She paused, then added. "And I hope he doesn't because I'm hungry, too."

Phil made a U-turn and brought the SUV back around. When they reached Maria's, he turned in to their small parking lot, which was on the other side from where Carlos sat. In the lot was a motorcycle and a beat-up Honda Accord. "Didn't Granny say Carlos rode a motorcycle?"

"Yes," Emma confirmed. "I'm glad it's after the bulk of the normal lunch hour so there won't be many others around." She pointed to a nearby trash can that was nearly full. "It looks like this place could be popular."

They parked and walked around to the front of the tiny structure. A man was at the window ordering food. He was dressed in business attire. At the curb, Emma noted a new-model sedan illegally parked with its engine running, the driver waiting behind the wheel. The passenger's side door was ajar. This was what passed as a drive-thru at Maria's Place.

Carlos noticed them before they got close. He sat up straight and squared his jaw as if expecting trouble. Dressed in jeans and a light gray T-shirt with a band logo on the front, he looked stronger and older than he had at the restaurant. The tattoos on his arms were also more obvious.

"About time you got here," Granny said to them.

"Hi, Carlos," began Emma, ignoring the ghost. "Do you remember me?"

He nodded, but said nothing for a couple of heartbeats. "You're that lady from the restaurant. The one who met with Rikki a couple of times about all that ghost BS."

Granny stomped her foot. "It's not . . . what you said."

"We'd like to ask you a couple of questions," Emma told Carlos. "It's very important."

"I didn't do anything wrong," he said with defiance.

"We don't think you did either, but aren't the police looking for you for questioning?" asked Phil.

"Let 'em look," Carlos said with confidence, spreading out his arms in a grand gesture. "I'm not walking into no police station, but I'm not hiding either. If they come to me, I'll tell them what I know."

"Like how you took money from Steve Bullock for a job of some sort that involved T.J., a man now lying in the hospital shot through the chest?" Emma didn't take her eyes off Carlos.

The young man's face turned dark and brooding. "I'd never hurt T.J. and I never did what Bullock wanted. I never intended to do it. I . . . I just took the money." Almost as soon as the words were out, his mouth fell open. "Hey, how do you know about that anyway?" Before they could answer, Carlos said, "Only two other people knew about that going down—T.J. and . . . another guy."

Everyone looked surprised, including Granny, who hovered next to Carlos. "T.J. knew about the payoff?" The ghost looked up at Emma. "That doesn't sound right. Do you think he's really involved and got shot because he knew too much?"

"Is the other guy Jeremiah Jones, by any chance?" Phil asked. "Aren't you working for Jeremiah?" Carlos didn't answer. He just watched them with the wary eyes of an animal not sure if he's met friend or foe. "Aren't you keeping tabs on Steve Bullock for Jeremiah as we speak?" Phil continued. He waved an arm in the direction of the Fiesta Time parking lot. "I'll bet if we checked, we'd discover that one of the cars in plain sight from this table is his, and that the money he gave you wasn't for watching his car."

"What do you want from me?" Carlos asked.

Phil looked at Emma. Granny looked at Emma. Emma realized they were waiting for her to make the next move in the interrogation. She sat down at the table and addressed the young man. "Listen, Carlos, we just left a meeting with Rikki Ricardo. She asked us to help her get to the bottom of what happened." She spoke calmly, laying out the facts that they knew so far. "We know that the Ricardo family has been good to you and that you wouldn't do anything to hurt them. We know that T.J. has been good to you and you wouldn't want to hurt him either. We're not thinking that you had anything to do with the shooting, but we need to know what happened." She glanced at Phil, then back to Carlos. "We saw you with Steve Bullock that day by the parking lot. We were leaving to go home and saw you accept an envelope from Steve. What was that all about? Did Steve Bullock pay you to hurt T.J.?"

After careful thought, Carlos took a deep breath, blowing out the air hard enough to stir the stack of paper napkins on the table. Instead of answering, he picked up his phone and made a call. "Hey, man," he said into the phone, "that ghost lady and her friend are here asking me questions. I don't know how they found me, but they did." He paused, then put the phone on speaker.

"Phil, Emma, what a surprise." It was Jeremiah. "I underestimated you."

Phil was leaning down close to Emma. She could feel him tense at Jeremiah's words. "Don't play with us, Jeremiah," Phil said into the phone. "This is serious business."

"I'm well aware of that, Phil. I just wanted to buy some time before telling you the whole story."

"Now would be a good time to begin," said Emma into the phone. "Start with the handoff of cash. You said you were hired by T.J. to follow Bullock. Is that true?"

"Yes, but Carlos here is who caused T.J. to hire me. Tell them, son. Tell these good people what started it all. They're cool."

"That handoff you saw was a setup," Carlos began after taking a drink from the straw stuck in his jumbo soda. The cup must have been close to empty, because his sucking resulted in a wet, empty sound.

"No," interrupted Jeremiah. "Start from the beginning when Bullock first contacted you."

Carlos shook the soda cup. The only sound it made was that of lonely ice, and not much of that. "I gotta get another drink first. It's hot out here."

"I'll get it," Phil said. "You keep talking. What kind?"

"A Coke."

"You want some food, too?"

"No, man. I had lunch." After Phil left, Carlos began. "It all started about two weeks ago. Bullock approached me at this gym I go to. He asked if I wanted to make some real money. I thought he meant something like drugs, so I told him to get lost."

Phil came back with Carlos's soda and iced teas for Emma and himself. "I've ordered us some lunch," he told Emma and left for the front window again.

"Keep going," Granny encouraged him, even though he couldn't hear her.

Emma smiled at the eagerness in the ghost's voice. Even

Jeremiah laughed, but Carlos only looked puzzled. "Go ahead, Carlos," Emma said. "Keep going."

Carlos unwrapped his fresh straw and stuck it through the hole in the lid on the top of the soda. "He didn't leave but told me he knew I worked for the Ricardos and that he had a job he needed done. He said that Felix had died holding something that belonged to his uncle Ramon, and the Santiagos wanted it back." He took a drink of his fresh soda. "I told him I wasn't a thief and turned away, but then he offered me ten thousand dollars and handed me his card. Told me to think about it."

Phil returned with their food. A burrito for himself and grilled shrimp tacos for Emma. "Bullock offered Carlos ten thousand dollars to steal something from the Ricardos," she told Phil.

"Seems like you're always catching that man up," quipped Granny. Instead of answering, Emma indicated for Carlos to continue. Then she picked up her taco and took a bite and nearly swooned. "These are delicious," she gushed, interrupting Carlos just as he got started again. Phil had his mouth wrapped around the burrito and grunted in agreement. Grabbing a napkin, Emma wiped her mouth and apologized, "I'm sorry, Carlos. Please continue."

"You two are acting like a couple of pigs at a trough," Granny said in disgust. Again Jeremiah laughed.

"Well, ten grand is a lot of money for a kid like me," Carlos said.

"For anyone," said Phil. He took a drink of his iced tea. "Had to be tempting."

"You don't know, man," Carlos told him. "My family needed that money bad. My mother's a single mom and she's been sick. My little brother and sister are too young to help out. Yesterday when I called in sick, I wasn't. I had to look after the kids while my mother went to some appointments. Usually my aunt does it, but she couldn't yesterday. Ten grand seemed like a gift from God." He spread out his arms. "Like it fell from heaven. So I asked him what he wanted. I was just supposed to sneak around until I found this agreement, then take it. That's all Bullock wanted."

"Guys," came Jeremiah's voice from the phone. "I already know all this and I have some people I need to talk to. Carlos, tell these people anything and everything they want to know. I trust them. I'll catch up with all of you later. And, Carlos, you can leave when you're done. Thanks for sitting there all day."

"Okay, man," Carlos said to Jeremiah. He ended the call and looked back at Phil and Emma, clearly uncomfortable about spilling his guts to them. He wiped the back of one hand across his mouth and continued, "For a day or two, even though I hadn't given my answer to Bullock yet, I did look for that agreement whenever I got the chance, but I felt like crap sneaking around like that. I need the job. I make good tips and they work around my school schedule. Sometimes I even pick up extra money working the food trucks when they need it." He shrugged. "Yeah, sometimes Rikki can be too strict with rules, but so was her old man, and everyone loved him. Rikki's a nice lady. She treats everyone good, with respect, no matter what your job there." He took another drink of soda. "I owe those people, and money or not, they deserve better from me."

Granny leaned over to Emma. "Fill me in later," she said to Emma. "I want to see what Jeremiah's up to. That okay by you?" Emma gave her a tiny nod. It was exactly what she wanted Granny to do.

"That's a very mature attitude," Phil told Carlos, "especially in the face of all that cash."

Carlos shrugged off the compliment. "I had to do the right thing, man. So I called up T.J. and told him I needed to see him in private. When we met, I told him about Bullock, the money, and what I was supposed to steal."

"Did T.J. seem surprised by the existence of the document," Emma asked, "or do you think he already knew about it?"

"He seemed totally surprised and determined to find out what was in it. All I knew to tell him was that it was a loan agreement and Bullock believed it to be at the restaurant." Carlos rotated his neck, loosening the tension settling in it. Every now and then he would glance over at the parking lot, continuing his surveillance. "I asked Bullock why the restaurant and not in a safe-deposit box. I mean, that's where I would keep such an important document."

"What did he say?" asked Emma. She'd finished her lunch, deposited her plate in a nearby trash can, and sat down again.

"He said the family didn't find it among Felix's personal things when he died. I found that weird."

"How so?" asked Phil after swallowing the food in his mouth.

"I wasn't sure if he meant the Ricardos or the Santiagos didn't find it. T.J. told me that Lucy and Bullock had become tight, so I just thought Lucy knew about it and wanted to find it before Rikki found out."

"What did T.J. do after you told him?" asked Phil. He took another drink of his tea and waited, totally absorbed in the tale. Emma was, too. Both listened with complete attention.

"I could tell he was angry after I told him, but he kept

his cool. The next day he and I met again after I got off work. This time Jeremiah was with T.J. Together we planned the setup. I would tell Bullock that I was in and set up the meeting for him to pay me half up front, the rest upon handing over the agreement. Jeremiah was to film and record the meeting. I even wore a wire."

"When I stumbled on the meeting," Phil said, "I overheard you say something about T.J. What was it?"

Carlos looked at Phil, a middle-aged, bald white guy, with surprise. "You speak Spanish?"

Phil gave him a grin. "Like a native, but the traffic muffled a lot of the sound."

For the first time, Carlos offered up a small smile. "I told Bullock that I wanted to make sure T.J. and Rikki would not be hurt, no matter what happened. He assured me they just wanted the document." He stretched. "After, I did what T.J. and Jeremiah told me to do, I stashed the money, but didn't look for that agreement again."

"When did you first hear about the shooting at Roble?" Emma asked.

"On the TV," Carlos said, taking another long pull on his straw. "Man, I freaked out. I called T.J. but he didn't pick up, so I called Jeremiah. He told me the cops knew about my meeting with Bullock so I should pack up and leave as soon as possible before they questioned me. He gave me an address where I could crash until it all got straightened out. As soon as my mother got home, that's exactly what I did. I haven't been home since. She's probably worried sick, but Jeremiah said I wasn't to contact her."

"But why did you run instead of just answering questions?" Emma asked. "You could have told the police what you're telling us."

Carlos shook his head and laughed, but not a happy laugh. "Lady, you were there the day Lucy accused me of being a *cholo,* and she's one of us. The cops would have been worse. They wouldn't have questioned me with respect like they probably did you. They would have cuffed me and dragged my ass in, deciding I was the shooter, and not looked any further for the truth. Jeremiah's black and a former cop. He knows how it is so he stashed me away except for today to watch Bullock."

Emma looked at the young man. Worry for his family was etched deep into his smooth face. "Give me your mother's phone number and address," she told him. "I'll contact her myself and let her know you're okay."

He shook his head. "No, the cops are probably watching her and the house. We just need to get this over with."

"Son," Phil said in a reassuring fatherly voice, "we're doing our best. We have some solid leads and so does Jeremiah. We're working together to find out who's responsible as quickly as possible."

Carlos looked from Phil to Emma. "How are T.J. and Chef Lupe?"

"Rikki says T.J.'s holding his own," Emma told him, "but far from out of danger. The police haven't been able to question him yet because of his condition. Lupe is doing better and recovering."

Carlos looked away, again at the parking lot next door, but he wasn't watching cars; he was lost in his thoughts. "T.J.'s like a big brother. I look up to him, you know?" He turned back to them, his face a block of anguish. "You have to find the mother—" He stopped, remembering his language, but the anger spoke volumes.

The table went silent for a few moments, then Emma asked, "What do you know about Isabel Gonzales?"

"Ana's sister?"

Emma nodded.

"She's a cold bitch," he said, not checking his words this time. "Ana is sweet but not the brightest. I mean, she's book smart but not street smart. Isabel is the opposite. You have to watch your back around her." He paused as a small, sad smile crossed his lips. "She's another Lucinda Ricardo, but without the power and money. Give her a few years and she'll be shooting at her sister, too." Carlos paused, then said, "Isabel is the real *cholo* here."

Phil and Emma exchanged glances, then Emma said, "Did you know she had a big crush on T.J.?"

"I'd heard about it once from Ana, but T.J. would never be interested in that, even if thrown at him." He stopped and looked at them as a light went off in his head. "Do you think Isabel shot T.J.?"

"We don't know," Phil told him, "but we suspect she had something to do with it. At least with setting it up. Did she have any ties to Steve Bullock and Fiesta Time?"

Carlos shrugged. "Not that I know, but he might have contacted her, too, especially if he and Lucy were tight. Lucy and Isabel had some sort of bitch connection thing going on. Maybe Isabel was plan B in case I didn't work out."

Emma filed the new information away along with the rest of it. She could see Lucy easily deciding on another course of action if Steve's idea didn't work out. Lucy knew Carlos had a sense of loyalty to her family and might back out if his conscience got the better of him. "Is it possible," she asked Carlos, "that Lucy could have made arrangements with Isabel or someone else, without Steve's knowledge? Her own secret plan B maybe?"

"I wouldn't put anything past Lucinda Ricardo," Carlos said with a curled lip, "or Isabel Gonzales. I don't know exactly what Lucy's relationship with Steve is, but both of those women only look out for themselves. Either would turn on anyone in a heartbeat."

Phil glanced at her, and Emma could see in his eyes that he was piecing together the same theory. Her next question was one that had been nagging at her.

"I know you weren't there the day T.J. was shot, Carlos," Emma asked, "but do you have any idea why he would just show up at the restaurant during its busy time to speak with Rikki? He told her it was urgent."

He hesitated and looked off again, then shook his head. "The corporate offices are so close to Olvera Street that the executives and office workers were always popping in for lunch, especially T.J. He liked to come by and have lunch with Rikki and sometimes with both Hector and Rikki, but usually he came later or early so not to disrupt the lunch service.

"It felt more like he was the CEO of the company and not Lucy. He and Rikki were really the ones who gave us a sense of being a team."

"Lucy didn't drop by like that?" Phil asked.

"Once in a while, but mostly she'd call and order her food to be delivered. Even in our busiest time, Isabel would call the order in for her and demand that the food be sent over immediately and someone would have to stop what they were doing and drive it over to corporate."

Phil scratched his ear, then asked, "Did you ever see Steve Bullock or Ramon Santiago at the restaurant?"

Carlos gave the question some thought, then answered, "No, at least not while I was working."

"Do you know Ramon Santiago?" Emma asked.

"Sure. He's the owner of Fiesta Time. And I knew who Steve Bullock was before he came up to me at the gym. Like the Ricardos, the Santiago family is well known in the Latino community."

With no more questions, Emma looked to Phil, giving him an indication that they should move along, but before they did, Carlos said, "Wait, I do know something else, but you have to swear not to get her involved."

· CHAPTER TWENTY-SEVEN ·

THE person Carlos wanted to protect was Christina, the receptionist at Roble Foods. It had turned out to be her and not Isabel who had alerted T.J. that Lucy was on the warpath at the restaurant the first day Emma met with Rikki. Thinking back, Emma realized that T.J. had never mentioned Isabel's name. It had been Rikki who'd made the assumption.

"You have to promise not to involve her," Carlos said, his voice tight and worried. "I can't get her mixed up in this. I can't do that to her."

Emma, who had already stood up to go, sat back down at the table at Maria's Place and looked Carlos in the eye. "I can't promise you that, Carlos. If she has information that could solve T.J.'s shooting, she'll need to be questioned." She paused. "Who is Christina to you?"

Carlos squeezed his eyes shut, then opened them. "She's my mother's best friend and my godmother. That's why she told me what was going on. She trusts me and now I'm about to betray her. I haven't even told Jeremiah this."

"You're not betraying Christina," Phil told him in a firm fatherly voice. "You're making a tough choice for the greater good. If this information can help find T.J.'s shooter, then that's the greater good. Christina will be part of the solution, and the sooner we get to the bottom of this, the better off she'll be. So how is Christina involved?"

Carlos considered Phil's words, then picked up his soda. For a few seconds, time hung in the air like it had no place to go. Carlos went to stick the straw of his drink between his lips, but at the last moment hurled the cup with all his youthful strength at the chain link fence. The cup hit the pattern of crisscrossed wire and exploded, Coke and ice bursting like wet fireworks before coming to rest with the cup, lid, and straw among the weeds at the base of the fence.

Emma and Phil didn't take their eyes off Carlos Fuentes. There were tears in his dark eyes, pooling but not spilling. He sniffed them back with a hard snort and wiped his nose with the back of his hand. But he stayed put.

"After the shooting," Carlos began, "while I was waiting for my mother to return so I could take off like Jeremiah told me to, Christina called my cell. She was upset and crying, saying crazy shit like she was responsible for T.J. being shot. She said she was leaving the office early and coming to our house to talk to me. I told her not to come but that I'd meet her somewhere. We decided to meet at a church not far from her home."

Carlos coughed and sniffed again. He was no longer the cocky young man with a chip on his shoulder. Now he looked like a child confessing to a playground prank. Phil got up and got him another Coke. "Thanks," Carlos murmured to the table top. Instead of unwrapping the straw, he took the lid off the big drink and chugged almost half of it down at one go. Then he belched, followed by an embarrassed apology like his mother probably taught him.

"Christina," Carlos continued, "was the reason T.J. showed up at Roble the day of the shooting, and she was blaming herself for what happened." He looked from Emma to Phil. "If T.J. dies, Christina will be devastated. She's a wreck now."

Emma remembered the attractive woman at the receptionist desk and in the ladies' room. She did look about to drop from a cocktail of stress and grief. Emma had chalked it up to the shootings in general, not to something specific like guilt, deserved or not. "We saw her at Roble today," Emma told Carlos. "She didn't look very good. I'm surprised she was there considering what you're saying."

"She didn't want to go in, but I convinced her to do it," Carlos told them. "I told her she needs to be business as usual. If she didn't show up, the cops might get suspicious and try to question her."

"And why is she afraid of the police?" Emma asked. "She hasn't done anything wrong, has she?"

"It's not the police Christina's afraid of," Carlos said. "It's Isabel and Lucy. They've both made a lot of people in the office miserable, especially Isabel. Like I told you, she's the real *cholo*."

"So what did Christina say to T.J. to send him flying over to the restaurant like a bat out of hell?" Phil asked.

Carlos took another slug of the soda. "She was in the bathroom and Isabel came in talking on her cell. Isabel didn't know Christina was there. According to Christina, it's a big bathroom with several stalls."

Emma nodded. "It is. I was in it myself today."

"Christina was curious. Very early that morning T.J. and Rikki announced their engagement via a company-wide e-mail and apparently Isabel didn't take it well, even though she tried to slap on a happy face."

"I heard the same rumor today when I was there," Emma confirmed.

"According to Christina," Carlos continued, "she pulled her feet up so if Isabel checked, the stall would look empty." He stopped, thought about something, then pushed forward. "I have to tell you something else. Isabel was Lucy's eyes and ears everywhere in that office. Her spy, although most everyone knew it. In return, Isabel got special favors."

Emma smiled to herself as another piece—a tiny piece—of the puzzle dropped in place. According to Granny, the younger woman in the bathroom complained about Isabel taking long lunches and not being around much during the work day with no consequences.

"Was Christina T.J.'s spy?" Phil asked, taking Emma's next question right out of her mouth.

Carlos nodded. "Yes. Although she says she only told him things about Lucy's movements. Christina said that T.J. didn't trust Lucy or Isabel at all. But she didn't tattle on the other employees the way Isabel did."

"But that day in the bathroom, the day of the shooting, Christina heard something really important, didn't she?" Emma pushed, moving the story along.

Again Carlos nodded, followed by taking several deep breaths. "Christina said she overheard Isabel telling some-one on the phone that it was all set. That Rikki was going to be out of everyone's hair forever."

Emma looked over at Phil and instantly knew he was

thinking the same thing she was, that they were right, that Rikki was the intended target all along.

Timing was everything in order to prove that Isabel had set up the shooting. "When in the day did Christina hear this?" Emma asked.

"It was early," Carlos answered, "sometime between nine thirty and ten, I think. It might even have been closer to nine, shortly after the office opened. Christina told me she tried calling T.J. on his cell, but he didn't answer."

Emma looked at Phil and said, "That would have been the morning after T.J. proposed. They went to Elena's house together to tell her the news. He might have turned his cell off the night before and forgot to turn it on or left it off while he was at Elena's."

"That's what he told Christina when he got to the office," Carlos reported. "She said T.J. came in close to lunch time all happy and smiling because of the engagement. He'd even stopped off and bought a bunch of cupcakes for the office to celebrate. She really hated having to tell him what she'd heard."

"So she told him and he took off?" Phil asked.

"Yeah. Christina said first he went flying out to Isabel's desk but she wasn't there. Lucy wasn't in either."

Emma nodded. "Lucy was at Santiago's having lunch with Steve Bullock."

"According to Christina, Lucy didn't come in at all that morning," Carlos told them. "They were doing some repair work in her office so she was working from home."

"Anything else?" Phil asked.

"One more thing," Carlos said as he rubbed his hands on the legs of his jeans. "Christina thinks Isabel is getting some big payoff. Isabel said to whoever was on the phone that she couldn't wait to get her money and leave town. She told the person on the phone to make sure it was all there and ready to go, or something like that." Carlos got up and picked up his helmet from the bench next to him. "That's it. That's all there is. Pretty screwed up, isn't it?"

Emma and Phil got up. Phil shook Carlos's hand. "You did the right thing, son. We'll work with Jeremiah to get this sorted out as quickly as possible so you can get home to your family."

Emma put a hand on each of the young man's strong upper arms and gave them a gentle squeeze, just short of giving him an embrace. "Go somewhere safe and stay there until Jeremiah tells you it's okay to come out. And leave me both your number and your mother's, just in case of emergency." Emma pulled paper and pen from her purse to jot down the numbers.

Carlos looked at his phone. "This is a burner. Jeremiah gave it to me."

"Still give me both numbers," Emma told him and he did. "And don't you call your mother," she warned. "Stay low. I'll let your mother know you're okay. I'm a mother myself. I know she's worried sick."

"Now what?" Phil asked Emma after seeing Carlos off. "Back to Roble's corporate offices?" They had remained at Maria's Place, drinking the last of their tea under the awning that shaded the tables.

Emma gave the idea some thought. "I'm worried that if we show up again today, someone will get suspicious. Lucy might have more than one mole in the place."

"That's an ugly thought," Phil said, making a face, "but a sound one. Do you think Christina is safe?"

"She is if no one knows she's T.J.'s snoop, but I'm very

worried about Rikki. If she was the intended victim, there might still be a target on her back. I mean, who knows where Isabel is right now?"

"We know Peter Bradford is somewhere between here and San Diego, so he's not a threat at the moment," Phil pointed out. "Do you think maybe he was the shooter?"

Emma weighed the possibility. "Maybe, but I'm inclined to think he was just a dupe. Someone Isabel manipulated to do what she needed done. I'm thinking someone else came in with the group and slipped upstairs. My money is on Isabel herself since she left the Roble offices about that time. Carlos is right—Isabel could have been plan B in the event he backed out. Or she could have been tasked with shooting Rikki while Carlos was in charge of finding the agreement. Two different people for two different jobs. They could even have been hired separately: one by Lucy and the other by Steve. It's also possible it was Lucy whom Isabel was speaking to on the phone in the bathroom. Lucy wasn't in, and if workers were in her office, Isabel couldn't go in there for privacy."

"But wouldn't people have recognized Isabel?" Phil asked. "She's Hector's daughter, and her sister works there."

"That is puzzling unless she wore a disguise. A wig and extra makeup could do a lot to change her appearance, especially if everyone was scattered about trying to get their work done and not paying attention." Emma gave it more thought. "The restrooms are by the back door and the staircase to the offices. She could have pretended to be a customer on her way to the ladies' room and slipped upstairs. She's probably been there lots of times, so would know the way. In fact," Emma tacked on, pointing her left index finger for emphasis, "I'll bet Isabel even worked there while in school like her sister does now. If so, she'd know the place inside and out, including how they work tour buses and crowds and where the office is."

"Excellent point, as usual," Phil said. He grinned at her. "I'm glad you're on the side of good and not evil, because you have a mind for this stuff. You and Granny could have quite a career in crime if you put your minds to it."

Emma chuckled. "Now there's a thought, but I don't think Granny would go for it. She can be touchy and annoying, but she's as honest as the day is long."

"And you're not?" Phil winked at her. "You and Granny are both a couple of Girl Scouts."

Emma shook her head and smiled, but didn't look at him. "Girl Scouts don't pimp their daughters to get information."

"Are you going to tell Jeremiah about this new development?" Phil asked. "Carlos said he didn't tell him. Only we know."

"I do think we need to share this but first I want to know what Jeremiah is doing. Jeremiah is obviously protecting Carlos from being dragged into this by the police." She looked over at Phil. "He will have to be at some point, but as a witness, not as a suspect. I think Jeremiah made the right call here."

"I do, too, honey." Phil took her hand, gave it a quick squeeze, and released it. "Being with Carlos makes me think of my boys and how I would feel if it was one of them in this situation."

Emma pulled out her cell phone and punched in the number for Carlos's mother. "That's why I insisted on getting his mother's number."

When a woman answered, Emma asked if it was Mrs. Fuentes. When the woman said yes, Emma said, "You don't know me, Mrs. Fuentes, but we're friends of Jeremiah's and we're helping your son." Emma paused while the woman gushed with questions. "I'm calling just to let you to know that Carlos is safe and healthy and this will all be over soon. Mother to mother, I'm telling you to stay strong. Can you do that?" Another pause. "Good. We'll be in touch soon." She ended the call. "She was very appreciative of the call, as I figured she'd be."

"If the cops trace that call, they're going to rain down on you, you know that?" Phil said with concern.

"Frankly, I don't care," Emma said, giving him one of Granny's signature head jerks of defiance. She placed another call.

"Now who are you calling? Jeremiah?"

"No, Rikki, but Jeremiah is next on my list." When the call went unanswered, Emma said, "That was Rikki's cell phone. It went to voice mail."

"Maybe she's in another meeting?" Phil suggested.

Emma left a voice message for Rikki to call her as soon as possible, then placed a call to another number and turned on the speaker. When that call was answered, she said, "Christina, this is Emma Whitecastle. I was in to see Rikki earlier today. Is she in? I need to speak with her. It's important." Emma was tempted to tell Christina to get out of Dodge but didn't want to panic the woman just in case she was being watched.

"No, Ms. Whitecastle," Christina said in a professional voice infused with forced energy. "Rikki left the office a short while ago and didn't say where she was going. Maybe she went to the hospital to see T.J."

"Thank you," Emma said into the phone. "If she returns, please ask her to call me right away."

She looked up another number and dialed it. When it was

answered, Phil looked surprised. Emma asked, "Is Mr. Bullock in?"

"Yes," said a pleasant voice, "who should I say is calling?" Emma disconnected.

"Were you checking to see if Bullock is where he's supposed to be and didn't give Carlos the slip?" Phil asked her.

"Yes," Emma admitted. "And it looks like he's still there." She pointed at the offices of Fiesta Time.

• CHAPTER TWENTY-EIGHT •

AS promised, the next call went to Jeremiah. Like Rik-ki's, his call also went to voice mail. Emma left a message to call her, then also texted him in case he was somewhere where he couldn't talk. Almost as soon as the text was sent, her phone rang. It was Jeremiah. "Hey," he said as soon as Emma answered. She put him on speaker and she and Phil gathered close.

"What's going on with you?" Emma asked.

"You don't know?" he laughed. "Your spirited spy has been shadowing me for the past hour hounding me to call and tell you what's going on. I figured she'd already popped in and given you a full report."

"Is she there with you now?" Emma asked.

"Sure is."

"Then she's not here telling me anything," Emma told him while Phil smiled. "Ghosts are like us, Jeremiah. They can't be in two places at once."

"Nice to know," Jeremiah said with a slight snort. "She can really be a pest, can't she? An itsy-bitsy pest, like a gnat."

Close by in the background, Emma heard Granny call out, "I heard that!"

"Wait until she really gets to know you," Emma warned him. "So what's up on your end?"

"I tracked down Hector Gonzales at the hospital," Jeremiah told them. "In fact, I'm still at the hospital. When I saw that you called, I went someplace to get some privacy. Earlier, Hector and I went to a corner of the cafeteria and had a little heart-to-heart. I honestly don't think he had anything to do with the shooting, but I think he has his suspicions."

"Are they related to his daughter Isabel?" Phil asked.

"He won't say, but I wouldn't be surprised because I think he's protecting someone. Who better than your own kid?"

"He might have seen her at the restaurant the day of the shooting and isn't saying," Emma suggested.

"I think that's a possibility," Jeremiah said. "When I told him we had a connection between her and the tour bus company, his body language definitely tightened up, like someone punched him, but he still didn't say anything."

"Where is he now?" Phil asked. "I hope you didn't let him out of your sight."

"Not a chance. I called Aaron and tossed him a bone. Told him what I suspect about Isabel. The cops took Hector in for questioning. This should take the heat off of their hunt for Carlos for the time being." He paused. "So what about you two?"

"We're tying up similar loose ends," Emma said. "Carlos told us something that also points to Isabel as not only being involved, but possibly the shooter or the one who hired the shooter."

"Really?" Jeremiah asked, surprised. "Something the kid didn't tell me?"

"Yep," answered Phil. He glanced at Emma and winked. "Never underestimate the power of a mother's inquisition, even if it's someone else's mother."

Emma smiled back. "Carlos told us that Isabel was overheard talking on her phone saying that Rikki would soon be out of the picture for good. That doesn't necessarily mean dead, but given the circumstances, I'd rather lean on the side of caution. Also she said something about receiving a big payoff and leaving town. That person told T.J. and that's what sent him flying off to the restaurant the day of the shooting. He went to warn Rikki to protect her and ended up face-to-face with the shooter himself."

"It didn't sound like T.J. had a clue about it going down that same day," added Phil, "just that it might happen."

"By the way, we know where that loan agreement is hidden." Emma tossed the information out and waited for a reaction.

"Did Carlos tell you he knew where it was?" Jeremiah asked, his voice swelling with irritation. "He told me he never found it and didn't know where it was."

"No, not him," Emma said.

"Wait a minute," said Jeremiah, his tone switching to amusement. "Felix told you himself, didn't he? I should have known. What else did he tell you that I don't know?"

"That was our only holdout," Emma said. "You gave us Carlos. We'll give you that."

"I didn't give you Carlos," Jeremiah conceded. "You

found him with Granny's help. That ghost is like a heat-seeking missile."

"She must have liked that comment," Emma noted, "because I didn't hear her grousing."

"Granny seems to have wandered off," Jeremiah said. "She's probably looking for newly minted ghost pals." He paused and Phil and Emma could hear people talking in the background. "All clear," Jeremiah said when the sounds drifted off. "I'll call Aaron when I get done with you and tell him what you just found out about Isabel. He'll probably put units on both Hector's house and Isabel's place as well as put out a BOLO."

"By the way," Emma added. "We checked up on Steve Bullock and he's still in his office. We were worried that somehow he snuck out past Carlos."

"Yeah," Jeremiah said, "if I were him with all this about to explode, I'd stick as close to my normal routine as possible. It's easier to plead innocence if you don't look like you're running from something."

"What kind of car does he drive?" Phil asked.

"Hang on," Jeremiah said. A few seconds later he read off a plate number and gave them the description.

Phil went to the fence and scoped out the cars. When he returned to the table, he said, "It's still there."

"I tried to call Rikki," Emma told Jeremiah, "but she didn't answer. You might see if she's with T.J. If she is, we need to get her somewhere safe. She's not as long as Isabel is on the loose."

"She's not there," Emma heard Granny say.

"Dammit, Granny," snapped Jeremiah. "Do you have to pop up like that?"

Emma grinned at Phil and whispered, "Granny just

startled Jeremiah by popping up." Phil covered his mouth and laughed.

"Do you mean you didn't see Rikki?" asked Emma for clarification.

"That's what I said," answered the ghost, who must have had her head next to Jeremiah's phone to hear. "She's not with T.J. or with Chef Lopez, who has a room full of visitors, including her wife and son. The only person with T.J. is his mother. Poor lady is just sitting there, running rosary beads through her fingers, waiting for her son to wake up. It's heartbreaking."

"Hold on, folks," said Jeremiah. "I have another call. It's Aaron."

Emma looked at Phil, locking eyes with him. "Are you thinking what I'm thinking?" he said to her.

"That Rikki went to the restaurant?"

"Uh-huh," Phil confirmed. "She doesn't know that Isabel is after her. She thinks she's safe because Lucy's still in jail, and once she learned about that loan document, she was hell-bent on finding it. Not to mention, her judgment's clouded a bit by that tequila."

"We need to get to the restaurant," Emma said, standing up and starting for their vehicle. She ended the call.

"What about Jeremiah?" Phil asked, following her.

"He'll call back when he's done with Aaron, and we can have him send the police there to find Rikki. In the mean-time, we can start heading over there ourselves." She glanced at her watch. "It's the beginning of rush hour, but we're head-ing into downtown, not out of it, so we might make good time."

When they were both in the SUV and heading for LA, Emma got nervous when Jeremiah didn't call right back so she called him. "It went straight to voice mail," she told Phil. "He's probably still talking with the police. "I'll text him our concerns and have him tell the police to get to Restaurante Roble."

"Good idea," Phil said as he urged the SUV in and out of traffic. "If Isabel is heading back over there, she'll probably wait until dark. At least that's what I'd do, and since it's summer, sundown isn't for a few more hours."

When they got to Olvera Street, they parked in the same lot they'd used before, but instead of a leisurely stroll down the quaint street, they strode with purpose to Restaurante Roble but not so fast as to draw attention to themselves. The street was only sparsely populated. It was the shoulder time of the day. The office workers were heading home and tourists were dragging back to their hotels after a day in the sun seeing the sights. Shopkeepers were cleaning up and getting ready for the next day's tourist action while waiting on straggling customers.

"Boy, this place closes up early for a Friday," Phil said.

"I think I read somewhere that most of it closes up by six or seven," Emma said. "The only day they're open late is Saturday. Rikki mentioned that there is only one other restaurant open for a late dinner and that's only on Friday and Saturday nights, like them."

"Not good," noted Phil as they walked. "It means if Isabel's coming, she might arrive before dark, knowing the street will be mostly shut up. I hope Detective Espinoza has already sent a unit to check it out."

When they got to the restaurant, it looked abandoned, except for an elderly couple dressed in shorts and colorful shirts taking photos through the bars of the lowered security gate of the front door adorned with police tape. The man looked at Phil and Emma as they came to a halt. "I wonder what happened here," he said to them.

Phil shrugged. "Too bad, we were looking forward to having dinner here tonight."

"So were we," said the woman. "We use their products at home all the time." She gave them a warm smile. "We're from Wisconsin. How about you, folks?"

"Locals," said Emma. "I've eaten here before. It's quite good."

"There were two nice policemen here a minute ago," the man said. He pulled out a white handkerchief and wiped the sweat off his brow. "But they wouldn't tell us anything. All they would say was that the place was closed for a few days for police business."

"I got my picture with them," gushed the woman. "Isn't that exciting? Real Los Angeles police officers, just like on TV."

Emma looked around, then asked, "Where did the police officers go?"

The couple shrugged simultaneously as if rehearsed. "They checked the security gate," the man said, "to make sure everything was locked up tight, then got a call on their radio and took off. It looked like they were just doing a check."

As the couple wandered off, Phil looked at Emma. "That woman and Granny would get along great."

"I think you're right." Emma backed up across Olvera Street and looked up at the windows of Rikki's office. "It doesn't look like anyone is there, but in daylight no one would need lights or a flashlight to look around."

"Maybe we were wrong," Phil said. He went to the gate and jerked it. It held tight. "Maybe Rikki didn't come here."

"Let's go around back and check that door," said Emma. She took off for the service alley with Phil on her heels.

The back alley was narrow and empty. The back door to the restaurant had a sign fastened to it announcing it as belonging to Roble. Next to it was a Dumpster. There was no police tape. Phil checked the door. "It's unlocked," he announced in a whisper. "Guess the police didn't have time to check back here."

"If Rikki is here," Emma said, "she would have come in this way and probably disabled the alarm."

"But if she's gone already, would she have forgotten to lock up when she left?" Phil noted.

"Who knows?" Emma said. "She's not exactly thinking straight by coming here in the first place."

Phil quietly opened the door. "You stay here and keep watch. Just in case Rikki's not here, where was the agreement again? She might not have remembered what we told her."

"You're not going in there," Emma told him in a forced whisper. "If you get caught, you'll be charged with breaking and entering, and it could put your law license in jeopardy."

"Well, you're not going in there alone," he hissed back at her.

"If Rikki's there, I'll text you to come in. If she's not, I'll check for the document and be in and out before you even know I'm gone," she told him. "Besides, you'd make a better guard than I would. If someone comes along, you can just say you stepped back here to pee."

"Right, like I pee in back alleys all the time."

"You're a guy," Emma cracked. "Guys pee anywhere that's convenient. I once saw Grant do it behind a potted plant at the Beverly Hills Hotel."

"And there's another good reason why you divorced him and are going to marry me."

Emma stared at Phil. "Are we really going to do this here and now?" She tried to look angry, but couldn't and started giggling. "Come on, Phil, out of my way. Let's get this over and done with. You know I'm the better choice to slip in there."

With reluctance, Phil finally gave in. "Okay, but if you're not out in ten minutes," he said to her, "I'm coming in, law license or not. And make sure you have your phone."

CHAPTER TWENTY-NINE

WITH no windows in the back of the restaurant, it was difficult to see at first. Emma moved cautiously until her eyes got used to the shadowy light. When she made her way from the back door into the hallway, diffused light drifted in from the restaurant's front windows, but it barely reached the back area. She put her hand on the wall for guidance, trying to remember exactly where the staircase to the upstairs offices was located. It was then she heard a noise. She froze. It was coming from upstairs. She strained to listen, shutting her eyes to concentrate. That's when she made out a voice. She was about to call out Rikki's name when she heard another voice. She stopped and got her bearings. The restrooms were on the left and the staircase next to them. To the right, just behind the large kitchen, was the storeroom and pantry she remembered from Rikki's brief tour of the place. She put out a hand and found a light switch but didn't dare turn the lights on. Nor did she want to use the light feature on her phone. Until she knew who was upstairs, she didn't want her presence known.

Finding the staircase, Emma took each step carefully, hoping none of them squeaked. Each had rubber safety treads on it, which helped to muffle her steps. At the top she poked her head around the corner into the hall. She saw nothing but could hear more clearly. One of the voices was Rikki's.

"I don't know what you're talking about," she heard Rikki say.

Another voice said something, followed by a loud slap and a cry of pain from Rikki. The other person was also a woman.

"Help her, Emma!" came an urgent whisper. She looked down the hall again and saw the hazy figure of Felix Ricardo. He was gesturing for her to hurry. "Please!"

Instead of moving forward, Emma pulled back and sent Phil a text: *Get help. Rikki & Iz.*

There was another hard slap and more cries of pain from Rikki. Emma again peeked around the corner. The sounds were coming from Rikki's office.

"Where is it?" the other woman asked Rikki.

"I told you I don't know what you're talking about," Rikki said in a frightened voice.

"The agreement. Where is it?"

"I don't know what you mean. I've opened the safe for you. Take what you want from it and leave. Go ahead. I won't say anything. I promise."

"You bet you won't." There were more muffled sounds.

Felix kept going in and out of the office, calling to Emma to help each time he came back out. He was upset and fading in and out, losing his power to materialize.

Emma stepped into the hall and melted into the wall. The

sounds were coming from the right, by Rikki's desk. As long as no one moved in front of the door, Emma might be able to sneak closer. She moved down the hall as fast as she dared in a sideways slink, keeping as close to the wall as possible, and barely breathing. She passed the closed doors of the employee lounge and Hector's office.

"Quick," Felix called to Emma, his voice growing weaker. "She's in the closet, now's the time."

Emma peeked around the door frame and only saw Rikki. She was tied up and sitting in her desk chair. Both sides of her face were covered with red welts, adding more damage to what she'd received the day before. Her nose was bloodied again. The place had been ransacked. Noises and curses were coming from the large closet by the desk. It was the closet where Felix said the loan agreement had been stashed, but apparently Isabel hadn't found it yet. When Rikki saw Emma, her eyes grew wide with relief and concern. Emma put a finger to her lips as she slipped inside. Looking around for a weapon, Emma quickly and quietly unplugged a lamp that sat on a small table next to the sofa. Hoisting it high, she leaned flush against the wall next to the closet door and waited.

Felix stood opposite her. "Her gun isn't in her hand," he told Emma. "It's in her waistband." Emma nodded to Felix to let him know she understood. "I'll let you know when to strike," the ghost told her, his hazy face serious but blurring. More noise continued coming from the depths of the closet. Things were being pulled from their places and tossed outside the closet, adding to the mess of the already searched office.

"Where the hell is it?" cried a voice that Emma now definitely recognized as Isabel's.

"I told you," Rikki said, half in tears, "I don't know what you're talking about."

"Almost," Felix told Emma, holding up a hand for her to be patient. Emma lifted the lamp up higher. "Now!" he screamed with his last bit of energy.

Just as Isabel's head emerged from the closet, Emma struck it with the lamp as hard as she could. The young woman staggered backward, then pitched forward out of the closet as her right hand fumbled to locate her gun through the searing pain. Before she was totally outside the closet, Emma grabbed her by the arm and slammed her face into the doorjamb. Isabel screeched, staggered more, and dropped the gun, which Emma kicked to the side. The younger woman was putting up a fight, screaming and throwing wild one-arm punches and kicking with her legs as her long hair whipped around her face. A few of her kicks connected with Emma's legs, but Emma held her tight. Grabbing a bunch of Isabel's hair in one hand, she yanked, forcing Isabel's head to snap backward. Her nose was dripping blood and she started coughing. Emma then kicked Isabel's feet out from under her and brought her to her knees. Letting go of her hair, Emma held both of Isabel's arms behind her back in a death grip. Isabel Gonzales might have been a lot younger, but Emma was in great physical shape and kept her cool as she subdued her opponent.

"It's over, Isabel," Emma told her. "It's all over."

"Ana," Rikki said, between catching her breath and her tears. She took a deep breath and made another effort. "Ana's here."

A shot rang out just as Emma realized what Rikki was trying to tell her. The bullet went high and wide and pierced the wall. Emma yanked Isabel to her feet and pulled her in front of her, then stepped backward until she reached Rikki, using Isabel as a human shield for the two of them as best she could.

At the doorway was Ana Gonzales. In her hand was a gun, but the gun was shaking and unstable. Tears ran down Ana's young face, which was puffy and red, and her eyes were ringed with smudged makeup.

"Don't do this, Ana," Emma said softly to the girl. "Don't throw your life away."

"She made me do it," Ana choked out.

"Shut up, you stupid bitch," Isabel screamed at her sister.

"You have so much ahead of you, Ana," Emma cajoled. "Put the gun down. We'll work it all out."

"You're pathetic," Isabel taunted Ana. "If you hadn't been puking your guts out while I tried to find that document, she wouldn't have been able to sneak in here." Isabel spit blood at her sister and sneered, "Daddy's little princess. You and Rikki should have been sisters. Both of you are worthless."

Ana steadied the gun and took aim. In a flash, Emma realized that Ana wasn't aiming at her or Rikki, but at Isabel. Another sister setting out to kill her sibling.

"No, Ana! Don't!" Emma cried, unsure of what else to do. She didn't want Isabel shot, but if she moved her out of the way, both she and Rikki would be in the line of fire. Taking a last-second gamble, Emma tightly held on to Isabel and turned them both so that she, and not Isabel, was in the gun's path. With her target out of the way, Emma hoped Ana wouldn't fire. She was wrong. The second shot missed, but not by much.

From the hallway came a loud grunt as Phil hurled himself at Ana, knocking her to the ground. The gun fired again, the third bullet taking out a window. Phil knocked the gun from her hand and grabbed it, holding it on her while she sniveled in a heap on the floor.

From outside came the scream of sirens. The cavalry had finally arrived.

CHAPTER THIRTY

TWO days had gone by since they'd rescued Rikki Ricardo, and Emma and Phil were enjoying their final evening together before Phil had to return to San Diego. When the front doorbell rang, Emma got up to answer it and found Jeremiah on her doorstep. She showed him into the den, where he took a seat across from the sofa. He declined a glass of wine.

"Where's Phil?" he asked.

"He just ran out to pick up something for our dinner tonight," Emma told him. "We're having Thai. Would you like to stay? We've ordered plenty."

"No, but thanks. I just stopped by," Jeremiah explained, "because I thought you two might want to know how everything is shaking out."

"We're assuming it was Isabel who shot T.J.," Emma said, curling her legs up under her.

"Sure was," Jeremiah confirmed. "Seems Bullock was

only involved in paying Carlos to grab the loan document. Lucy had her own game going on. She claims she didn't know about the deal between Bullock and Carlos, and Bullock claims he knew nothing about any deal with Isabel. Lucy was paying Isabel to steal the document. Isabel set up the diversion with the tour bus crowd, sneaking in with them and up the stairs during the confusion of lunch. She was apparently in the closet trying to open the safe when T.J. surprised her and she shot him."

"So it was kind of an accident?" Emma asked. "Rikki wasn't targeted."

"There's a difference of opinion on that," Jeremiah said. "She was supposed to die according to some accounts, and only the document was to be stolen according to others. Again, Bullock is claiming no knowledge of any of this." He stretched his legs out. "My personal opinion is that Isabel was hired to do both, but whether that can ever be proved is another matter."

"What about Ana?" Emma asked. "She really didn't seem all that on board with it."

"Ana claims she was coerced, but we're still not sure about that either. Isabel says Ana was in on everything from the beginning. Ana also claims they were only going to steal the document. She was in the employee lounge tossing her cookies when you came in." The left side of his mouth turned up. "If Ana had the nerves of steel needed for crime, you might have been looking down the barrels of two handguns when you broke in there."

"Did Hector know about any of this?" she asked.

"He admitted that he saw Isabel at the restaurant the day of the shooting. He wanted to confront her himself, but couldn't reach her, then everything happened so fast."

"Have either Lucy or Rikki heard from their mother yet?" Emma asked after taking a sip of her wine.

"Not yet," Jeremiah answered. "But Lucy conceded that her mother knew about the plan to steal the agreement. I doubt that Elena Ricardo is very anxious to return to California."

"We heard from Rikki this morning," Emma told him. "She said T.J. is going to be fine and that the restaurant is not going to be sold to anyone."

"So I heard." Jeremiah laughed softly. "The publicity over the two shootings will probably even help business."

"Thank you, Emma," came a voice from near the fireplace. Emma and Jeremiah both turned to find the ghost of Felix Ricardo standing there. With him was Granny.

Emma sat up straight. "Felix, I didn't expect to see you again."

"I wanted to come by and thank you for helping Ricarda." He looked at Jeremiah. "You, too, sir. You saved her life and our family business." The pleased look slipped from his face. "Although I am very sad about Lucinda and about Hector's girls. Hector and his wife are beside themselves with shame and tragedy, as I am about Lucinda. Whether she realizes it or not, she will always be my daughter." The ghost floated about as he thought about what to say next. "And now I am going to return to where I belong. I do not wish to stay like your Granny here. Too much sadness. I want to rest in peace, as the saying goes." The ghost smiled at Emma. "I wish you and your man, Phil, a long and happy life together."

"Thank you, Felix," Emma said just as the spirit disappeared.

Granny looked at Jeremiah. "Did you tell her yet?"

"Tell me what?" asked Emma.

Granny came close and Emma could see how excited she was. "Jeremiah asked me if I would help him sometimes. Is that okay with you?"

Emma looked at Jeremiah, then at the ghost. "He offered you a job?"

"More like a partnership," Granny said with pride. "He wants to learn more about working with spirits. I told him that he needs to talk more with you and with Milo, but that I'd help with some of his cases. Imagine, Emma, real detective work!" Granny was about to pop with excitement.

"She'd be a great asset," Jeremiah said with a laugh. "As long as you're okay with it, Emma. I wouldn't want to step on any toes."

Emma laughed. "Sure, why not?" she said to Granny. "Go have some fun. Do you start this . . . um . . . partnership right away?"

"No," Jeremiah answered. "I'll be busy helping the police clean up this Fiesta Time mess for a bit."

"And I want to go down to Julian and spend time with my man, Jacob," responded Granny. "I miss Julian when I'm away for very long. I'm going there now unless you'd rather I stick around here?"

"Go on, Granny, you deserve it. Phil and I are just going to be hanging out having some alone time tonight."

"Yeah, I know what that means." The ghost winked at Emma and left.

Granny and Jeremiah hadn't been gone long when Emma heard the doorbell again. She'd almost drifted off to sleep on the sofa, so it took two rings of the bell to get her attention. Thinking Jeremiah must have forgotten to tell her something, she padded across the hardwood floors and answered it. This time she was surprised to find Grant Whitecastle standing on the other side of the door.

"Hi, Emma, do you have a minute?" he asked, looking sheepish and uncomfortable.

"Um, I guess. What's this about?" She showed him into the den, where he sat in her father's favorite chair while she took her spot on the sofa.

Grant looked around. "Kelly told me your folks are in Julian. Did Phil go back home, too?"

"No, he didn't. He's out rounding up some dinner." She hesitated. "You're making me nervous, Grant. Is Kelly okay?"

"She's fine," he said. Grant had been slouching but now sat up straight. "I wanted to talk to you, Emma, alone. About us."

"Us?" She didn't try to hide her surprise. "What about us?"

Grant leaned forward and clasped his hands together between his knees. "I don't want you to marry Phil, Emma."

Emma sat at attention, her back ramrod straight. "I don't think that's any of your business, Grant. Not in the least."

Grant Whitecastle, TV showman and aging celebrity bad boy, took a deep breath. "Don't marry him, Emma. Remarry me instead."

Emma hopped to her feet. "Have you been drinking, Grant? Is this some kind of booze-initiated joke?"

"It's no joke, Emma. I made a huge mistake leaving you. Carolyn and I are getting a divorce. I want us—you, me, and Kelly—to be a family again."

Emma waved a hand in the air. "That ship has sailed, Grant. Trust me on this."

"Give it a chance, Emma." He got up and looked her square in the eye. "I'm a changed man. I want to go back and correct the biggest mistake of my life. Please, Emma, come back to me. It's not too late."

He reached out to her, but before he could touch her, Emma backed up. "I don't love you anymore, Grant. I love Phil." She started walking to the front door. Reluctantly, Grant trailed behind her. They met Phil in the hallway. He'd come in through the back and had dropped the food off in the kitchen.

"What's going on?" Phil asked, eyeing Grant with suspicion.

Emma stood next to Phil and put an arm around his waist. Automatically, his arm went around her shoulders. "Grant was in the neighborhood," Emma explained, "and stopped by to ask me something. He was just leaving."

"Good," Phil said to Grant with no frills. "Don't let us hold you up. I'm sure you're a busy man." He twitched his mustache to punctuate the comment.

Grant started to say something, but checked himself. On the way out the door, he turned to Emma and said, "We can discuss this more fully later."

Emma shook her head. "There is no later, Grant. Not in a million years."

As soon as Grant was out the door, Phil asked, "What was that all about?"

"He came by to propose to me," Emma told him as she started for the kitchen. "Let's eat."

"Now hold on," Phil said, stopping her. "What was he proposing? Something about his show?"

"No, Phil, he proposed marriage to me. Grant wants me back."

Phil stared at her, then turned around and went out the front door. Emma started to go after him, then changed her mind. Instead, she went into the kitchen and started pulling food containers from a plastic bag. A few minutes later Phil came in. He went straight to the freezer and pulled out two bags of frozen peas, holding one against his left eye with his left hand, and resting his right knuckles against the other.

Emma stopped what she was doing and stared at him. "What happened?"

Phil shrugged. "Not much, but I think I changed his mind about that proposal."

Emma came around the counter and stood in front of Phil. She took the bag of peas from his eye and inspected the bruised area just below it. It wouldn't be long before the eye blackened.

"I hope you didn't hit him too hard, Phil. He has to be on camera, you know."

Again Phil shrugged. "Not my problem, and I'm sure he employs a lot of very good makeup people."

"I should be very angry with you," she said to him, staying close.

"But you're not?"

In answer, Emma very lightly and very carefully kissed the bruise.

Phil tapped a finger against his lips. "Grant missed these, you know."

Emma wrapped her arms around Phil's neck and planted a long, hard kiss on his mouth. Dinner could wait.

WELL-CRAFTED MYSTERIES
FROM BERKLEY PRIME CRIME

- **Earlene Fowler** Don't miss these Agatha Award–winning quilting mysteries featuring Benni Harper.

- **Monica Ferris** These *USA Today* bestselling Needle-craft Mysteries include free knitting patterns.

- **Laura Childs** Her Scrapbooking Mysteries offer tips to satisfy the most die-hard crafters.

- **Maggie Sefton** These popular Knitting Mysteries come with knitting patterns and recipes.

- **Lucy Lawrence** These brilliant Decoupage Mysteries involve cutouts, glue, and varnish.

- **Elizabeth Lynn Casey** The Southern Sewing Circle Mysteries are filled with friends, southern charm—and murder.

M5G0610